A PROMISE

"I guess I'd better be leaving." He thought it better to make an exit while he could control himself. He didn't know how long he could continue to ignore the longing he had for her.

"I enjoyed dinner." Tonya walked him to the door. She reached for the doorknob and he grabbed her hand.

"Wait . . . there's something I've been wanting to do all evening."

He cupped her face in his hands and gently kissed her on the lips. It had been a long time since she had felt a kiss so soft.

"Why did you want to do that?"

"I couldn't help myself. You don't realize the effect you have on me."

The kiss began to deepen. He didn't realize the effect *he* had on *her!*

The more she thought she didn't want anything to happen between them, the more she yearned for it.

She could feel his lips trailing down her neck. She could feel the buttons of her blouse being undone. Why wasn't she stopping him? A low moan escaped from her throat.

His body began to tremble with excitement as his lips touched the swell of her breast. She could feel the rapid beating of his heart or was it her own heart? She had to do something.

"Dexter, this has to stop. We don't know each other well enough." Instead of pushing him away, she held him closer to her.

"Well," he murmured as he massaged her shoulder, "you're about to get to know me well enough in a few minutes and that's a promise . . ."

BOOK YOUR PLACE ON OUR WEBSITE AND MAKE THE ARABESQUE ROMANCE CONNECTION!

We've created a customized website just for our very special Arabesque readers, where you can get the inside scoop on everything that's going on with Arabesque romance novels.

When you come online, you'll have the exciting opportunity to:

- View covers of upcoming books

- Learn about our future publishing schedule (listed by publication month and author)

- Find out when your favorite authors will be visiting a city near you

- Search for and order backlist books

- Check out author bios and background information

- Send e-mail to your favorite authors

- Join us in weekly chats with authors, readers and other guests

- Get writing guidelines

- AND MUCH MORE!

Visit our website at
http://www.arabesquebooks.com

FOR LOVE'S SAKE

Rochunda Lee

ARABESQUE
BET BOOKS

BET Publications, LLC
www.msbet.com
http://www.arabesquebooks.com

ARABESQUE BOOKS are published by

BET Publications, LLC
c/o BET BOOKS
One BET Plaza
1900 W Place NE
Washington, D.C. 20018-1211

First Printing: November, 1999

10 9 8 7 6 5 4 3 2 1

Printed in the United States of America

Prologue

Was she mad at the world? Was she angry at her parents for providing her with a nice, sheltered life? Was it their fault that she was naive enough to believe every syllable that rolled from some man's lips? No, she loved her parents because they only wanted the best for her and her two brothers.

She was a victim of the "nice girl next door" syndrome. She could never do anything wrong, she had to be prim and proper at every moment. When her parents found out that she was sexually active her sophomore year of college, it was like a fall from grace. They wanted to know just who was corrupting their daughter. That man turned out to be David, the man she planned to marry. It was just that—a plan.

Tonya's two siblings had turned out to be close to nothing, so her parents refused to lose with their last child. She was expected to be an overachiever, and her goals in life reflected that. She'd wanted to go to college, graduate, and get a good job. She had done that and also graduated from law school.

Her two brothers never wanted anything out of life. They both dropped out of school and pretty much did nothing for a long time. Reggie, her oldest brother, got his GED two years after he dropped out and finally went to barber college. Her next to the oldest brother, Kip, didn't pursue anything except for becoming a drunk by the time he was twenty-four. He said he was a professional alcoholic.

Most of her friends thought her family lived an easy life because they lived in the prestigious Lillian Estates subdivision. Yes, they lived a nice life, but it hadn't come easy. Her father, John Locksley, was in the export business; he imported and exported food products to and from major grocery centers throughout the world. Her mother, Ruth Locksley, was a teacher at a well-known private school, Roswell High, the same school that Tonya had graduated from. Neither of her parents received any financial aid during their college years and worked full-time jobs to pay for their educations.

Tonya couldn't understand why her brothers felt that everything should be handed to them on a silver platter. Reggie's philosophy on life was that he would eventually get married and become a househusband. In other words, his wife was going to take care of him. That outlook on life changed when he met and became involved with a woman no one in the family liked, by the name of Ramona but, Tonya loathed Ramona. If there was one thing she couldn't stand, it was a loud-mouthed woman with gold teeth and bad diction. Talk about being ghetto, she put the "g" in the word. Ramona would fight with Reggie when he refused to give her money to get her weave done. Since he and Ramona lived together, she would put him out when she couldn't have her way. It came to be a ritual that every two weeks when it was beauty shop time, Reggie would be homeless. Kip believed that he didn't need a woman to take care of him, as long as he had his liquor and their parents, he didn't have a thing to worry about. Her brothers always argued that Tonya was their parents' favorite. They could have been right in a small way, but maybe if they gave their parents something to be proud of, they would get the same treatment.

Tonya could understand her parents' feelings about Kip because he did nothing at all, except drink. Reggie was a different story. He may not have graduated from high school, but he did get his GED. He may not have gone to college, but he had one of the most popular barber shops on the north side of town. Their parents gave him no credit, however, Tonya did and to her that's all that mattered. He pretended like it didn't matter, but she knew that deep down inside, he wanted their parents' approval.

Shortly after Tonya graduated from law school, she took the bar exam and passed on her first try. In three weeks, she would start her new job at Freeman and Reynolds, a large, black-owned law firm. She had clerked there every summer while she was in law school. Tonya wasn't going to get too excited about the job because it was just a stepping-stone for her. The idea of having her own practice was starting to sound pretty good. That was later on down the road. She had to establish herself in a firm before branching out on her own.

Her life was on a definite path and she didn't need anyone or anything distracting her from what she wanted to do. She had a plan for success and avoided everything she had written on her "deterrent list." This list included friends, foes, and men. She wasn't letting any friends, foes, or men get in the way of her success. Of course, this list wasn't in that particular order; men were at the top of the list.

She had been through a bad relationship once and wasn't anticipating jumping into another one. Her ex-boyfriend, David, had taken her through enough changes and heartache. He was the man she had hoped to marry. He was perfect in her eyes—handsome, intelligent, and his career as a financial analyst was thriving. She and David dated through three of their four undergraduate years and through her last year of law school. It was just a matter of him proposing to her. Just when she thought she had him where she wanted him, she caught him in bed with a man. He was no ordinary man, he just happened to be one of David's fraternity brothers. He was supposed to be at work, so she had decided to stop by his place and surprise him with dinner and a little something special for dessert. She turned the key to the door and headed to the kitchen when she heard voices coming from the bedroom. She put the bag she had in tow on the counter and armed herself with a butcher knife from the drawer. She picked up the phone and dialed 911 and told them there was an intruder in her boyfriend's apartment. She was petrified and couldn't move from the spot where she stood in a corner. From that corner, she had a direct view of the closed bedroom door. The only thing that stood between her and the bedroom was the counter and very little space. She moved only when she heard the sirens pulling up outside. She forced herself to meet the police at the door and would let them surprise the thieves. She opened the door and pointed toward the bedroom. She could vividly remember telling the police, "They're in there," and following close behind the man and woman officers as they positioned themselves outside of the door.

"Freeze, police," they called out before kicking the door in. Not only were David and his fraternity brother, Ken, surprised, so was Tonya. When the police said *freeze*, they froze in exact position. She would never forget the scene that took place before her very eyes. Tonya could remember screaming and taking her ring off and throwing it at David before running to her car. He had the nerve to run after her, insisting that he wasn't gay or interested in this man that he had been seeing the last *three* months of their relationship. He referred to his experience with Ken as something to give him another level of excitement. Excitement—he had thrown their relationship away because of excitement. It killed her to think that she wasn't exciting enough for him, especially since he was with another man. In her opinion, their sex life had been excellent.

He sent flowers and cards, but she wouldn't accept any of them. Finally, he got the message and the phone calls, flowers, and unannounced visits ceased. Her parents loved him to death, and she was too embarrassed to tell them the reason for the breakup. The only person she told was Reggie. Reggie was a bit trifling, but he was still her brother and he promised not to tell a soul. That turned out to be a lie, he told everyone he could think of except their parents.

She wasn't ready for another man to get close to her any time soon. Heartache was something she didn't plan to feel again . . . ever. There were many opportunities for her to become involved with someone, but she preferred to be alone. Men—you can never trust them. Why bother with a relationship when you already knew what was going to happen? You'd fall in love, put all of your trust in him, give him the benefit of the doubt, then he'd mess up. You'd find out that he had someone else the whole time. You'd start putting two and two together and it all starts to add up. You'd wonder why he didn't call you back, after paging him four or five times. You'd think about how he never showed up when he was supposed to come over. You'd even think about all of the times he couldn't take you out because he was broke. You give beyond your best and he gives his worst. No, that's not something she needed in her life right now.

Kiera, her best friend, always had men in her life, even though she didn't take any of them seriously. Sometimes Tonya envied her because she was able to remain so unattached to the men she got involved with. They would break up and all she would do is move on, as if nothing ever happened.

Tonya always thought Kiera was an attractive person. She had long, thick, dark brown hair. She had the smoothest brown skin that Tonya had ever seen and had a shape that men died for. Yet, she was always complaining. "Girl, my hair is just too nappy; I need a serious perm." Then she would go as far as to say, "I need to lose a few pounds; I'm getting too fat." There wasn't an inch of fat on that girl and she knew it. She just liked to hear how good she looked, just to build up that ego of hers.

As far as looks were concerned, they were like night and day. Kiera was kind of on the thick side and Tonya was on the slim side. Tonya had smooth dark skin and medium-length hair and didn't consider herself skinny because skinny people didn't have shapes. She had small waist and hips and long shapely legs. A lot of men liked to see her going as well as coming. So, even if there was a major difference between them, they both got their fair share of men.

They had always done things together. They went to elementary school through high school together. The only thing they didn't do was go to the same college. Kiera went to the University of Texas and majored in chemical engineering, while Tonya attended the University of Houston. At first, they both had the same majors, then they kind of found their own identities. Kiera worked for Epson Corporation. Tonya loved the fact that Kiera didn't have to depend on anybody, and in a few weeks, she would be doing just that—starting her own independence.

Her first step toward that goal was moving out of her parents' house. Most of the time, it was only three of them there. She felt it was time she had her own privacy, as well as letting her parents have theirs. Mr. and Mrs. Locksley insisted on helping her get an apartment. It turned out to be a graduation present. They surprised her with a fully furnished condominium in a neighborhood they considered nice enough for their daughter. The one thing it had a lot of was windows. Mrs. Locksley knew how much her daughter loved windows and decided it was perfect. The living room furniture consisted of a leather crème couch and love seat and an oriental rug with crème and teal designs. Actually, the bathroom and bedroom were of the same colors. Those colors weren't Tonya's particular favorites, but she loved it anyway.

One

The buzzing of the alarm clock brought Monday all too soon. Mechanically, Tonya's hand with perfectly polished nails moved to the snooze button. Her entire weekend had been spent moving into her new place. Of course, she had to have a housewarming party. After hitting the snooze button twice, she decided to get out of bed. She hated the idea of getting up, but she was anticipating the beginning of the first day at her new job. She went to the kitchen and put on a pot of coffee since there would be no time to go by Starbuck's to get her morning latté. She had decided on wearing a navy blue suit with a long slim skirt. The jacket was tapered at the waist. She had always liked that suit because it made her look classy, but sexy. After a nice hot shower, she dressed and a look at herself in the mirror gave pleasing results. After a final glance in the mirror, she picked up her briefcase and headed for the door. The ringing of the phone halted her exit. She quickly answered it and heard her best friend's voice on the other end.

"I just called to say good luck today." Tonya could hear static on the phone and knew immediately that Kiera was on her car phone.

"Thanks. I was just about to walk out the door." Her friend could be long-winded and this morning was not the time for dragging out a conversation.

"Well, I wouldn't want you to be late on your first day. So go get 'em."

"You know it. Talk to you later." She needed the moral support because today began a turning point in her life.

Thirty minutes later she entered the plush office building. There were leather chairs in the waiting area and deep, thick, burgundy carpet. All of the tables and end tables were made of cherry wood. Mr. Freeman happened to be at the door when she walked into the office.

"Good morning. I see you've made it." He smiled.

"Good morning. Am I late?" she asked nervously. Several passersby looked at her curiously.

"No. Did you have any problems finding us today? I remember when we interviewed, you ran into some difficulties."

"No. I found the building just fine. I did have trouble parking though."

"Oh, we have a garage. I'll give you all of those details later. Let me show you to your office." As he led the way, he stopped to introduce her to other staff members they passed along the way. Her office was very nice. It wasn't too large or too small. It was perfect. There was an ivy plant in a brass pot at the left corner of her desk.

"This is your office. Feel free to decorate it as you please. You'll be spending a lot of time here and I want you to be as comfortable as possible." His smile didn't quite reach his eyes.

"Thank you, I will." She smiled the same empty smile.

"Well, I'll leave you to your work and welcome aboard."

That work consisted of briefing cases, researching background information, searching for information on clients, and worst of all, filing. If there was one thing she hated most, it was filing. She hadn't been assigned a secretary as yet, therefore, she had to do her own filing, copying, and typing. Freeman and Reynolds had the largest filing rooms that she had ever seen. There were what seemed like hundreds of rows with shelves and shelves of files.

She wondered why Mr. Freeman had seemed so aloof. Since he was from the old school, maybe he didn't think that she would live up to the Freeman and Reynolds standards. He'd coined the phrase, "Good grades in law school do not guarantee one will be a great attorney."

Mr. Freeman was a nice-looking gentleman. She thought him to be in his mid to late fifties. There was a touch of gray at his temples, but otherwise, his curly hair was jet black. His skin was a caramel color and it was apparent that he had been a real looker in his younger days.

After leaving the file room, she returned to her office. She hadn't taken the time to familiarize herself in her new surroundings and she checked out her office. She tried out her chair by slightly bouncing up and down on it. Someone rapped softly on her door, interrupting her. She looked up to see that a woman had stepped inside. She could only imagine what she must have looked like and was embarrassed to have been caught.

"Oh, I didn't know anybody was there." Tonya said, slightly breathless. The woman smiled at her.

"Trying out your chair? I'm Rita. I'm an associate in the litigation section." The woman extended her hand to her.

Rita was very pretty and down-to-earth. She was brown skinned with very long hair, which she had pulled away from her face. Her voluptuous lips curled easily into a dazzling smile. Tonya had a strange feeling that they were going to become close. She felt comfortable with Rita and liked her immediately. Rita began filling her in on all of the office gossip and who was dating who.

"Girl, you should see Mr. Freeman's son, Dexter," Rita said, whispering slightly as she leaned across Tonya's desk. "He is so fine and good-looking. Women in this office and in buildings all down the street want to get with him. But, I don't believe he wants to get caught."

"Why do you say that?"

"He hasn't made it a secret. He doesn't want a woman until he gets himself together. I guess he wants to have the house, the car, and all of that before he settles down."

"What's wrong with that? He sounds like a winner to me." She found herself getting caught up in the gossip that Rita so vividly described.

"Nothing's wrong with it. He's just taking too long and the man loves children. He's always spending time with orphaned children. He's also very active in that big brother program. He was thinking about adopting a little boy through the program. I don't know if he's still considering it." Rita sat in the chair, fanning herself as if she had just run a marathon.

"He does seem like a nice catch. I take it you have plans for him yourself?" Tonya asked, looking down at her polished nails.

"Girl, I'm happily married. If I wasn't, he'd have been mine a long time ago." She laughed.

"Does he work here?" She asked with vague interest. For some reason Tonya believed that if Rita was single, she definitely would have had him.

"No, he works at a law firm in Atlanta, but he does a lot of work for his father here in Houston and he's here quite often."

"I'm sure if he's all that, he has someone in his life. At any rate, I won't get my hopes up. A man like that can just pick and choose any woman he wants. Has he ever been married?"

"I don't know. I haven't heard anything about a marriage. But, you shouldn't count yourself out, you never know. Anyway, I'm sitting around here like I don't have any work to do. I've got to be in court in less than an hour. I'll talk to you later." Rita said, walking out the door.

"See ya'," Tonya called after her.

It was well after six and she had been working on Westlaw all day when her passcode decided it didn't want to give her access anymore. Then, she found out that it wasn't her passcode, it was their service and it wouldn't be working again until later that evening. Her first day on the job and she was already working long hours, the thought of leaving any work undone just irked her nerves. The office was almost empty when she was forced by the interruption to call it quits. She sat on the edge of her desk, trying to decide whether she should take some of her work home or leave it until the next day. She decided to leave it and leaned across the desk to turn off her computer. Just as she hit the power button, someone stopped at the door.

What a great pair of legs! he noticed as she leaned across the desk. "You must be Ms. Locksley," a deep sultry voice said.

She rose quickly. *Oh my God! Who is this gorgeous man?* The tall, lean, but fit frame relaxed in the doorway. Parted lips revealed perfectly straight teeth and he had the deepest dimples. She could almost see her fingers touching that lovely dark skin or going through that wavy hair. She was mesmerized.

"Excuse me, are you Tonya Locksley?" he asked again.

She snapped back to attention. "Yes. I'm Tonya Locksley." His eyes were averted to her skirt, which had risen when she stretched over the desk and she self-consciously tugged it down.

"I'm Dexter Freeman," he said, extending his hand as he walked into her office.

Why was her heart beating so fast? Why was she so nervous? "It's nice to meet you," she said, holding out her hand and embracing his. He held it for a moment before letting go. She wondered if he could tell that she was nervous. Why wouldn't he just go away? What was with all of the small talk? *Go away.*

"So, how was your first day?" Dexter asked, towering in front of her.

"Great, the people here are very nice." She licked her lips nervously. The act hadn't gone unnoticed by Dexter.

"I wouldn't want anyone to make you feel uncomfortable or nervous," he said, laughing slightly.

He had to know that *he* was making her nervous. It was obvious that he liked watching her squirm, because the more uncomfortable she became, the more he lingered.

"Thanks," she said, rubbing her sweaty palms across her skirt. She began organizing the messy piles on her desk and grabbed her jacket. The room wasn't cold, yet there were goose bumps on her arms. That disturbed her. She quickly donned the jacket and hoped he got the message that she wanted him to leave.

He quietly observed her and after a long pause spoke. "I'm sure you're in a hurry to get home after such a long day. It was nice meeting you and I'll be seeing you soon." With that, he was gone. The only thing that he left behind was the scent of his cologne. *I don't know about that, Dexter Freeman, I don't think I want to see you too soon.*

All the way home she couldn't get his face out of her mind. It was etched in her brain. She knew this feeling very well and she didn't like it. Every time this feeling crept up on her, she ended up falling for someone when it wasn't convenient. No, she wasn't going to let this happen again.

She walked into her apartment and began checking

her messages. There was one from her mother, one from David, and one from Kiera. It had been months since she'd heard his voice. She knew that her mother had probably given him the number. She wondered why he'd decided to call her after all of this time. He knew it was over and there was nothing else to talk about. His message was the only one that she erased. After placing a frozen dinner in the microwave and changing clothes, she returned Kiera's call.

"Hey, I got your message. What's up?" Tonya walked into the kitchen and retrieved the dinner that was warming in the microwave.

"Nothing much, I just wanted to know how your day went. Anything new happen?"

"Girl, I worked my butt off. I'm just getting home." The couch rumpled as she flopped down. She idly flipped the channels on the television screen and picked over her zesty spaghetti frozen dinner. *I've got to learn how to cook!*

"Well, you can never work too hard. How do you like your new boss and coworkers?" Kiera asked.

"Mr. Freeman is *so* nice and I like him a lot. I even like most of the other staff. There is this one lady that I really like. Her name is Rita, and she's *extremely* nice. I think we're going to become good friends."

"That's nice. I'm glad you're making new friends." Kiera rolled her eyes up in her head. Tonya always thought everyone was nice. She could meet a mass-murderer and she would think he was nice.

Tonya kind of got the feeling that Kiera was jealous of her potential friendship with Rita. "You would not believe who called me today." She was amazed that David had the nerve to call her after everything that had happened.

"Who? You know you don't have that many friends outside of myself, so this could be a hard one to figure out." Kiera said it on a light note, but she knew Tonya had a limited set of friends. She didn't have a problem with this because it made their friendship even more special.

"Very funny—David!"

"David—ugh! Not friction booty. What did he want?"

"I don't know. As soon as I heard his voice on the answering machine, I erased it. As long as he isn't calling me about his health, I'm fine." She had gotten tested for everything when she found about David's *invisible life*. Everything was fine, but she still got tested every six months. Her health was one thing she wasn't playing around with.

"I doubt it, he probably wants to reconcile." Kiera made a yuck face every time David's name was mentioned. It kind of looked like she had gotten a bad taste in her mouth when she thought of him.

"Speaking of friends," Tonya was eager to change the subject. She removed the fork from her mouth and swallowed some spaghetti. "I met Mr. Freeman's son, Dexter."

"You met Dexter Freeman—*the* Dexter Freeman?" Kiera gasped. She made a low whistle.

"Yeah. He came into my office tonight and introduced himself. Now that I think about it, I probably made myself look like a fool." *If I didn't make a fool of myself, I sure felt as if I did.*

"He introduced himself? Girlfriend, you were in the company of Atlanta's and Houston's most wanted man. Yours truly wouldn't mind having her some Dexter Freeman."

"It's not that kind of party. I'm there to do a job, not to look at men. It doesn't matter how good they look."

"So what happened?" Kiera asked.

"He just asked how I liked working there and if I was comfortable with the staff. It was a casual conversation. I'm not making anything big out of it. If anything, I was trying to rush him out of my office. I was ready to jump on the first thing smoking to my place."

"Why? You should've been trying to keep him in there

as long as you possibly could. Girl, get him. Go after that man. If he seems interested, why not give it a chance?"

"It wasn't like he was asking me out. He just stopped by to introduce himself, nothing more. Besides, I don't want anybody in my life right now. If anybody else wants him and they want to participate in the hunt, they can have him." Tonya wasn't big on the idea of chasing down a man. Going after a man like she was desperate, made her feel like a floozy. She believed in being subtle about the chase. There are many ways to chase a man without letting him know he's being chased. That was one area where she and Kiera were different. Kiera didn't mind letting any man know she was interested. Kiera called it being bold. Tonya called it being desperate.

"Give me a good man. I'll show you what to do with him," Kiera said more to herself than to Tonya.

"I don't know what for. You can't even deal with the two you have already," Tonya reminded Kiera. She cringed at the thought of Kiera winning Dexter over her. Kiera always got the good ones, leaving her with the leftovers. Ever since she and Kiera had been friends, it had been that way. She quickly banished the thought.

"I know that's right. I need to deal with these two before looking for another one." Having to deal with two men was worse than having two jobs and Kiera was getting tired of keeping up with all of the details.

"Now, you know Reggie always wanted you. Now that his barber shop is successful and all, you might want to go on and get with him." Tonya's brother had liked Kiera for as long as she could remember. She never knew whether Kiera felt the same about him. If she did, she never mentioned it to her.

"Girl, you know Reggie is darn near married. That woman won't let him get two feet away from her."

"You know it. But seriously speaking, you need to choose between Anthony and Myron before you get somebody killed. I worry about you and that situation. I don't want anything happening to you."

"Don't worry about me. I'm a grown woman. I can take care of myself."

Tonya let out an annoyed breath. Why wouldn't Kiera listen to anything? "Okay, Ms. I can take care of myself, what are you going to do when it all hits the fan? Don't come crying to me because after I get through boo-hooing with you, I'm gonna' say *I told you so.*"

Kiera laughed at her crack. "I might as well tell you that I've made a decision. I plan to be with Myron. I'm telling Anthony tonight. Girl, the confusion at the job is driving me crazy." Kiera turned on the water in the bathtub and poured in some bubble bath. She didn't want Tonya to know just how much the situation bothered her.

"How did you come about that decision?" Tonya asked. She knew her friend was one confused person. She's probably dumping Anthony for convenience purposes, Tonya thought to herself.

"I drew straws." Kiera laughed. "I've gotta go, tonight isn't going to be pleasant. You know breakin' hearts ain't easy."

"Well, good luck heartbreaker. I hope things work out like you've planned. Don't forget to let him down easy." She placed the phone back on the receiver. She was still worried about that situation. Those men had invested a lot of time and money in Kiera. Just letting her go might not be that easy.

Two

Twenty minutes had gone by and Tonya continued to stare at the blank computer screen. For some strange reason, she couldn't get started on her work. Mr. Freeman had assigned Rita as the attorney she would be working with and she had her doing all kinds of research on wills and estate planning. This morning, work wasn't on her mind. The phone rang and interrupted her thoughts. She pressed the intercom button. "Tonya Locksley," she answered.

"Ms. Locksley, I would like to visit with you a moment, if I may." Mr. Freeman's baritone voice boomed over the intercom.

She quickly picked up the phone. "That will be fine, Mr. Freeman. I'll be right down." She wondered nervously if there was anything wrong. She got up from her chair and pressed the wrinkles out of her linen skirt. *Am I not doing something right? Am I not doing enough? Am I wearing my skirts too short?*

It was only a short walk from her office to Mr. Freeman's, but it seemed like ten miles. She rapped softly on his door.

"Come in." Mr. Freeman was puffing on a cigar when Tonya walked into his office. She didn't tell him that she couldn't stand smoke. His office was huge and there were trophies of stuffed animals throughout the office that he had killed on hunting trips. *Is it a testosterone thing or do men always have to prove their manhood?* Oddly enough, she saw none of his degrees lining the walls. The two chairs at his large cherry wood desk were burgundy leather and there was an enormous window directly behind him that overlooked downtown Houston.

"Have a seat," he said, leaning back in his chair, cigar in hand.

"Thank you," Tonya said in a low voice as she sat in the chair.

"I know you're wondering why I've asked to see you," he said, taking a long puff from his cigar and exhaling.

She stifled a cough. "Yes, sir. I was wondering just that." If she stayed any longer, her eyes would begin to water.

"I know that you've already been working with Rita and I hear that you are doing excellent work. How do you like it so far?" She could hardly see his face for all the smoke. It was like being in a dense fog.

"I like it very much. Is there something wrong?" She had to know. The suspense was killing her.

"No, no. It's quite contrary to that. I was thinking of assigning you to another attorney."

She sighed in relief. "Oh, really? When?"

"I don't know if you've met my son. He's going to be here for a few weeks helping me with a relatively large probate case."

His son! No. I can't work with him. "Yes, I've met him. I don't know about that Mr. Freeman, Rita keeps me pretty busy. I don't know if I can handle the extra workload." There she was turning down an assignment from the big boss because she didn't want to work with his son. She amazed herself.

"You're quite capable of handling it. You're very intelligent, and I'm sure you'll do just fine."

"When will he be in the office?" She might as well make the best of this. She fanned her hand in front of her face. The smoke was thick, and she knew the smell would be in her hair and clothes.

"He should be in early next week, perhaps on Monday." He noticed her fanning motions.

"Oh, is my smoke bothering you?" Mr. Freeman asked, taking the cigar from his mouth, exhaling.

"No, not at all," she lied. Tears streamed down her cheeks and her eyes burned.

"I'm sorry, I didn't know the smoke bothered you." He extinguished his cigar. "That was the only thing on the agenda. You're free to return to your office, unless there is something else you would like to discuss," he said with a question in the angle of his eyebrows.

"No, sir. I'm fine."

"Okay, keep up the good work." He looked down at the papers in front of him. Tonya took that as her cue to leave.

She hadn't seen Dexter since he'd introduced himself and she had assumed that he had gone back to Atlanta. She hadn't wanted to ask about him because people might start to get the wrong idea. She would see him soon enough. *Why am I thinking about him anyway?* Every spare moment she had was spent with him on her mind. *Girl, you only met him once. Thank God its Friday!* She'd known working in a law firm would be tedious, but she didn't quite expect her first days to be so hectic. She plopped down at her desk and began comparing cases that could be used in their defense strategies. Once she got started, she couldn't stop. There was no question about it, she loved law.

An e-mail interrupted her constant pecking at the keyboard. These people e-mailed all day long! What was it now? E-mails annoyed her. She considered it something to deter her from work. Half of the time, the e-mails weren't anything of importance. Reluctantly, she placed her hand on the mouse and clicked on open. It read:

Ms. Lockley,
    *I'm having a party at Ritzy's tonight and a lot of people
are going. I would be happy if you could make it, too. It
starts at nine and keeps going until . . . ! If you don't
know where Ritzy's is, give me a call and I'll give you
directions. E-mail me back if you can make it.*

                                                    Keith

A party! She hadn't been out in a long time. She
drummed her fingers on her desk, trying to recall who
Keith was. With a snap of her fingers it came to her. He
was the attorney who worked on the floor above her, in
the real estate section. *He's kind of cute!* She moved the
mouse to accept and clicked. She definitely knew where
Ritzy's was. It was the club of the elite. Its crowd included
professional football and basketball players and other lo-
cal celebrities. It also included everyday professional people. David had taken her there for her twenty-fifth
birthday. Things were perfect then. Even though she and
David had been apart for over a year, it still hurt to think
about him.

She had made up her mind that she was going to that
party. There was no way she was going to work late on
this day. Rita called and told her that she was going and
they decided to meet at the party. Kiera had plans for
going out with Myron, so there was no need to invite her.
She needed to go out more often instead of staying home
making it a Blockbuster night. Things had to change in
her social life. Instead of mulling over work that wouldn't
be finished, she made a beauty shop appointment and
made a mad dash for the door.

Her first stop was the mall. There was no need of going
to a party in an old outfit. What could she possibly wear?
She couldn't wear anything too skimpy, because that
wasn't her style. She felt uncomfortable wearing really
short, tight skirts or dresses. Her eyes quickly darted to

a cute little number. It was black, tight, and short—everything she didn't want. It had the spandex top, made like a sports bra that extended down to the rib area. Then, there was this see-through material from the rib area to the hips, the spandex picked up again and completed the skirt. She tried it on. This just wasn't her style. She looked at herself in the mirror and kinda liked what she saw. She couldn't possibly . . . she ended up buying the dress. Her timing was perfect. She made it to the beauty shop earlier than expected, surprising her beautician.

"Girl, I can't believe you're early," Casara said, as she gave her hair the once over. She motioned for Tonya to sit in the chair and draped a smock around her. She ran her fingers through her hair to see if she needed a perm.

"You aren't the only one who's surprised. I made it here earlier than I expected."

"Whatcha' gettin' done? Is it time for you to get permed?" she asked.

"Now, you know I got a perm the last time. What are you trying to tell me—that my hair is nappy?"

Casara laughed. "You know this hair is always on the nappy side. I'm gonna' give you a spot perm. What are you getting all doodied up for anyway? You aren't due in until next week."

"I'm going to this party tonight so I need something cute. I guess I'll get a wrap with a lot of curls," she said, thoughtfully.

"What about a bob?" asked Casara. "You've never had a bob before."

"Do you think it'll be right for me?" She looked in the mirror, trying to imagine her hair in a bob.

"Yeah, you'll have a classy look. I'm going to have to shave you in the back."

"You're just cut happy, Casara. Every time I come in here you say, 'I gotta' cut ya.' " She laughed.

"You look good though. That's the whole point. You look good." Casara laughed.

She left the beauty shop at six and as usual, Casara was right. She did look good. The change from the curly to the straight look complimented her features. The party started at nine and she planned to get there around ten thirty so that left her with more than three hours to transform herself.

After getting home, she ran her bath water and poured some Wings bath gel into the water and soaked for an hour. The more she thought about it, the more she dreaded putting that dress on. *What was I thinking?*

After dressing, she liked the outcome. It was as if a totally different person was standing in the mirror. The dress wasn't as sleazy as she'd thought, maybe there was a such thing as wearing skimpy stuff tastefully.

She got to the party around ten forty-five instead of ten thirty and noticed a lot of people staring her way. *Do they think I look like a slut or do they think I look nice?* She made her way to the bar and ordered her favorite drink, champagne and cranberry juice. There were a lot of guys who asked her to dance and she accepted most of them. After the dance they tried to stick around and make small talk. She wasn't in the talking mood, so she sat at the bar and waited for Rita who hadn't shown up yet. She glanced around the room for the umpteenth time—still no Rita. As she sat there sipping her drink, someone sat beside her. She didn't bother turning to look at him. Besides, he might have gotten the impression that she was interested.

"What are you drinking?" The person asked as he settled onto the stool next to her.

"Champagne and cranberry juice," she answered without facing him. The bartender was throwing wine bottles up in the air and catching them behind his back and pouring drinks. *Show off!* Although she stared intently at the clean-cut man behind the bar, she was thoroughly aware of the pair of eyes watching her.

"That's different. I'm always open to trying something different," he said. He glanced down at the pair of shapely legs in front of him. From one encounter, he could tell that her taste in clothes was expensive. He appreciated the way the short dress clung to her small shapely frame. A well-dressed woman—he liked that.

"That's nice," she said. Why couldn't he get the hint and leave her alone? She allowed her eyes to scan the room for Rita. She was over an hour late.

"You've been out on the floor all evening. You seem to be pretty popular around here. But, then," he said, looking her up and down, "I can see why."

"Is that right?" she asked dryly. Who was this guy? Some people can't take a hint. She turned to face him.

"I see we meet again." Dexter gave a slight nod of his head.

She could feel herself losing her composure. She couldn't start falling to pieces now. "Yes . . . we do meet again." The calmness in her voice surprised her. She took a sip of her champagne and gently placed it on the counter. She was afraid the shaking of her hand would be apparent if she continued to hold the drink.

Dexter looked nice in his dark blue Armani suit and a crème silk shirt. She was a stickler for heels. If a man had run-over shoes, she was turned off. She stole a glance at his shoes—immaculate!

"So . . . where's your date?" he asked, casually looking around. "I don't want to get into anybody else's business." He knew very well that she was there alone, although she kept looking around the club as if she was expecting someone to arrive any minute.

"I'm my own business. Now, if you will excuse me, I have some mingling to do," she said as she started to walk away.

"I guess it's safe to say that you're here alone." He stood up as she attempted to leave. There was no way she was getting away tonight.

"You could say that." She turned her back to him and began moving through the crowd. Dexter followed in close pursuit.

He loved the way she moved gracefully through the club and realized that he wasn't the only man who appreciated her good looks. A tall slender guy in a very nice suit grabbed her by the hand. Dexter watched closely as she engaged in conversation with him. She didn't seem like she was too happy to be in his presence.

It was like the rerun of a nightmare. In front of her stood the very appealing David. Nothing had changed. The hazel eyes, flashing smile, everything was still perfect.

"Tonya, I'm surprised to find you here." He leaned over to plant a kiss on her lips, but she dodged out of reach.

"Not as surprised as I am," she said sarcastically. Her heart still flipped when she saw him. How could she still have feelings for him?

"You look well. Time has been very good to you," he said as he looked her over.

She felt violated and shuddered under his gaze. How could he give her such an intimate look? How dare he? She snatched her hand away from his. "Yeah, you look the same, too." She cleared her throat in annoyance.

"I called to tell you I've moved back to town. I guess you didn't get my message. Why don't we talk? We still have a lot we need to discuss—some unfinished business."

She couldn't believe him. There was nothing to discuss. The frown on her face let him know how she felt about the subject. "You know there is nothing left to talk about. I've got to be going." She turned to leave but the grip on her arm halted her.

"Tonya, please, let's talk." He gave her his most charming smile.

"Go find the *person* you were in bed with. Where is *he*? What do you need me for?"

Dexter'd had enough of the scene and felt like he had to do something to help her out. He stepped in between Tonya and David. "I can't let you get away without getting one dance from you, can I?" He quickly took her by the hand.

The man seemed annoyed and shot Dexter a scowl, to which, Dexter returned an I don't give a damn look. He reluctantly turned to leave when he realized Dexter wasn't going anywhere, but not before turning once again to Tonya. "We'll have our discussion." With another dirty look to Dexter, he left.

"Do I have a choice?" she asked Dexter, half smiling. She was relieved he'd come to her rescue.

"As a matter of fact, you don't." He grinned, taking her into his arms. He loved the way she felt in his arms. She was perfect. They swayed to the music and his arms found the small of her back and he caressed her softly.

She was compelled to thank him for rescuing her. "I want to thank you for what you did back there. I wasn't all that nice to you earlier."

"Consider it a favor. Maybe one day you can return one to me. Did you know that guy?" He didn't know why he felt jealous of the man who had just left. The scene that played out in front of him suggested that he knew her a lot more than as just a friend.

"Unfortunately, yes." She didn't want to think about David anymore. What was worse, she was in the arms of another dangerous man.

"Is he *close* friend of yours?" His curiosity was getting the best of him. The dim lights and soft music made him feel bold enough to ask her such personal questions. Under other circumstances, he would have never questioned

her. He could feel the tension in her back when he
brought up the subject.

"No, he's not a close friend." At least she wasn't lying.
He used to be close to her, but not anymore. *I shouldn't
be here with him. He's been on my mind too much already.*
Dexter held her close enough that she could smell the
subtle scent of his cologne. She noticed how smooth his
dark skin was. He was even better looking up close. She
wondered if his hair was naturally wavy. Nah . . . it was
probably an S-curl, she doubted it though. Although
David was temporarily out of her mind, the current situation was getting too dangerous and she had to get away
from Dexter as soon as possible.

"I did thank you for rescuing me—didn't I? If not,
thanks." It was the first time that she looked in his eyes.
She'd never noticed that they were a lighter brown than
she'd thought.

"Is that the only reason you said yes? Would you have
danced with me otherwise?" He hoped she would say yes.
He didn't know where his fascination with Tonya Locksley
was coming from, however, he didn't try to fight the feeling.

"Of course, but I really must be going," she said, stopping in mid-dance.

"Going?" he said, glancing at his watch. "It's only
twelve o'clock."

"I have a lot of work to catch up on. There are mounds
of documents I have to review before Monday." Of
course, this was the truth—partly. She did have a ton of
work to do, but it wasn't necessarily due on Monday.

"Is there anything I can help you with? I'm sure you
don't want to spend your entire weekend with your nose
behind some books and papers." He didn't want her to
leave, not now that he was getting to know her. He had
to think quick. He took her hand into his and quickly

released it. He didn't want to come off like the man he'd seen her with earlier.

"If you're starting to feel stressed by the job, let me help. I can be a great stress reliever."

Talk about a line! It was a unique one, but still a line. "No, thanks. I think I'll tough it out. Besides, I'll be thoroughly familiar with everything if I do it myself. Enjoy the rest of your evening." Without giving him a chance to respond, she disappeared into the crowd and the music faded as she left the club.

She needed some fresh air. The atmosphere was suffocating. She leaned against her car. *What is wrong with me?* She got in the car and drove home.

Rita hadn't shown up at the party, and Tonya couldn't wait to get her hands on her. The blinking red light on her answering machine reminded her to check her messages. Rita's voice was the first message that she heard. Speak of the devil!

"I'm sorry I can't make it to the party. I came down with some kind of stomach virus and I've been running from both ends, if you know what I mean. I hope you have a good time. Talk to ya' later."

Here I am wanting to kill her, and she's already half-dead. She undressed and pulled her mauve and green comforter sheets back and hopped into bed. Maybe if she closed her eyes, she wouldn't see that face haunting her. She was wrong.

She dreamed that someone was ringing her doorbell or was she dreaming? It rang again. She turned over and looked at the clock. *Five o'clock! Who could be at my door at this hour?* She got out of bed and put on her robe. She looked through the peephole and saw Kiera standing in front of her door.

"What's wrong?" Kiera stood outside with an angry expression on her face.

"Can I come in or not?" she snapped at Tonya.

What's with her attitude? "I'm sorry, yeah, come in. It's really early. What is all this about?"

"I was out with Myron last night and we were having dinner. I wasn't very hungry and pretty much picked at my food. He got all upset and accused me of wanting to be with Anthony." She sat down on the couch while Tonya stood glaring at her.

What does that have to do with you being at my apartment at five in the morning? She rubbed her fingers at her temples impatiently. "Okay, where is all of this going? I have a date with my bed."

"Well, a lot of things came out during our dinner last night. He also explained about the little rendezvous the two of you had one night." Her eyes shot darts through Tonya and her tone was clipped.

"That's just *crazy!*" She wanted to break out into laughter because it was so stupid, but her friend's chilled expression checked her. "I know you don't believe that."

Kiera got up from the couch and stood face to face with Tonya. "That's just what you would want me to believe, isn't it?"

"Of course, that's what I want you to believe. It's the truth." It was her turn to sit on the couch.

"You know, at first, I couldn't believe it. Then, the more I thought about it, the more it made sense. You kept urging me to make a decision between Myron and Anthony. Then you kept saying you didn't want anybody in your life. Maybe it was just like Myron said. Maybe you didn't need a man because *he* was your man. How could you do such a thing?"

"It's obvious that he's lying, Kiera. He just wanted to upset you."

"Quit covering up. Why don't you tell the truth for a change? You always liked to pretend you were a goody-two-shoes. The truth is that you're an undercover whore."

Now that was something she wasn't going to tolerate.

"Since you prefer to believe him over me, your best friend, it's time for you to leave. When you feel like talking about this without making accusations, call me." She moved over to the door and opened it. Kiera hesitated before moving.

"You don't have to ever worry about me calling you. Call Rita. I'm sure she'll do just fine as your new best friend until you backstab her. How could you let me down like this?" With a pained expression on her face, she walked out without looking behind her. Tonya closed the door and sighed in relief.

As soon as the alarm clock buzzed, Dexter turned it off. There was no need for him to have it on since he had been awake for hours. Dexter wondered why Tonya Locksley interested him so. She seemed as if she didn't want to give him the time of day and hell—he liked it! He was tired of having women throw themselves at his feet and do just about anything he asked them to do. *Sit! Roll-over! Play dead!* Most of them acted as if they didn't know how to make a logical decision. These women weren't bimbos either. They were lawyers, doctors, judges, and so on. Some were very intelligent, but when it came to relationships, they were so pliable. You'd swear they were on remote control. He could imagine himself flicking the switch to the friend channel, maid channel, cook channel, and most of all—the playboy channel! Yep, he could get them to do just about anything he wanted, and that was boring.

When his father mentioned that there was a new associate in the office, he wasn't interested in going in to meet her. He wasn't afraid to admit that meeting her wasn't high on his list of priorities, but when he happened by her office door and saw her—he *had* to meet her. He knew he was playing a dangerous game, but he didn't mind the distraction.

Tonya Locksley was the subject of every conversation he came upon at the office, especially from the male attorneys. They ranted and raved about how attractive this woman was supposed to be. He couldn't take their word at face value because some of those brothers were straight up desperate and a witch in daisy-dukes would look appealing to them. When he met her, he was inclined to agree with them.

He found out from one of the attorneys that she would be at Keith Lexington's party and he decided to go. He wondered what Tonya would look like outside of her crisp office appearance and what he saw, he thoroughly approved of. It was five o'clock in the morning and he was lying awake thinking of her. He wasn't used to feeling that way. There *had* to be something wrong with her— some flaw. Either she was all beauty and no brains or all brains and no common sense. *Nah, she's a graduate from law school, she* has *to have intellect.* Maybe she was another remote control woman. Dexter threw the covers off. He could see his ex-wife, Melissa, vividly in his mind and he thought, *All remote control.* Why he thought of Melissa, he didn't know. If anything, he wanted to get as far away from her as possible. She was a nice woman, but she couldn't get it through her head that when the divorce decree was signed, their marriage was officially *over.*

More than likely he wouldn't see much of Tonya Locksley again. On the other hand, maybe he would. Since he would be working on a case for his father, he would be in Houston a while and that would be his chance to get to know her better. When he went to Houston, business in Atlanta stayed in Atlanta and vice versa. Although he was born and raised in Houston, Atlanta was his real home. The city was beautiful, the people were nice, and most of all, Atlanta is where his reputation as one of the best litigation attorneys had begun. He stood on the balcony of his plush BuckHead high-rise and watched the sun come up. He enjoyed waking up early to watch the sunrise. There was very little traffic on the Atlanta streets and the fragrant smell of fresh bread was in the air from the bakery across the way. Maybe he would get some fresh bagels after his morning jog. The idea of hot bagels with cream cheese was very appealing. It would be nice if he had someone to share those bagels with him. As much as he didn't want to admit it, he was lonely. The more he thought about the guy from the club, the more he wanted Tonya Locksley.

Three

It didn't matter that she had gone back to bed after Kiera left. Her next door neighbor began blasting his music at six o'clock that morning. She lay in the bed until she could tolerate it no more. Kicking back the covers in frustration, her feet hit the floor and she sprang out of bed. She stepped into her slippers and headed out the door. The music reverberated throughout her body as she stood in front of the neighbor's door. She knocked impatiently. *This makes no sense, just because you're up, doesn't mean the rest of the world is.* She knocked several times before a tall, dark-skinned guy with a clean shaven head opened the door. He had on black jogging pants, no shirt, and a white towel was draped around his neck. His well-defined chest glistened with sweat and music blared as he stepped out. She had left her apartment in such a haste that she didn't realize she was standing in front of a complete stranger with nothing on but her night shirt and slippers. The stranger smiled a wicked grin as his eyes drank her. Too late now, she thought.

"I sure hope there's something I can help you with." He took the towel from around his neck and wiped the sweat from his face. She crossed her arms in front of her chest defiantly.

"As a matter of fact there is something you can help me out with. How about turning that loud music of yours down for starters? It's too early in the morning to hear that crap," she yelled over the top of the music.

"I'm sorry. I didn't mean to disturb anybody. I was just getting my morning workout done. I work out to music every morning. I hadn't realized anyone had moved in next door. If I had known that, I wouldn't have had it up so loud. When did you move in?"

He seemed to be rather nice. She was almost sorry for jumping on his case the way she had. Almost—she decided she wasn't apologizing. "About a week and a half ago. It's cool, I know a brother has to get his workout on, but let's try it a little more quietly next time." She smiled to soften her steely tone.

"Since we haven't formally introduced ourselves, my name is Warren. I would shake your hand and all of that, but I'm a little too sweaty." He wrapped the towel around his neck and held onto it with both hands. He was nice-looking. He kinda' reminded her of the guy on the Ford Mustang commercial with the bald head. He wasn't her type, he looked more like a ladies' man.

"I'm Tonya Locksley. I hate that we had to meet under such strained circumstances. Maybe next time will be a better occasion." She waved as she went back to her apartment. The heat from his glare stung her back, but she didn't look back.

She spent most of the morning contemplating everything Kiera had said. She couldn't figure out what happened. She came home from the party, went to sleep, and the next thing she knew, Kiera was knocking at her door. Why would Myron tell such a lie? The whole accusation about her sleeping with him was unjustified. Her apartment was clean from top to bottom, yet she fussed with the pillows on her couch. She rearranged them, fluffed them, and put them back the way they were before. By the time Rita called, she was in a complete funk. She began to recount the previous night's events. After hearing how upset the was, Rita told her she would come over. She promised to go by Starbuck's and pick them up a latté.

When she opened the door for her, Rita came in like a burst of energy. She literally shoved the coffee into Tonya's hand and sprawled across the couch, ready to get into gossip mode.

"Girl, now what happened again? You were talking so fast on the phone that I missed all of the details. This was your best friend right?" She blew on her latté before taking a sip.

"Yes, my *supposed to be* best friend came over and accused me of sleeping with her boyfriend. Now, mind you, she was dating two guys at the same time and just decided to wipe the slate clean and be with just one of them." She fumed at the idea of Kiera believing such lies.

"Where would she get an idea like that? I mean, did she just come up with the accusation or did she have a reason for saying it?"

"*He* told her that's what happened. She believed him over me—her best friend."

Rita clicked her tongue in disbelief. "Why would he lie like that?"

"I don't know. They were out at dinner or something and he accused her of wanting to be with the guy she broke up with. It was probably an act of revenge. I don't know. Who knows how these brothers think." The doorbell rang and interrupted their conversation.

"Were you expecting anybody?" Rita stood up. "I'll get that if you want me to. I know you probably aren't too excited about the idea of seeing your friend, if that's her. I can tell her you're in the shower or that you're not here."

"You can get it. If it's her, let her in. I want to get to the bottom of this." Rita went to the door and looked through the peephole. There was a guy waiting out front.

Rita turned to Tonya. "There's some guy out there. He's medium height, brown skinned, and get this girl—it's darn near ninety degrees outside and he's wearing a starter jacket."

Tonya's body shook with laughter. "That's probably my brother, Reggie. Let his crazy behind in."

Rita opened the door and Reggie looked her up and down. Slowly, a wide grin spread across his face as he walked in. Shades covered his face as his eyes focused on Rita.

"Damn, Tonya. Why don't you ever introduce me to any of your fine friends like her?" he said, looking at Rita.

"Get on in here, silly, and you can quit that lying because I introduced you to Kiera." She knew that she would get a reaction from that statement. He claimed he didn't have those kind of feelings for Kiera, but she knew better.

He looked at her over the rim of his shades. "Now you know she don't count. I said some of your *fine* friends, not that chicken head." He took off his shades and ducked before getting hit by a pillow.

"While you're taking off your shades, you need to take that hot jacket off, too," Tonya said, laughing.

"Now why ya' gotta' talk about my jacket." He smiled, wiping invisible lint away from the white jacket. "A brother just trying to be all that and a bag of chips and you trying to mess his wardrobe up." He sat on the couch next to Rita. A little too close for her comfort.

Before the two could continue with their sibling games, Rita interjected. "I hate to run off, but I've stayed longer than I intended and I have to go home and get dinner started for that husband of mine."

"Now, you don't have to run off. You don't have to leave just because that pipsqueak of a brother of mine dropped by."

"Yeah, Rita, you *don't* have to go. Since Tonya didn't properly introduce us, my name is Locksley, Reggie Locksley." He held her hand in his. "Did you catch my James Bond impression?" He leaned over to kiss her on the hand. She snatched it away before his lips could touch it.

She eyed him narrowly. "Yes, James Bond, I caught it. My name is Rita *Happily Married*. It's nice to meet you." She turned to Tonya. "See ya', girlfriend, and I hope you and Kiera can patch up the friendship." She grabbed her purse and headed toward the door.

"I'll walk you out," Reggie offered.

"No, thank you. I can find my way out."

After Rita left, Reggie gave a low whistle and clapped his hands together. "Whoo-weeee, that woman is *ffff-fine*. You never intro me to your friends like that." He sat back down on the couch.

"Reggie pl-lease. Ramona will kick your butt if you go out with a *real* woman. You need to stop bargain-basement shopping and get you some quality merchandise."

"Don't go bringing Ramona into this. Ramona *is* a real woman."

She gave him the "talk to the hand" motion. "Whatever floats your boat, to each his own, as you like . . ."

"Enough with the clichés. What did she mean by you and Kiera patching up the friendship?" By this time, the starter jacket was off. Even *he* wasn't cool enough to keep that hot jacket on.

"We sort of fell out. She came over here early this morning accusing me of sleeping with Myron."

"What do you want with him? She didn't try to come up in here swingin' did she?" Tonya loved the way her brother could describe a situation and she laughed at the thought.

"No, she didn't try to come up in here *swingin'*."

Reggie looked at her and smiled. He went to the

kitchen and grabbed a coke from the refrigerator. He laughed out loud and almost doubled over with laughter as he walked back into the living room.

"What is so funny?" Tonya asked, smiling.

"I mean—I would hate to have to tell my boys that you got your butt kicked in your own place. No family of mine gets beat down in their own crib."

"Now you know the deal. I can't go out like that. By the way, have you talked to Kip? I haven't talked to him since I moved."

"Man, Kip is too busy running around with them winos. He doesn't have a job and ain't looking for one. Don't worry, he'll call when he needs some money."

"I just worry about him. Actually, I worry about both of you. At least you have your barber shop—even if you don't go to work."

"Hey, partner, I've been going to work. Oh, and guess who came in to get his hair cut."

Tonya frowned, trying to think of someone she would know. "I don't know. Is it someone I know well?"

He finished the last of his coke. It was amazing how little time it took him to finish a can of Coke and it took her almost half an hour. "Yeah, you know him very well. I know it's killing your brain to have to think so hard so I'm going to help you out—David."

"David? I should have known. You know, I ran into him at the club last night."

"I thought he moved to Chicago or New York or somewhere. What's that punk doing looking you up?"

"I don't know. He said he wants to talk about some unfinished business."

Reggie's mouth dropped in disbelief. "Unfinished business? Doesn't he know that his business with you went bankrupt over a year ago?"

"I'm trying to tell you." Tonya agreed with Reggie. *How*

*could David just waltz back in and think he's going to pick up
where he left off?*

"You probably want to go out with him—huh? You
know how soft you can get."

"No, I don't. I don't miss David at all." She wondered
whether she was telling the truth or not, but figured it
didn't matter since she wasn't going back to him.

"You must have someone to go out with. Are you seeing
somebody, 'cause if you are, I need to check the brother
out. You know, we need to have a man-to-man talk." He
flexed his muscles as he said this or at least as much of
the muscles as he had.

She knew it was coming. Reggie could never leave without bringing up the subject of her and who she happened
to be dating.

"As a matter of fact, I'm not seeing anyone. I don't
have time to get involved." She couldn't look him in the
face. She wanted to get involved, but was too afraid of
being hurt. Just when you think you know someone, secrets come out that hurt everyone involved. She couldn't
take any more secretive behavior.

Reggie looked at her out of the corner of his eye. "I
know that look. You've found someone, haven't you?"

She tried to suppress a smile. "Not really. We haven't
gone out or anything."

"Tell me about him. What does he do? Does he have
a criminal record? Better yet, get his social security number so I can look the brother up. But most importantly,
please, *please*, make sure the brother has his sexuality in
order cause you know there's a lot of half-n-half brothers
running around. You know—half man, half *wo*-man," he
said, shaking his hand sideways.

"Oh, please. I'm pretty sure he's not half-n-half. His
name is Dexter and his father owns the firm that I work
for. He probably has women all over him."

Reggie stared at her dreamy look and shook his head.

If she hadn't already fallen for the guy, she would soon. He listened to her ramble on and on about why he wasn't right for her or why she wasn't interested in him. "You like him. I don't even want to hear about his faults or he's too this or that. You like him. So, does he have a last name?"

"Of course, silly. His last name is Freeman. What do you want to know for? It's not like you know him or something." The chances of Reggie knowing Dexter were slim, since he liked hanging with neighborhood lowlifes.

"I wouldn't say that because you know my shop is a pretty happening place for the big-time brothers, too. I don't discriminate, everybody's money is green. That name sounds familiar. I think I cut his hair sometimes. Isn't he from out of town somewhere?"

There is no need to worry! Its probably not the same Dexter. "As a matter of fact he is. But we could be talking about two different people. I just can't believe the world is that small."

"Well, we'll see in a few seconds. You can tell me if it's a different Dexter or not then." Reggie took out his wallet and pulled out a tan-colored business card and handed it to Tonya.

She took the business card and looked it over before handing it to him. They were definitely talking about the same person. "Okay, maybe the world is small."

"Nah, girl. Just admit that we travel in the same circles." Reggie laughed.

"Whatever, Reggie. We don't travel in the same circles. You never see me hanging around the corner store. Our circles just overlapped briefly, that's all."

"You are in denial. They all say that admittance is the first step to recovery. Now repeat after me. We travel in the same circles . . . we travel in the same circles . . ." he said, laughing as he looked into Tonya's eyes as if he were trying to hypnotize her. He couldn't stop laughing.

"I've always known you had a mental problem, Reggie. Please don't make me have to admit you into Charter Hospital," Tonya said, smiling. "So, you cut his hair sometimes."

"Yeah, he comes in to the shop every now and then. He won't let anybody cut his hair, but me. He said he lives out of town. When he's here, he makes his way into the shop or I go to him. You know I'm not at the shop that much, so I gave him my pager number."

She didn't know why she was surprised. She criticized her brother about being trifling, but his barber shop was doing pretty well. Maybe that's why he wouldn't go to work—maybe he didn't have to.

"Man, Reggie, do you have to know everybody?" Tonya whined.

"Don't hate me 'cause I'm popular." They both erupted with laughter. "But, listen, sis, I have my reservations about that brother. He seems like he's a few years older than you and like he's been around the block a little more. I just think he's running games. Don't get me wrong, he's cool, but I don't know about him. He doesn't seem like a one-woman man."

Maybe he knows something that I don't. "Why do you say that?" She knew her brother was only trying to protect her. Sometimes she felt he went too far.

"He's just too suave for me—a pretty boy. A dude like that, with all the paper he makes, I just can't see him with one woman. Don't get me wrong when I say this, but he probably won't settle for the average-looking woman—not that you're average. I'm talking about a *beautiful woman.* A brother like him is going to have him a runway model kind of woman. You understand?"

"I hear what you're saying. I won't waste my time." *Who am I trying to convince, him or me?* A gut feeling told her that he was right.

"Yeah, right. I told you not to get involved with that

punk David. But, did you listen? Look, sis, I don't want to see you get hurt again."

It touched her when either one of her brothers showed how much they cared. They would walk around, trying to be so hard. Whenever she caught a rare glimpse of their sensitive side, she relished it. She went to her brother and gave him a big hug. "I know you're just looking out for me. Thanks."

His masculinity emerged and he wriggled out of her embrace. "Alright, girl, that's enough of that. I don't want you getting me all wrinkled." His pager went off before she could respond. He pulled the pager off and looked at the number, frowning. "Man, it's Ramona. I gotta' go."

Tonya took the pager from him. "Where are you going? How high did she ask you to jump? What's up with that? Looks like *somebody* runs things."

He took the pager from her, stuffed it in his pocket and put on his jacket. "Don't even go there. You already know who runnin' this relationship. Ain't but one somebody wearing the pants." He tugged at his jeans.

"Yeah, I know—*she is.*"

He opened the door and gave his sister a good-bye hug. "Now you think about what we talked about. What's the new word we learned today?" That was a game that she and her brothers had shared since they were kids. When one learned a new word, they shared it with the others.

"What—*half-n-half*?" She laughed at her own joke. She knew very well what the word was, but she didn't want to hear it.

"Nah, goofy. The new word of today is—*player*. See ya' later and call Mom before she has a cardiac arrest. Remember—*player*. Leave him alone. Gotta' run."

She closed the door behind him. Slowly but surely, she was beginning to believe that Reggie knew more than he let on. She hoped Reggie wouldn't tell their mother about this. He had such a big mouth and couldn't keep water to himself. She went to the kitchen and grabbed a champagne glass from the shelf. She had been saving a bottle of Dom Perignon for a special occasion. *I guess this is as gooda time as any.* She watched the liquid bubble as it filled the glass and savored the taste as it touched her tongue and slid down her throat. She grabbed the bottle and walked slowly into the living room. The phone began to ring. She contemplated not answering it. *What if it's Mama?* She didn't want to worry her, so she picked it up.

"Hello."

"Tonya, what's going on over there? Reggie called me and told me something about you and Kiera fighting. Are you okay?" Her mother asked. *Man, Reggie just left and Momma's calling already!*

"I'm fine, Mom. It's not as bad as it sounds," she said sluggishly. "We didn't have a physical fight, only an argument." The champagne was starting to take effect. The room was starting to spin slightly and she sprawled across the couch.

"What was this argument all about? Knowing Kiera it had to do with some man."

She knew that Reggie had told her what it was about. He probably added extra hype in to make it sound good. "What did Reggie tell you?"

"He said that Kiera came over this morning and accused you of sleeping with some man she was seeing and she slapped you and that he had to come over and what was the word that he used? *Regulate.* He said he had to regulate and call the police."

She knew it. *That lying Reggie.* Her mother rambled on and on. She took the receiver from her ear and looked at it before replacing it. She closed her eyes. "Mama, you know how Reggie is. The arguing part of it all is true, but the fighting is a lie. There is no way I'd do something like that."

"That lying Reggie. Lord have mercy, I don't know where he gets it from. He's been lying since he was old enough to talk. I was just about to say that that didn't sound like something Kiera would do. Still, two best friends arguing over something like this is silly. Maybe you need to reevaluate who you consider to be your friends. This shouldn't have happened to best friends. I'm very disappointed in both of you."

"It wasn't my fault. I haven't a clue as to what she was talking about. She went out to dinner with this guy and let him fill her head up with lies, what was I to do? I told her to leave and when she calmed down, call me." Her mother was completely silent as her daughter explained details of the argument.

"That's just crazy. What was she thinking about? While she's out fighting and making a fool of herself, he's in the arms of some other woman. You should never lower your standards for anybody or anything. Oh, well, I guess I won't be seeing her around anymore."

"I don't know. How can you be best friends with someone you don't trust? I know you liked Kiera, but this is going to take a little time." Her voice slurred when she spoke. She had to get off the phone or else.

"I understand. I'll let you go. Get some rest while you're moping around the house and put the champagne down. I think you've had enough for the evening."

"I will. I love you, Ma."

"I love you, too, baby."

She finished off the bottle of champagne and didn't remember falling asleep.

Four

The next morning she woke with the worst headache that she'd ever had. Was she dreaming or was the phone actually ringing all night? She had spent the night on the couch and there was the lingering taste of alcohol on her breath. *Ooh . . . dragon breath.*

She walked into the bathroom and picked up her toothbrush. As she was brushing her teeth, the phone rang.

"Not again. It's too early in the morning for sales people to be soliciting anything," she said agitatedly and grabbed the phone. "Whatever you're selling, I'm not interested." After the night before, her personality wasn't one that someone would welcome.

"I haven't offered anything yet," a male voice responded.

"You don't have to offer anything because I'm not interested."

"Gee, that's too bad. I was hoping maybe you wanted to go to lunch."

This was the strangest sales call she had ever received before. It made her go *hmmm!* "Do I know you?"

"This is Dexter Freeman. Did I catch you at a bad time?" He knew he was taking a chance by calling her, nothing hurt but a try. After she ran out on him at the party Friday night, he wondered if he had done something to offend her.

She couldn't believe it. The man was so persistent. "No. It's not a bad time." She still had toothpaste in her mouth and had to rinse it out. "Actually, I need you to hold on for a moment." She ran into the bathroom and rinsed the remaining toothpaste from her mouth.

He had been apprehensive about calling her. The guy that was giving her problems at the club didn't seem to want her to give anyone else any attention. Maybe that guy was her ex and he had finally gotten back in her good graces. He strained his ears to see if he could hear the sound of a male voice in the background. He heard nothing except the sound of running water. That was a good sign.

"Sorry about that." She returned to the phone, puzzling over what his call was regarding. Maybe he was calling about Mr. Freeman assigning her to work with him for the next week. She quickly ruled that out, because she knew of no one who would waste a perfect weekend worrying about the upcoming work week.

"That's quite alright. I was wondering if you were okay. After you ran out the other night, I started to get worried about you. You know, my offer still stands to help you with any work you need to get done."

Her mind reeled with suspicion. How did he get her number and why was he so concerned? She knew it wouldn't take this long for him to call and check on her if he was *supposed* to be so worried about her. "I don't mean to be rude," she said, "but, how did you get my home number?"

"Someone from the office gave it to me. Do you mind? I hope it's not a problem."

Yes, I do mind. "That depends on who that someone is." Had she known he was calling, she would have let the answering machine pick up. A small investment in a Caller ID would have been nice just for a time like that.

"If you socialize enough, you'll have connections. Let's just say that I have my methods."

"I guess stalking is one of your methods."

"Stalking is a bit extreme, don't you think?" he asked.

"Why go through so much trouble to get in touch with me?" All of the game playing was starting to get old. *Just what do you want?*

"Believe me. It was no trouble at all. Actually, I called to see if you would like to go to lunch today." He cleared his throat to remove the feeling that his words were choking out of his throat. Maybe he was pushing it. It was bad enough calling her up out of the blue for something other than business. If she hung up on him, he would feel as though he had gotten what he deserved.

He talked with too much confidence for her. Tonya was sure that he wasn't used to being rejected. He probably thought she would jump at the chance to go out with him. Well, she wasn't going to be another woman on his bandwagon. "Actually, I'm going to be busy. I've already made other plans." She was anxious to see how he would respond to that.

Her answer took Dexter by surprise, but he concealed it quickly. He consoled his ego with the fact that she didn't actually come out and say the word no, only that she had other plans. Maybe she was playing hardball. She didn't need to worry because he wasn't going to be brushed off that easy. "I guess your friend from the other night would be upset if you went out with another man."

She didn't necessarily agree with Dexter referring to David as her man, however, she wasn't going to leave the door open by saying she wasn't involved with anyone. "I'm sure he would, some men can be really jealous." In a small way, she wanted to say yes to Dexter's lunch invitation. Out of consideration for her heart, she couldn't risk getting involved in something she was sure wouldn't work.

"Is that right?" he laughed.

Tonya failed to see any humor in what she said. Maybe he laughed because she didn't sound convincing enough. "That's right," she answered curtly.

"Well, I wouldn't want to interrupt your plans," he said. "I'll give you a call later when I think you're free." He hung up before she could tell him not to call her again. He didn't want her to get the impression that he was going to put his life on hold until she broke up with the person she was seeing. There was something about Tonya that made him beside himself.

Tonya's hands were sweating and she felt clammy. She cursed herself for getting all worked up over a phone call. How could someone she's known for such a short time have that kind of control over her?

The next week went by quickly. She hadn't heard anything from Dexter since that Sunday. Part of her wondered why he hadn't called her since then. After all, this was the week that she was supposed to start working with him. Tonya found herself *wanting* to work with him and checked her voice mail regularly during the day to see if he had called. She almost felt bad about brushing him off the way she had.

First-year associates are the low man on the totem pole and didn't have the luxury of turning down assignments. Their main purpose is to assist upper-level associates and partners with their workload. Thus, when Tonya was asked to assist in the medical malpractice section, she had to go. The attorneys in medical malpractice were preparing to go to trial on a plastic surgery gone wrong case. It was affectionately called *The Joker Case*. The Joker Case was a medical malpractice case that involved a lady who wanted plastic surgery done on her face to remove skin wrinkles. Well, the surgeon removed the wrinkles, but he pulled the skin too tight. She was stuck with a permanent smile, a smile that looked exactly like the Joker from Batman. She had to have several surgical procedures to make her look normal again.

Assisting the med mal group turned out not to be too much of a big deal. It was mainly what Tonya considered time-passing work. Time-passing work was just adding the finishing touches to the trial preparation. The only time-consuming thing was the trial notebooks, of which there had to be several copies.

Tonya didn't mind the time-passing work because she didn't have to think about personal issues. Kiera was one issue she hadn't allowed herself to deal with. However, on this particular afternoon, she couldn't get Kiera off her mind. Since she and Kiera had been on bad terms, Rita was the only friend she had to talk to about her problems or just to talk to in general. Tonya mused that it just was like Kiera not to call her. Kiera more than likely realized that she was wrong and hated to admit it. Then, it could be, Kiera really did hate her.

More than Tonya wanted to admit, she missed her best friend—if she could still call Kiera that. Tonya tried calling Kiera, but the answering machine kept coming on. Tonya called late at night in an attempt to catch her at home. When that failed, she called her early in the mornings. All of her attempts to catch up with Kiera failed. Tonya hoped nothing had happened to her. A knock at the door interrupted her thoughts.

Tonya welcomed the sight of Rita with a smile. "This is a pleasant surprise. I thought you put me down since I had to go to the malpractice section."

"Nah, you're still on my team. How are things going?" Rita sat in the chair in front of Tonya.

"I think the Joker case is going to settle." Tonya was a little disappointed because she wanted to go to trial. She wanted to know the joy of winning.

"That's good. How much money are we talking?"

"Oh, not that much, just eight million dollars."

"The things I could do with eight million." Rita laughed.

"I'm trying to tell you. Have you seen Dexter around? I was supposed to work with him this week. I think it's kind of strange that he hasn't surfaced yet."

Rita looked at Tonya with a smug expression on her face. She knew her friend wanted to know Dexter's whereabouts for other reasons. "No, I think he went home until Thursday. I heard through the grapevine that he was at some charity event the other night."

Tonya didn't want to ask the question that was nagging at the back of her mind, but she was going to anyway. "Was he with someone?" She tried to be as nonchalant about it as possible.

Rita looked at her and smiled a knowing smile. "Yes. My source said that he was with some woman. I'm not quite sure who she was though."

Tonya could feel her heart drop to the pit of her stomach. He didn't waste any time before he found someone else to go out with. There she was waiting around for him to call or wishing he would drop by her office and he wasn't thinking about her. Reggie was definitely right about Dexter not being a one-woman man. He'd probably had a backup plan all along.

"That's good." Tonya forced a smile and leaned back in her chair.

"You like him, don't you?" Rita seemed to be certain that Tonya had a thing for Dexter and was only confirming what she thought.

Tonya's face began to warm. For some reason, she couldn't look Rita in the face. "Please! Why do you say that?" Was it that obvious? She was certain that her blushing would give her away.

"I can tell by the way you're acting. You can't look me in the face."

"You've got it all wrong. I didn't approach him, he approached me. He called me last Sunday wanting to know if I wanted to go to lunch." She smiled at the recollection of his call.

"Did he?" Rita clasped her hands over her knees. "Where did you have lunch?"

"I didn't go." Rita's unbelieving stare compelled her to explain her inactions. "I didn't want to look like I was starving for a date, so I told him I had other plans."

"What? I know you left the door open for lunch at another time, right?"

"I told him that my ex and I had other plans."

"You did what?" Rita covered her mouth with her hand, as if Tonya had made a big mistake. "Why? You're not dating anyone, are you?"

"Of course not. I didn't want Dexter to think I was willing to change my plans to accommodate him. I'm not desperate. I do have a life, you know."

"I think you're being too uptight about this. It's obvious something about him appeals to you. He seems to be interested in you and you in him, you should have said yes. Unless, of course, you don't take him seriously. You never know, you two probably could have had something special. But, you'll never know until you try. He could be Mr. Right."

"Or Mr. Wrong."

"Exactly—or Mr. Wrong. Don't lose any sleep over it. If it's meant to happen it will all work out. I would love to finish counseling you on your love life, but I've gotta' run. I've got a million things to do and only a couple of hours to get them done."

Tonya returned home to the emptiness of her apartment. She decided to get some cleaning done and picked up clothes and sorted them to be washed. She scrubbed the bathroom and cleaned the kitchen. She had been thinking about getting someone to clean up for her twice a week, but if she did, she would have nothing left to do. It was pitiful that her life had no excitement besides cleaning her apartment. After her cleaning and scrubbing were done, she picked up the phone to call her mother. She placed the phone to her ear and heard no dial tone. There was a voice on the other end of the line.

"Hello." She frowned. The phone didn't ring.

"Hi. It's Dexter."

Her heart skipped a beat. *Don't get too excited, play it cool.* "Hi." She picked up the base of the phone and noticed that the ringer was off. It must have been switched off accidentally.

"I'll get straight to the point. This call is not about business and I know it's a week night, but I was wondering if you were busy tonight." He didn't realize he was rambling.

"No, I'm not busy," she answered.

"Would you like to go out, you know, if you're not busy or anything?" He didn't know what he would do if she turned him down again. He wasn't going to beg, but having a tantrum wasn't beneath him.

Something deep inside of her told her to say no. *Player, player!* Her brother's words echoed in her mind. Her voice of reason overruled the warning. What could one date hurt? "I'd like that. What did you have in mind?"

He couldn't believe she said yes without him having to coerce her into going out with him. He was nothing short of prepared to throw a fit if she said no. "Maybe we could have a late dinner. How about I pick you up at nine?"

She gave him the directions to her apartment and mulled over what she was going to wear. She didn't want to wear anything seductive, so she decided on a long black and white skirt that reached her ankles. It was a slim-fitting skirt that complemented her figure. She chose a black sleeveless top to match. She combed her hair into place and added a touch of magenta mist lipstick as a final touch. It was just right.

Dexter arrived at nine on the dot. She didn't open the door until he knocked. He was wearing a black shirt that clung to his well-defined chest and stone-washed jeans that emphasized a firm butt and muscular legs.

"Hi," she said with a smile. She was smiling so hard, the muscles in her face hurt.

"Hi, yourself," he said, smiling down at her. "You ready to go?"

"Yes. Let me get my purse and we're off." She went to the couch and grabbed her purse. "Where are we going?"

"It's a surprise. You'll see." His arm draped casually across her shoulders as he led her to his champagne-colored Acura.

The sweet smell of leather filled her nostrils as she eased into the seat. The sunroof slid back and the night air poured into the car. The melodious sound of Brian McKnight was soothing to her ears. She watched him handle the car with ease. *He's definitely sure of himself.* He caught her stare and smiled that darling smile at her. Her heart melted. *So, what if he's a ladies' man? So, what if he wants the runway model kind of woman?* Tonight he was with her and that's all that mattered.

The car pulled into the garage of the Mills High-Rises. These apartments were some of the most luxurious in Houston. The gray marble floors of the lobby glistened. They took the elevator to the very top floor. He opened the door to the penthouse. It was beautiful. There was a white spiral staircase leading upstairs encased in glass. The stars and moon could be seen clearly through the skylight. It was definitely a bachelor's place. They walked across a black and white marble checked floor on to snow white plush carpet. He led her into the living room where a romantic, candlelight picnic was waiting.

She had to admit that she was impressed. A huge picnic basket was placed on the edge of the blanket and there was a bottle of wine chilling.

"Wow, you really know how to surprise your women." She shouldn't have said that. She knew she wasn't his woman, at least not yet.

Dexter took her by the hand and led her to the picnic. "Does that make you my woman?"

"That didn't come out right." She laughed nervously as she stepped onto the blanket.

Dexter stood in place, pulling her away from the blanket. "The rule is, we take our shoes off before we sit. May I?" He squatted and reached for her gold sandal. She was a little reluctant having a stranger play around with her feet, but didn't object. He removed one sandal and then the other before helping her ease down on the blanket. She thanked God that she had recently had a pedicure. He sat down opposite of her.

"This is a lovely place you have here."

"Thank you. This is my home away from home. This is where I spend most of my time when I'm here in Houston. I'm glad you like it. Would you like some wine?" He held up a wine glass.

"Yes, please." She curiously eyed the large basket. "May I?" She gestured toward it.

"Yes, be my guest."

She opened the basket and emptied out it's contents. There was smoked salmon, fresh bagels, cream cheese, strawberries, grapes and other goodies. The basket was filled to the max.

"This looks delicious. I have just one question." She looked at the massive spread as he fumbled with the cork on the wine bottle.

"What question might that be?" He stopped fussing with the bottle long enough to hear the answer to his question.

"Just who is going to eat all of this? This is so much food."

He laughed at the question. At first, he was slightly tense because of her expression, but he was relieved to know she was thinking on the light side of things.

"I didn't know what you like or dislike, so I put together a variety of things to choose from. You might not have liked salmon, so I decided to put in a little bit of everything just to be on the safe side."

That was a good sign. It was a sign that he was a planner and she liked that in a man. After her second glass of wine, she felt comfortable with him and pretty much felt free to ask him whatever came to mind.

"So, what is a man like you doing single? Why aren't you attached?" There was an unreadable expression on his face before he answered. He seemed to be choosing his words carefully. She hoped she hadn't asked the wrong question.

"I think that before a person, not just myself, but before anybody decides to make a commitment to someone, they should make sure that the person they are with is the right one." Dexter wished he had thought of that before he married Melissa.

Tonya noticed how he had danced around the question. *What does his answer mean? Does it mean that he's looking for a permanent relationship?* "So, I take it there isn't anyone in your life right now?" She wanted to know. There was no need for her to get involved with him if he wasn't available. Again, there was the unreadable expression and a moment too long of silence before he answered.

"No, there's no one in my life right now." He quickly changed the subject.

She didn't pursue the subject and was content letting him control the conversation. He went on to ask her about her educational background, her likes, and her dis-

likes. Time passed quickly and when they finally looked
at the clock, it was twelve forty-five.

"I didn't realize that it was so late." Dexter looked at
the clock on the wall and back to Tonya. He hadn't
planned on keeping her out so late, especially since it
was a week night. If it wasn't a shame he would ask her
to spend the night. Knowing what her answer would be
to that suggestion, he opted not to ask.

"I guess I should be getting you home."

"I guess so. I've got to be up early tomorrow." The
ride home was pleasant and he walked her to her door.

"I enjoyed dinner. I've never been to an indoor picnic
before, it was lovely."

"As I've told you once before, I'm always willing to try
something different."

When she turned to unlock her door, Dexter fought
with the thought of kissing her lips. If he did, she might
get the wrong idea about him—well it wasn't all wrong.
Should he, shouldn't he?

"Am I something different?" *Why did I ask that question?
He probably thinks I'm throwing myself at him.*

By this time, he was looking down into her eyes. "Oh,
most definitely." Those were the words he murmured as
his lips touched hers.

Just as the kiss began to deepen she heard the door
open behind her. They broke apart and she turned to
see David standing in her doorway. She could not believe
it. "What are you doing here?" She was confused. How
could this happen to her, especially when her date with
Dexter had gone so well? David looked from Tonya to
Dexter.

David's eyes focused on Dexter. "I used my key and it
looks like I came out just in time."

"Your key? What do you mean your key?"

Dexter remembered his face as that of the man from
the club. For some reason he couldn't put his finger on,

he didn't like him. He was reluctant to leave her with this man, although he knew she had a history with him. "Tonya, do you need me to stay?" He glared at David. Dexter was beginning to see this man one too many times.

"Ah, ah . . . no. I think I can handle this," she stammered.

"You didn't seem to have a problem handling it last night," David said with a sneer.

"Last night?" Dexter looked from Tonya to David. "What's going on here?"

"What do you mean last night? I haven't seen you since that night at the club. Don't even try it, David." She faced Dexter. "There is nothing going on here, he's lying. Just let me handle this, okay?" She was pleading for him to understand. As messed up as it looked, she hoped he would understand.

"Alright." Dexter raised both hands up and backed away. "I'll call you later."

David quickly answered for Tonya. "Nah, she won't be receiving any phone calls tonight, she'll be busy."

Tonya stood with her mouth gaped open. This was unreal. Dexter walked away before she could reassure him that it was okay for him to call. She couldn't begin to imagine what it must have looked like to him. She was filled with rage. How could David do this to her?

"What is going on and why are you in my apartment!" She was literally yelling at the top of her lungs? He ushered her inside, as if he didn't want to make a scene.

"I told you that we were going to talk. I knew you wouldn't take any of my calls and you wouldn't let me come by to see you. I *had* to do this."

"You had to do this! How did you get in here?" She threw down her purse. She was angry enough to slap him.

"Just calm down, okay. I told the manager that you hadn't been answering your phone for a few days and that the family was worried about you. I told him I would lock up when I left."

"You did what? Who were you supposed to be? You aren't in my family?"

"I told him I was your brother. I know you're angry, but hear me out. I need to talk to you. Would I do something like this if I wasn't desperate?"

"Desperate or not, this is unacceptable and I'm about to call the police." She moved swiftly to the phone and picked it up.

"Tonya, please don't do this. I love you and I need to know if you still love me. If you can look at me and honestly tell me that you don't have any feelings for me I will leave and never bother you again."

She looked him directly in the eyes. "There is nothing left between us to talk about."

He closed the distance between them and placed the phone back on the receiver. "Who was that man? Is that who you're seeing?"

"Yes, that's who I'm seeing and actually, it's none of your business." She knew she was lying. But anything would do in order to get this man out of her apartment.

"I'm sure he's nothing more than a rebound relationship. We've only been apart for a year. You can't possibly be serious about him so soon unless . . ."

"Unless what? You were the only person in our relationship doing the cheating." He had some nerve, trying to accuse her of ever being unfaithful to him. "How dare you try to come back into my life after a year has gone by? You've always had perfect timing. Just when I was about to put my life back together you show up." She went to the door and opened it for him to leave.

"I know it's been a long time and I should have tried to talk to you sooner but I'm here now. I see you need time to think about this, so I'll leave, but I'm not giving up on us." He headed toward the door.

"Oh, David."

"Yes?" He stopped short of the door.

"Give me the key."

"What key?"

"The key you asked the manager for." She held out her hand, waiting for him to put the key in her palm. He smiled because he knew she wouldn't let him get away with it.

"You don't miss a thing, do you?" He took the key out of his pocket and placed it in her hand. He raised the closed fingers to his lips. "You haven't changed at all. You're still smart, beautiful, and everything that you were before we parted." His arm slid around her waist.

"No, David, that's where you're wrong. The difference between then and now is that I've matured." She slipped out of his embrace and waited for him to walk out. She closed the door behind him. What if David had rummaged through her things? She could see him now—making himself at home in her apartment. *Nightline* had just done a special about people planting bugs in other people's homes. What if David had bugged her place? She checked her bedroom and bathroom, everything was in place except for the seat on the toilet being raised. When she made her round to the kitchen, she noticed that a wine glass had been placed in the sink and so was a plate. He had made himself so at home that he cooked himself an omelet and helped himself to a glass of wine—her wine! She threw the dirty dishes in the dishwasher. There was no need for him to get comfortable because he wasn't getting back into her life. David's presence had wiped thoughts of the lovely evening she had shared with Dexter out of her mind. A dream date, that's what it was. Possibly a dream that would turn into a nightmare and all because of David's intrusion. There was no excuse for her apartment manager to have given David a key to her apartment. What would have happened if they had let someone into her apartment she barely knew? What if that person turned out to be a murderer or a rapist?

The more she thought about it, the more upset she became. She picked up the phone and called the front office. She knew no one was there, but she was going to leave a message for the manager to call her.

To her surprise, someone answered the phone. "Sugar Creek Associates." The woman answered in an automated tone.

"I know it's late, but I was wondering if I could leave a message for Mr. Schultz. It's imperative that I speak with him at his earliest convenience."

"If this is an emergency, I can page Mr. Schultz and have him call you as soon as possible."

"Yes, that will be fine," Tonya said.

The woman took Tonya's name and phone number and promised to have Mr. Schultz call her as soon as possible. She paced around the living room, waiting for the phone to ring. After ten minutes of waiting, the phone rang. She answered it on the first ring.

"I received an emergency message and I'm calling to find out what the problem is," Mr. Schultz said.

"Mr. Schultz, this is Tonya Locksley. I live in apartment number twenty-five."

"Oh, yes, Ms. Locksley. Your brother was wondering if you were alright. He seemed to be very concerned about your well-being."

"That's just it, Mr. Schultz. The man you gave a key to my apartment is not my brother, he's my ex-boyfriend."

He seemed to be shocked by Tonya's statement. "What? He swore he was your brother and he said your family was worried about you. He promised he would give the key back after he had checked on you."

Tonya was not about to let Mr. Schultz off the hook. He made a mistake that very well could have cost her life. He made a careless mistake that could have had serious results. "Did you bother to check his identification?" There was a pause on the other end of the line. She took that to mean no. "How could you have let someone who claimed to be my brother into my home without identification?"

Mr. Schultz seemed to get frustrated. "Well, Ms. Locksley, what good would it have done to have his identification? I don't know who your brother is."

"First of all, Mr. Schultz, you shouldn't have given anyone a key to my apartment. You should have opened the door and walked with him through my apartment and escorted him out when it was apparent that I wasn't home. Second, all you had to do was look on my reference sheet, which is attached to the application that my parents filled out. I'm sure both of my brothers, as well as my aunt and uncle, are listed on that sheet."

"I apologize. I actually thought he was your brother. He seemed so desperate. I hope my actions didn't inconvenience you."

"I was most definitely inconvenienced by your actions. I want my locks changed. This incident was enough to make me want to relocate."

"Oh, no. We appreciate your business. What can we do to make this up to you?"

"There's nothing you can do to make it up to me. Change my locks and don't let it happen again."

"We'll get those locks changed for you and we can assure you that nothing like this will ever happen again."

"Make sure it doesn't." She clicked off the phone. She was tired of listening to him grovel on the other end of the line. He was probably afraid she would sue the properties. She should sue the properties, just to teach them a lesson. *Nah, it's not worth it. It will take up too much time and money.*

Five

"You're going to be working with me today," Rita told her when she burst into Tonya's office.

"Well, good morning to you, too. I've been working with you ever since I started here, in case you've forgotten." In spite of the bad ending to the previous evening, she was in a good mood.

"No, I haven't forgotten, but you've been with those malpractice people." Rita frowned as if she had eaten something bitter, then smiled. "Today, I'm meeting with a new client and I want you to be in the meeting, also."

Tonya hadn't expected to hear that. This meant that she would actually get to be involved if Rita took on this client. "Really, who is it and what is it about?"

"Now, don't faint when I tell you who it is."

"I promise. Who is it?"

"James Tanner." Rita waited for a response from Tonya, who stood with a blank expression on her face.

"Okay." *Who is James Tanner?*

"Well, aren't you excited?"

Tonya stared at Rita and waited for her to explain who James Tanner was. "Forgive me if my enthusiasm doesn't quite reach yours, but who is James Tanner?" She didn't want to seem like a recluse but she honestly didn't know who the guy was.

"Jimmy Tanzent! Jimmy Tanzent is going to be our client!" Jimmy Tanzent was a multimillionaire fashion designer famous for the Tanzent clothes line, Tanzent Productions, and JT eye wear.

"I'm sorry about the James thing. James uses Jimmy Tanzent as his business name. Where he got the name, I don't know."

Now Tonya could feel the excitement. "What does he need Freeman and Reynolds to do?"

"It appears that his mother married a wealthy man who owned an oil company. There was no prenuptial agreement and he was no longer working. The mother died, leaving a trust for Mr. Tanzent and his two sisters. After a certain age, which was thirty, they would get the money. Mr. Tanzent is thirty-five and has already started to receive his portion, but his two sisters won't start until the end of this year and mid-next year. They have no problem with the money, except the issue of community property. Do you know what that problem might be?"

Tonya put a finger under her chin and thought about the question. "Okay, they have community property and there's a trust. Well, wouldn't her half of the community property go to the children?"

"Gee, you're brighter than I thought. The catch-22 is, he had stocks and all other kinds of assets that were accruing interest. It's true that there was no income because he was retired, but there is always the interest on the income he had prior to retiring."

"So, what Mr. Tanzent and his sisters are getting doesn't include interest?"

"Exactly. We're talking millions of dollars in interest from a twelve-year marriage. This case could be big for Freeman and Reynolds. This could be the beginning of a very promising career for you. He's going to be here at eleven, so come by my office a little before the hour; then we'll meet Dexter and all go to the conference room together."

She wasn't too thrilled about seeing Dexter since their date ended on such a bad note. She'd waited for a call from him, but that call never came. However, she was a little curious as to what his reaction would be when he saw her again.

At ten minutes to eleven, Tonya met Rita in her office. Shortly after she arrived, Dexter walked in. "Are you ladies ready to meet with the client?" His eyes met Tonya's briefly before he stepped aside and waited for them to exit the office.

"Yes, we are," Rita answered for herself and Tonya.

"Then, let's do it." He made the statement, looking directly at Tonya.

Jimmy Tanzent turned out to be a polite as well as a handsome man. Tonya liked the charisma he emitted. He made it plain that he did not want to cause a family dispute with his step-father. The only thing he did want was to assure a secure future for his sisters.

Dexter controlled the flow of the meeting. Tonya had never seen Dexter work his magic in a courtroom or a meeting for that matter. This was her opportunity to see firsthand how intelligent the man was. Even though he was in the presence of one of the richest men in the world, he did what he did best.

Dexter scribbled some notes on his yellow notepad. "Mr. Tanzent, as you are well aware, we can make no guarantees as to the result of this action. However, we can assure you that our team will do our best to give you a pleasing outcome.

"We are going to have to contest the will, and right now it appears there is no clause in your mother's will that prohibits contestation. After reviewing all the facts, I would say that you have a good case and we understand your professional status. My colleagues and I will try to be as discreet as possible about this suit."

Jimmy smiled and took a sip of water before speaking.

"I have great confidence in all of you and I don't care how much money it takes to go through the process. I just want what rightfully belongs to my family."

They concluded the meeting and Tonya headed back to her office. Rita asked her to have lunch with her and they would talk more about Jimmy Tanzent.

Dexter seemed to be anxious about something. "Excuse me, Ms. Locksley, may I speak with you privately for a moment?" He told her he would call but in light of the way the evening ended, he thought maybe she would call when her visitor left. He had waited for her phone call in vain. Several times he resisted the urge to pick up the phone to see if she was okay. The only thing that kept him from calling, was the obvious need for her to speak with the guy waiting in her apartment. Maybe Tonya never called because her guest ended up spending the night. He was determined to find out where her head was.

Tonya wasn't sure Dexter would care to see her again. There was no telling what thoughts were running through his mind about David. "Sure, we can talk. Rita, I'll see you at lunch." She followed Dexter to his office. He closed the door behind them.

"I wanted to tell you that in spite of the way last night ended, I had a good time."

"So did I. I had a wonderful time, thank you."

Maybe if he talked to her for a while, she would clear up the misunderstanding at the end of their evening. "Oh, anytime. I hope we can get together again soon."

"That would be nice." Maybe another date would be an opportunity to tell Dexter the history of her and David.

He couldn't stand it anymore. "I . . . are you okay? Did everything go alright?"

"Yes, I'm fine. It was a strange situation, but I finally got him to leave."

He secretly sighed in relief. "I didn't know what to think after last night. That was the guy from the club, right?"

"Yes, that was David. Everything went as well as could be expected."

"I'm just concerned." He was stalling. He was sure she had enjoyed herself while she was with him, yet he was hesitant to ask her out again. *Where am I getting this shy thing from?* "Ah, Tonya, I was wondering if you would be free tomorrow night, maybe we could go to dinner."

"What time should I be ready?" After everything that had happened, she was delighted.

"Is eight fine?"

"Yes, eight is great." *Great, I'm rhyming now.* "I hate to cut our visit short, but I promised Rita I would meet her for lunch." She left his office, wondering why she wanted to go out with him so much. Reggie had warned her about him, but he didn't seem so dangerous to her. She would never know what kind of person he was if she didn't allow herself to get to know him, right?

"Ready to go to lunch?" she asked Rita.

"Yes, I'm ready. What did Dexter want?" Rita didn't miss a beat.

"It wasn't business related." Tonya couldn't help smiling when she told her this. Rita eyed her suspiciously.

"Then it was personal?" She led the way to the elevators.

"Rita! Come on. It had nothing to do with the office." Tonya knew Rita wouldn't give up until she found out. *Maybe the elevator will be crowded and I will be off the hook.* She pressed the button for the down elevator.

"I take it this is something maybe you don't want to discuss." The curiosity was about to get the best of her.

"Is it the attorney in you or are you just nosey?"

"I'm just plain old nosey." Rita laughed. "So . . ."

"Okay, he asked me out to dinner." Tonya stepped into the elevator.

"Well, it's about time." Rita smiled. "See, I told you not to count yourself out. How did all of this come about?"

"Actually, this will be our second time going out." She knew she was going to hear it then. Rita would be upset because she wasn't told about it first thing that morning.

"What? Why didn't you tell me? When was this?"

"Last night. We had a picnic at his penthouse last night."

"You work it then, diva! A picnic at the penthouse. Might be the one for you."

"I don't know about all of that. I'm not getting serious about it."

Rita took one look at Tonya and could see through that lie. "Yeah, right. Whatever you say. Let's go to lunch."

Six

Dexter wasn't supposed to pick her up until eight, but she was excited and started dressing over two hours early. It was typical Houston weather, hot and humid. The less clothing she wore, the better. She put on a fuchsia silk spaghetti-strap dress. It wasn't much of a dress, since it was only thigh length.

When she stepped out the door, Dexter stood motionless before asking her if she was ready to leave. She didn't know whether that was good or bad. It had to be all good, because she knew that dress was a hot number when she put it on.

"Excuse my expression, but you look really good tonight." She sure did look good to him. He almost asked her to order in dinner.

She grinned from ear to ear. "I'll excuse you this time since it was for a good cause."

"I hope you like seafood," he said after they were both in the car. "I was told about a good place to get some fresh seafood."

"Seafood sounds delicious. Where is it?"

"You're not in a hurry to get anywhere are you?"

"No, I'm in no hurry."

"Good, you'll see when we get there."

They drove forty minutes outside of Houston to Kemah, Texas. The restaurant turned out to be Landry's on the Lake. There was a thirty-minute wait before they were seated at a table on the patio, overlooking the water.

The waitress came over and asked them what they would like to drink. Tonya was reluctant to order anything stronger than a soda. She wanted to have full thinking capacity while out with this devilishly handsome man. If anything happened between them, she wanted to be fully conscious of every detail. Not that she planned for anything to happen, but if it did, it did.

"I'll have a coke, please," she told the waitress.

Dexter looked at her in disbelief and grabbed her by the hand. "Come on, it's Friday. Live a little. How about some chardonnay?"

"Maybe just one glass." Alcohol had a way of making everything funny. The world could be coming to an end and she wouldn't have the slightest care.

He couldn't take his eyes off her. The fuchsia complimented her chocolate features and the neckline of that dress dipped low enough to drive his imagination into overtime. Those full lips had been kissed by him only once and he longed to feel them over and over again. What was wrong with him? He wanted desperately to have her in his life, even if it was for just a little while. A little while was all he could hope for. Actually, a little while was too much to hope for.

She could feel his gaze wash over her face and down to her breasts. Somehow, she felt like she was the epitome of sensuality. There was no question about it, there was definitely chemistry between them.

Tonya's only problem sleeping with him would be the risk of giving up her heart as well. That was something she wasn't ready for. Sensuality was one thing, but love was another thing. Love was something that she wasn't capable of giving, not that either were looking for love.

Dexter had figured out that David was the reason for

Tonya's reserved attitude. He was no psychiatrist, but he hoped that if she talked about it, she could release some of her tension.

"Do you mind if I ask you a personal question?" Her easygoing attitude and light flirting ceased as soon as the words fell from his lips.

"That depends on how personal the question is." Why was it that people asked you *can I ask you something personal* shortly before probing into something they know is a touchy subject? Instead of looking at him, she played with her salad.

"Did you and this David person date long?" That wasn't so personal. Yet, an expression of pain crossed her face for a fleeting moment.

"Long enough. We were together a little over four years." She hated talking about David. The very mention of his name made her uneasy.

"What happened?" He, at least, wanted her to confide in him as a friend. They could be friends if nothing else. "If you don't want to talk about it I understand."

It took her what seemed to be a millennium to answer him. She noticed the other people dining. They were all huddled close to one another, sharing intimate glances and laughing at jokes, in which, only they found humor. The waters on the lake were calm, which was an enormous difference to how she felt inside. This was something she hadn't felt in what seemed like ages—the closeness and intimacy of a lover and a friend.

"Tonya, are you okay?" The voice gently called her back from the black depths of sadness.

"What?" She answered him with her eyes remaining fixed on the calm waters of the lake.

"I asked if you were alright." Where had her mind gone to that fast? Now he was certain that this David person was the source of her pain.

"I'm sorry. My mind just went out to sea, I guess. Do you mind if I don't answer that question?"

"I know we're not at the point where we have a trusting relationship, but I hope that one day you will trust me enough to tell me about your pain. Maybe one day you will consider me a friend. Who knows, maybe one day I'll tell you about my pain."

Tonya laughed softly. "I'm sure you haven't experienced pain before. Maybe a little disappointment, not pain."

Dexter laced her fingers between his. "We're all human and we all experience pain at some time in our lives. Trust me, I've experienced pain, though it may be a different kind of hurt. Enough of the past relationships, we have to concentrate on the relationship developing between us."

"Is that what we're working on—a relationship?" Those were his words, the only thing she wanted him to do was confirm what he said. She didn't want to be guilty of misconstruing anything he said.

"I would hope so. I don't want anything you don't want. If you think we can work out a relationship then that's fine with me. Don't think I'm trying to pressure you. We can start out as friends and if anything comes out of it we'll deal with it. Okay?" He released her hands and took a sip of his wine. He needed a strong drink after letting those words leave his lips. He was digging himself in deeper and deeper with Tonya every day. One day he would be buried alive by his very words. What was he going to do when everything started to fall apart?

"Okay." That was the end of that conversation and her plate of blackened fish over a bed of rice pilaf and his seafood platter was a welcome interruption. There was no way that she would be able to come out of her emotional shell anytime soon. Breaking open that shell would be something she had to work on. If he wanted her, he would have to want her for the person she was.

She no longer envied the secret smiles of others dining in the restaurant because the same smiles they had were hers to share at that moment. It was her turn to huddle up with someone special on the way back home. He walked her to the door.

"You've never really seen the inside of my place, would you like to come in?" She didn't want him to take her invitation as one to her bed. It was just a friendly gesture.

"I'll come in for a little while." That was all that he could stay. He wouldn't be responsible for his actions after that point.

She gave him the "Tonya grand tour" of the place.

"It's lovely," he said, looking around. "Did you do your own decorating?" As if he was interested in her decorations.

"Actually, my mother picked out everything. None of this," she said moving her arm in a sweeping motion around the room, "is me really, except for the windows. I have a thing for a lot of glass."

"Your mother has wonderful taste. I think she did a great job." Was his mind playing tricks on him or was that dress getting shorter every time he looked at it? His hormones were starting to work overtime.

"I'll be sure to tell her."

"Yes, do that."

Tonya glanced around her apartment, making a mental note of how much she enjoyed living there. An image of David lounging all over her furniture, making himself right at home dashed out the cozy image in her mind. It was then that the thought of David bugging her apartment sent chills up her spine. She had no idea what a bug looked like, but since Dexter was there, maybe he could look around for anything suspicious.

"Dexter, since you're here, would you mind looking

around my apartment for anything that seems suspicious? I can't get over the idea that David may have planted some sort of bugging device here."

"Bugging device?" Dexter laughed. "It seems to me that you've been watching too much television."

"I'm serious." Tonya slapped him playfully on the shoulder. "I wouldn't put anything like that beneath David."

"Okay, I'll take a look around." He agreed to look around only because he noticed that Tonya was truly disturbed by the thought of this David guy bugging her place.

After searching every place he thought perfect for a bugging device, Dexter concluded her place was bug free.

"Well," Dexter said, turning to Tonya, "it seems to me that there are no bugs here. I honestly don't think you have anything to worry about. Unless this guy is really sick, I think you can rest peacefully tonight."

Tonya sighed in relief. "Thank you. I feel so much better now. If a person would tell a lie to get into your apartment, there's no telling what else he may do."

"That's true," Dexter agreed. "This day and time, you never can be too careful."

"Can I get you anything to drink?"

"No, I'm fine. I guess I'd better be leaving." He thought it better to make an exit while he could control himself. He didn't know how long he could continue to ignore the longing he had for her.

"Okay, I enjoyed dinner." Tonya walked him to the door. She reached for the doorknob and he grabbed her hand.

"Wait . . . there's something I've been wanting to do all evening," he said. He cupped her face in his hands and gently kissed her on the lips. It had been a long time since she had felt a kiss so soft. She was taken off guard by that move. In actuality, she was expecting him to give her a hug instead of a kiss.

"Why did you want to do that?" She backed away slightly, trying to shake off the intoxication of his kiss.

"I couldn't help myself. You don't realize the effect you have on me." He kissed her again.

The kiss began to deepen. He didn't realize the effect *he* had on *her!* She could feel her body beginning to betray her. The more she thought she didn't want anything to happen between them, the more she yearned for it. She could feel his lips trailing down her neck. *This is starting to feel too good. This has to stop!* She could feel the buttons of her blouse being undone. Why wasn't she stopping him? A low moan escaped from her throat. *Traitor!* His body began to tremble with excitement as his lips touched the swell of her breast. She could feel the rapid beating of his heart or was it her heart? She had to do something.

"I've been thinking about this moment since I met you," he whispered.

Everything was happening too fast. They were only on their second date and they didn't know each other well enough. *Who was that woman you were with at that party?* What if she was his other woman? She wanted to know, but was too afraid to ask. Every question in her mind refused to manifest itself in her voice.

"Dexter, this has to stop. We don't know each other well enough." Instead of pushing him away, she held him closer to her.

"Well," he murmured as he massaged her shoulders, "you're about to get to know me well enough in a few minutes and that's a promise."

Dexter took her into his arms and carried her to the bedroom. After laying her gently on the bed, he began removing her clothes with such precision that Tonya knew he had known many women intimately. Her skin burned wherever his fingers touched.

After he had successfully removed all of her clothes, Dexter rolled onto his back, taking her with him. It was her turn to remove his clothes. Tonya let her fingers roam all over his body, memorizing every detail. She felt bold under his gaze. Just as she imagined, Dexter's body was perfect.

He planted hot kisses all over her body, letting his tongue taste and tease. When he tasted the center of her being, Tonya could have sworn that fireworks were bursting all around her. She found herself begging for more, begging to be released.

"Tell me what you want," Dexter commanded.

"I want you to make love to me." Tonya heard herself saying. David had never asked her what she wanted, he never expressed himself during their lovemaking. With Dexter, she felt free to say what she felt, free to unleash the passion she had been holding back for so long.

Dexter placed a long, passionate kiss on her lips. His fingers traced the outline of her brows. He caressed her face with his hand. "Are you on anything?"

Tonya's eyes popped open. "You mean the pill?"

Dexter smiled. "Yes, that's what I mean."

"No, I mean, I haven't exactly . . ."

"That's okay, I understand." Dexter interrupted. "I have some."

Tonya watched Dexter take a condom out of his wallet and open it. "I know you're not going to do that *here.*" She covered her eyes with her hands as he put it on.

"Why not? I know you're not shy."

"No, I'm not shy." Tonya peeked between her fingers. "I just thought you would, you know, turn your back or something."

"I'm a grown man, you're a grown woman, there's nothing to hide," he said as he slid into her embrace. "See, I told you that you would get to know me better."

And she did get to know him. She was familiar with all

six feet two inches of him. What was supposed to be a fifteen-minute tour of her apartment turned out to be all night, and what a night it was. She kept hearing a little voice saying, *He doesn't seem like a one-woman man.*

Seven

Tonya's mother was satisfied to see her daughter happy again. She knew Tonya had been hurt by David and she never expected to see Tonya happy again so soon. She insisted on preparing dinner and wanted Tonya to bring Dexter with her. Tonya wasn't sure Dexter was ready to meet her family at this point in their relationship. Tonya knew how much it meant to Ruth Locksley to meet her latest love interest and hoped Dexter wouldn't mind meeting her family. Tonya casually mentioned having dinner with her parents to Dexter and to her surprise, he accepted. Usually, when a woman invited the man she was seeing to meet her parents, the man would assume it meant marriage and chicken out. Not Dexter, he didn't bat an eye before saying yes to the invitation.

Dinner was scheduled for seven thirty. As usual, Dexter was on time. Of course, Tonya had a key to her parents house, but since Dexter was a guest she decided to ring the doorbell. Dexter, who was dressed casually nice, seemed to anticipate meeting Tonya's parents. He shifted the flowers he had in his arms to plant a light kiss on Tonya's lips. Just as he did so, Tonya's mother opened the door.

"I see all is well between the two of you." Mrs. Locksley smiled. She extended her hand to Dexter. "Hi, I'm Ruth."

Dexter took her hand. "I'm Dexter and these are for you." He handed the flowers to Mrs. Locksley.

"Oh, you shouldn't have." Mrs. Locksley took the flowers, smiling. "This is so nice of you." She opened the door wider. "Don't just stand out there, come in."

"Thank you." Dexter waited for Tonya to go into the house first before following.

"Dinner will be ready shortly. " Mrs. Locksley turned to Tonya. "Why don't you help me in the kitchen? You can show Dexter to the sitting room. You father is in there, I'm sure they'll be fine without us women hanging around."

While Tonya spoke with her mother, Dexter busied himself looking at the family pictures lining the Locksley walls. There was a picture that had a little girl, he presumed to be Tonya, with two little boys. The two boys appeared to be a little older than Tonya. They had what seemed to be a very nice family. There was a warmth about the Locksley household he never had at home.

The Locksley household was, by comparison, more inviting than his family's home had ever been. It had that lived-in appeal. Dexter's family's home looked more like a house out of *Better Homes and Gardens,* it appeared to be a showcase and very much like it hadn't been lived in. He let his finger slide over a brass frame with a picture of Tonya's family inside. The picture reflected what he thought to be genuine happiness. There were no snapshots in his home. Every picture taken in the Freeman home were professionally done. Dexter couldn't say there were no happy moments in his family, because there were many moments of happiness, but standing in Tonya's parents' home brought a certain sadness to his heart. It made him realize that his relationship with his parents seemed to be more of a business relationship than anything else. Dexter continued to finger the picture. His mind was long gone when Tonya returned to his side.

"You seem to be deep in thought." Tonya smiled and wrapped her arm around Dexter's. "What are you thinking so hard about?"

Dexter was overwhelmed by the sudden onset of loneliness he felt. He blinked quickly to hold back the trace of tears lining his eyes. He cleared his throat. "Ah, nothing. I was just admiring the pictures of your family."

Tonya got the feeling something was more than wrong. There seemed to be a sadness about Dexter she had never seen before. She decided not to press the issue with him. If there was something on his mind he wanted to share with her, he would do it in his own time. She gave his arm a comforting squeeze. "Let me take you in to meet my dad. He's in the sitting room watching the game."

Dexter didn't answer, he merely followed her lead to the sitting room, where Mr. Locksley was waiting.

Tonya went over to her father, who was sitting in his favorite recliner and gave him a hug. She turned in Dexter's direction. "Daddy, this is Dexter."

Mr. Locksley rose from his chair and extended his hand to Dexter. "Hi, I'm John Locksley. It's a pleasure to meet you." When Dexter took Mr. Locksley's hand and gave it a firm grip, Mr. Locksley smiled. Mr. Locksley took a firm handshake as that of a person who was very secure.

"The pleasure's all mine." Dexter noticed that Mr. Locksley was in great shape. He was nothing like he thought Tonya's father would be. Her father was very young looking for his age.

Tonya excused herself to help her mother in the kitchen. Mr. Locksley motioned for Dexter to have a seat. "You have a very nice handshake. A person's handshake tells me a lot about them. A firm grip shows self-assurance. A loose grip shows a lack of confidence. If there's one thing I can't stand, is a sloppy handshake. You're confident, I like that."

Dexter took a liking to Mr. Locksley immediately. He didn't know what it was about him, only that he liked him. "Thank you. I've never thought about it that way."

Mr. Locksley was about to answer when his basketball team did something he didn't agree with. His eyes were glued to the television. "That darn team is going to give me a heart attack. Every time the Rockets come back from halftime, they struggle to keep their lead."

Dexter laughed. Some people were so serious about their home teams. "I take it you're a die-hard Rockets fan." Dexter could identify with Mr. Locksley's enthusiasm because he was a big sports fan himself.

"I sure am. I can't be a fair weather fan. I'm a fan when it's all going good and I'm a fan in times like these. If the Sacramento Kings are giving us hell, you can imagine what those Bulls are going to do."

"I just think the Rockets are tired. You know, they've played back to back the last three games. I think since we've got a pretty good starting team, we'll do okay against the Bulls. Rudy should let those rookies play in the first half and pull out the more experienced legs in the second half. Our bench players are pretty good, but they don't get enough playing time to get more experience."

Mr. Locksley took a sip of lemonade and smiled a wide grin at Dexter. "That's what I'm talking about. There's nothing like an optimistic fan. Why can't everybody think like that? I agree with your theory. Rudy T. should let those youngsters play the first half. They have younger and stronger legs. These other teams are all young. We're an old team and can't be running the full forty-eight minutes. Those other teams will run us to death. The forth quarter is what kills us."

"I know what you mean. Are you going to the game on Sunday?"

"Nah, the tickets were all sold out. You know how Chicago can pack an arena. It would be something to see though, especially since Houston is the underdog in the series."

Dexter thought for a hard moment before continuing the conversation. "Well, I have season tickets. I was planning on going to the game myself. You're welcome to go with me, if you like." Dexter could tell he had struck a nerve with Mr. Locksley, it was the only time his eyes reverted from the television for a long moment.

"I couldn't impose. I'm sure there's someone else you're more acquainted with who would like to go."

"No, there's no one else. You wouldn't be imposing at all." Dexter hoped Mr. Locksley didn't get the impression he was trying to get in on his good side to be close to Tonya. Actually, Dexter could have gone to the game with his own father, but he didn't want to be in his company.

"Well, okay. I would love to go. Should I meet you at the Compact Center on Sunday?"

"How about I pick you up? It will be much easier for us to ride together." When Dexter thought about it, he was starting to look forward to going to the game with Tonya's father.

"That sounds like a plan."

"What sounds like a plan?" Tonya and her mother entered the sitting room at the end of the conversation.

"Dexter and I are going to the game on Sunday. I was just telling him how I wanted to go to the game, but it was sold out. It turns out that he has season tickets."

"That's so nice of you," Mrs. Locksley said to Dexter. "You don't realize what you've done. John is a sports fanatic. You'll never get rid of him now."

Dinner went as smoothly as could be. There wasn't a shortage of conversation all evening. After three hours of talking about everything from politics to work, dinner finally concluded.

"I think what you're doing for my dad is sweet," Tonya told Dexter on their way to her apartment. "You didn't have to offer to take him to the game, but you did and I think that's good of you."

Dexter's smile exposed the dimple in his cheek. "Well, you know, I'm just a good kind of guy."

When they reached her apartment complex, Dexter had that far-off look in his eyes again. "I'll call you later," he told Tonya, not looking in her direction.

"You're not coming in?" Tonya was starting to get worried about him.

"Nah, I think I'll pass tonight. I'll walk you to your door." Dexter opened the car door for her and waited for her to get out. He was walking so fast that he practically walked off and left her. He glanced back at her as if she were walking too slow.

"Is something wrong, Dexter?" Tonya caught up with him at her door. Dexter seemed so aloof. She had thought they had a good time at her parents' house, maybe she was wrong.

"Nothing is wrong. I'll call you when I get home."

Tonya touched his arm. "Dexter, if something's bothering you, please tell me. More than anything, I'm a friend. If you're in pain about something, share it with me."

Dexter found it hard to resist such an honest request coming from her. "I don't want to burden you with my problems."

Tonya breathed a sigh of relief. At least he was starting to open up to her, even if it was just a little bit. "Isn't that what friends are for? Aren't we supposed to be a shoulder to lean on in times like this?"

"I would never want to put anything so heavy on your shoulders. I'll call you when I get home." He kissed her on the cheek and left.

Just like that, he was gone. Tonya couldn't imagine

what could be troubling Dexter to such a great extent. She waited to hear the sound of his car cranking before closing the door. Maybe it was something she'd said.

Eight

Dexter's promised phone call never came. She called him at home to see if everything was alright, but his answering machine kept picking up. She was pacing around her apartment at two in the morning, wondering if he was okay. Tonya's breath caught in her chest. *Oh, my God! What if he was in an accident?* She immediately picked up the phone and called him again. There was still no answer. Her worry turned into anger. It was very inconsiderate of him not to call and let her know he made it home. Maybe he didn't go home. On second thought, maybe he was home and wasn't answering the phone. He probably saw her number on the Caller ID and refused to pick up the phone.

She threw her hands in the air. She gave up, she was going to bed. Tomorrow she could worry about him all day, but now she was going to get some sleep.

Her sleep was restless, yet she managed to dream. It was all so clear. She and Dexter were at a restaurant and this woman appeared out of nowhere. The woman walked up to Dexter's side of the table and asked him how could he hurt her the way he had. Dexter recognized the woman and an uncomfortable expression was on his face. He told the woman what they had was over and he wanted to know why she insisted on hoping for something that would never take place. The woman's eyes began to cloud and she stared at Tonya. *If it weren't for you, Dexter and I would still he happy.* The woman walked away from the table and left the restaurant.

Tonya asked Dexter to explain his relationship with the woman who had just left their table. He tried to make no big deal of it and swore it was all in the past, but Tonya refused to believe it. Tonya left the restaurant and headed to her car, where Dexter cut her off. She could remember every detail vividly.

"If you cared anything about me, nothing like this would have ever happened," she yelled at him.

"You already know how I feel about you. I told you, she was in my past," Dexter explained.

"I don't believe you."

This particular part, Tonya remembered as if it were in slow motion. Dexter reached into the right pocket of his slacks. "I see you're not going to let it wait until tomorrow, like I planned. I guess I'll have to do it now." He pulls out a small, black, velvet box. Tonya's eyes focused on the box and she automatically knew what it was.

"What is it?"

Dexter smiled and placed the box in the palm of her hand. "Tonya, you already know what it is. I just need to know your answer."

It was a moment of sheer happiness. Dexter was proposing to her. Tears of joy streamed down her cheeks. She remembered standing at the altar on her wedding day. The first two rows on both sides of the church were filled with friends and family. After those first two rows, the faces of the people in the audience were blurred. Her soon-to-be husband took his place at her side. When she went to gaze into his eyes and say "I do," she couldn't see his face. His face was hazy, but the body and other outlying features were Dexter's. Tonya was sure the man standing next to her was Dexter. There was no doubt in her mind.

Suddenly, the haze began to clear, but not before she woke. She couldn't even remember what the ring looked like. The least she could have done, was remember what the ring looked like. It was so real. She could have sworn she felt the velvet material caressing the palm of her hand. Although it was a dream, the tears staining her pillow were very real. What did the dream mean? It was certainly a dream with much more clarity and realism than any other dream she ever had before.

Nine

By the time the Sunday of the game arrived, Tonya had yet to hear from Dexter. The game was the first of a doubleheader on NBC that started at twelve thirty. It was apparent that something had happened to him. Tonya was afraid she was going to have to call her father and tell him Dexter might not pick him up for the game. She didn't want her father to be dressed and waiting for Dexter if something had happened to him. Her mother called her before she had a chance to see if her father had gone already.

"Mom, I haven't spoken with Dexter and I don't know if he's still going to pick Dad up for the game. He was supposed to call me when he got home after dinner the other night and I haven't heard a thing from him."

"Dexter just picked up your father a moment ago. Did you two have a disagreement?"

Tonya was relieved to hear that at least Dexter hadn't let her father down. "Not that I know of. I don't understand. He was acting a little weird when he brought me home, but he didn't want to talk about it. Well, at least he kept his word to Dad and that's all that matters."

"I'm sure that whatever it is, he'll tell you about it in time. It's probably nothing to worry about."

Tonya sighed. "I hope you're right."

"Of course I'm right, you'll see. I agree with you on

one thing, he is a man of his word. I tell you they both seemed eager to get to the game. They had on their jeans and Rockets shirts. You know how your father is. I was calling to let you know they were off to the game and don't worry about Dexter. He just probably needed some space."

"You're probably right. I'll talk to you later."

After hanging up from talking to her mother, Tonya walked outside on her balcony. It was a beautiful and sunny afternoon. Although the temperature was a pleasant eighty degrees, Tonya felt a chill wash over her. The game would be on shortly. She would go inside after the tip-off. She had to resist the twinge of jealousy threatening to manifest itself. She was a die-hard Rockets fan, but Dexter didn't ask her to go to the game with him.

Why hasn't he called? She had given up calling him the night he left her apartment. If he had gone home, he would have seen she had called him several times. She had also left him a message letting him know she was worried about him. She assumed he would call her when he received her message. He could at least have left her a message telling her something. *I'm dead or I'm alive, something!* But did he call? No.

Tonya looked to her left and could see her neighbor having a few friends over to watch the game. He shuffled by his open patio door lugging a cooler in his hands. He caught her looking in his direction and flashed a quick smile, to which, she waved.

It was a miracle. The Rockets won by three points. She knew her father probably had a wonderful time at the game. A couple of hours after the game was over, Tonya's father called her.

"That was some game. That was one of the best games I've ever gone to," Mr. Locksley told his daughter excitedly.

Tonya was happy her father enjoyed the game. "Was it really? How were your seats?"

"Do you know we had courtside seats? I could see every move made. That friend of yours is an okay fellow. We had a good time."

Tonya didn't agree with that at the moment. At this point, Dexter was on her deterrent list. "Yeah, he's okay." He was fine, until he pulled his disappearing act on her.

"Well, I guess I better go. I had one too many drinks at the restaurant." Mr. Locksley yawned. "Isn't that pitiful? Now, I'm ready for a nap."

They went out to eat, too! "What restaurant?" Tonya asked. Dexter could wine and dine her father, but couldn't pick up the phone and say hi.

"We went to that seafood restaurant. Pappa . . . something? They had pretty good food."

"Pappadeaux?"

"Yes, that's it. Anyway, babycakes, I'll talk to you later."

Tonya heard a soft knock at her door. "Okay, Dad. I'll let you go, someone's at the door."

She opened the door, but a dozen roses blocked the facial view of the person holding them. The flowers and the person carrying them, moved close enough to violate her spatial needs. When the flowers were lowered, she could see Dexter's face lingering over hers. He leaned down to kiss her, but she moved abruptly.

Her anger took control of her. "I assume those are for me." She looked at the roses in his hands. He leaned on the jam of her door and held out the flowers for her to take them. She took the flowers and set them next to the door. There was no way he was going to make up with her by giving her flowers. Flowers couldn't take away the concern and worry she'd felt over the last few days.

"Aren't you going to invite me in?" He continued to lean in the doorway and crossed one foot over the other.

She glared at him. "No, I'm not going to invite you in."

"My flowers are on the other side of the door, why can't I be?"

Tonya held up her index finger, pointing it at him. "Correction. You gave the flowers to me, now they're mine. Anything that belongs to me, belongs on *this* side of the door."

Dexter uncrossed his feet and walked inside her apartment. "Then, I guess I belong on *this* side of the door, right?"

Tonya gave in to the relief that was begging her to yield to it. "Why haven't you called? I was worried about you. You could have, at least, called and left a message saying you were fine."

Dexter could see how much he had upset her. Her top lip was trembling ever so slightly. He took her in his arms and held her close. "I'm sorry. I never meant to upset you like this. There are so many things I want to tell you, but I can't right now. I don't think you will understand."

Tonya pulled her head away from his chest and looked into his eyes. "Why don't you try me? You never know what I might understand."

A single tear rolled along her cheek. His thumb wiped away the wet trail from her face. He let his body relax against the wall and leaned Tonya against him. He could smell a sweet lemony scent in Tonya's hair. Dexter felt an overwhelming sense of guilt. A feeling of guilt that would only worsen with time. "There are some things I can't explain, but the things I can, I will."

"I'm listening."

Dexter shifted his weight to the other foot. "When I was at your parents' home the other evening, there were so many things that were different from my parents' home. I saw the way you and your parents got along, the bond between you. I realized that I never had that kind of relationship with my family. Everything was always according to a plan, more like business plans. I've always longed for a close relationship with my mother and father. There was always someone else there helping them do their job in raising their child. They were rarely around for the special moments in a child's life. It was often someone else." Dexter paused before continuing. "Although they were off living the high-profile life, they managed to plan what my life would be. By the time they had slowed down enough to spend the quality time I needed, I was practically a grown man. When I was younger, I would do things just to get their attention. They were so blind they didn't see beyond the act to the real problem. My father wouldn't tolerate deviation from any of his instructions. His word was the law. I blocked out all of the bad memories by never talking about it. I never had to deal with it. There has always been this empty void in my life and I never knew what it was, until I visited your parents' house."

Tonya could hear the pain in his voice. She was afraid to make eye contact with him because she was afraid of what she might see. "I didn't know. I'm sorry, Dexter. That must have been so painful for you."

"That's where I'll stop." Dexter had never told any one what he had just told Tonya. Part of a big weight had been lifted from his shoulders. Part of it, that is. He couldn't tell her the other thing on his mind because she most definitely wouldn't understand. "The other part, trust me, you won't understand. But, for the most part, that's it."

Tonya was afraid of the thing he claimed she wouldn't understand. Her main concern was, was it something that would concern her? "Dexter, I don't know why you don't think I will understand. It must be something awful. Is it something that I should be worried about?"

He lifted her chin. "You trust me, don't you?"

"Of course, I trust you."

"That's all that matters, right?"

"I guess so."

Dexter gave her a tight squeeze. "I know so. If we don't have trust between us, what do we have? I'm sorry for not calling you. I needed some time to think and face some old ghosts. You forgive me?"

After what he had just shared about himself with her, how could she not forgive him? "I forgive you. But, the next time you need space to think, just say so."

Ten

That night was the beginning of a wonderfully intense relationship. With a newfound trust, there wasn't a day that went by that wasn't spent in Dexter's company or in which a telephone conversation didn't take place.

Tonya finally had hope that one day she would be a total person. Total meaning being happy spiritually, mentally, and emotionally. It was amazing what a relationship could do to your whole outlook on life. She was on a natural high and walking on cloud nine. There was nothing that could bring her down, not even the thought of Reggie's long-unheeded warning.

Sometimes she wondered if it were all too good to be true. You know when things are going too smooth, something is bound to happen to mess it up or you find out it was never as good as you thought it was. This was her secret fear, but she refused to be held hostage by her fears. Just when she was about to be swallowed up in doubt and anxiety, Dexter would do something wonderful to make her forget about all of the crazy thoughts that circled around in her head.

At other times, she found herself analyzing conversations they'd had or how he'd reacted to certain things she would say. One particular conversation Tonya had with Dexter stuck in her head. They were at lunch one afternoon when he brought up the subject of them dating and their work environment.

Dexter seemed to be slightly uncomfortable before bringing up the subject. He stirred his tea a little too much and some of it spilled onto the tablecloth. "Tonya, I've been doing a lot of thinking about us lately and I hope you're as excited about what's happening between us as I am."

Tonya's face began to warm and her heartbeat accelerated. Excited, the word excited was an understatement as far as she was concerned. "Of course, I'm excited about us, Dexter." She smiled.

"Good, I'm glad. I just want to keep what's going on between us as just that—between us."

He wants a commitment! "Well, of course, Dexter. This *is* just between us, there's no one else involved. I'm not seeing anyone but you." She was happy he wanted a one-on-one relationship because that's what she wanted, too.

Dexter gave a nervous laugh before continuing. "Well . . . that, too, but that wasn't exactly what I was speaking of."

"Oh?" She arched her brows. "What exactly were you speaking of?" She was beginning to get a little concerned and embarrassed for thinking along the wrong lines.

"I just think that we should keep quiet around the office about what's going on between us." He cleared his throat. "You know our firm has an unwritten policy that there be no dating going on between attorneys." His eyes were focused on the glass of tea.

The smile that was fixed on her face melted away. "So, in other words, you don't want anybody knowing about us." Her voice rose an octave and a few people dining at other tables glanced in their direction.

Dexter loosened his tie nervously. "I don't mind people knowing about us, as long as those people don't work with us."

"Just admit it, Dexter. You, for whatever reason, don't want anybody knowing about us, whether it's at work or not." By this time, her fork was down and her dinner napkin was lying on the table.

"It's not like that. All I'm saying is that we should keep our business to ourselves. Nobody has to know everything we do."

"What are you hiding from? You've never worried about firm policies before, besides, your father owns the firm."

"I have nothing to hide. Where's your sense of reason?" he had asked.

Reason, he wanted her to be rational about the situation. Her sense of rational wasn't functioning that day and she left him in the restaurant with his explanations. Needless to say, he apologized and she had let the conversation drop. She promised herself she wasn't going to let his undercover behavior worry her.

It sometimes bothered her when she heard rumors about Dexter going to different events with other women, but there was no way she could attend too many affairs with him without people wondering what was going on behind closed doors. When she wasn't pondering things of that nature, there was nothing that could bring her down.

Eleven

Tonya's mother begged her to invite Dexter to the next family function. Mrs. Locksley thrived on spearheading any upcoming family event. In this case, it was the family reunion. It took a lot of effort on Tonya's part to keep in good standings with her family and with Dexter. It seemed like every time she turned around, there was some get-together planned. Of course, she was expected to attend all of them—or else! The upcoming weekend was the family reunion. Tonya's father was pressuring her to bring Dexter so her aunts and uncles could meet him. She was hesitant about it because they never failed to embarrass her.

Tonya was expecting the reunion to be one big fiasco. Her cousins from Philadelphia, on her father's side, would be there. Her father's side of the family was kind of weird at times. She had a cousin, Vince, who she gave the alias *Alien,* because he was one strange character. Vince decided to join a cult that believed the human race was brought here by aliens and that one day the aliens were coming back to pick them up. Recent gossip was that he had just ordained himself as a minister to this religion or cult. Vince said he had to spread the word about this religion by any means necessary. Tonya's guess was that he planned to hijack a news station and give a sermon about the return of the aliens.

Then there was the other cousin, Kim, Mr. Locksley's niece who had been in jail since Tonya was a freshman in high school. Tonya didn't want to introduce Dexter to her father's extreme side of the family. It wasn't that she was embarrassed, it was her fear of them doing something that would shock everybody that had her a little hesitant.

I can't go through with it. I can't let Dexter think that the rest of my family is looney. She decided to call her mother and tell her she wasn't going to the reunion. As she waited for someone to pick up the phone, she contemplated the excuse she would use. Her parents wouldn't take work as an excuse. *I'm sure you won't be working all day.* She could hear them say.

"Hello." Mr. Locksley answered.

"Hey, Daddy. Where's Mom?" Tonya asked.

"She's gone to the store. Want me to tell her you called?"

"That's okay. I didn't want anything in particular."

"You are still coming to the family reunion—aren't you?"

Why did he have to ask that question? "I don't know. I was thinking that maybe I should go into the office and finish up on some last-minute stuff for a project I'm working on."

"Don't even try getting out of this. You bring that fella' of yours so that everybody can meet him. You know your uncles are going to want to see David's replacement."

Dear God, here we go. "Dad, tell Uncle Roosevelt not to embarrass me."

"Embarrass you! Oh, I guess you're ashamed of your family. He's going to have to meet the rest of your family one day. It may as well be sooner than later."

"Dad . . ." she whined.

"I don't want to hear anything else about it. You're coming and you're bringing him. I'll talk to you later.

The least you can do is show up. You know your brothers won't show their faces."

It was no use. When she mentioned it to Dexter the next day at work, he eagerly accepted. During lunch, she sat there staring at him.

"What's wrong, Tonya?" Dexter asked.

"You don't have to go to my family reunion. I'm sure you've got other things you can do," Tonya said hopefully.

"Is there a reason why you don't want me to go?"

"Some of our *weird* relatives are going to be there. They always do or say something crazy. I can only imagine what they're going to do this year."

"Your family can't be all that bad. I think you have an overactive imagination. Everything will be fine. You'll see."

"I hope you're right. Don't get me wrong, I want you to meet the rest of my family. My immediate family—that is. When we start talking about the extended family, we start to have problems," she said, looking across the restaurant.

"Look, everybody has black sheep in the family. My family has its share of alcoholics, drug addicts, and just plain old lazy people. What's the big deal?"

"I know you're right. I guess I'm not very sociable when it comes down to it."

"Yeah, you're being downright *antisocial* about this."

"You didn't have to agree. You've made me feel a lot better," Tonya said sarcastically.

The day of dread finally arrived. Things were going to kick off at noon. Of course, Tonya was going to arrive later than that. Besides, Dexter had to pick her up. It was such a pretty day for disaster to strike. The sky was cloudless and it was in the pleasant eighties, yet she felt as if ice had been dumped on her back.

She and Dexter rode along in silence. She was starting to think her tension was rubbing off on him.

"Don't worry, everything will be fine," he reassured her with a troubled expression on his face.

"I'm not worried," she lied.

They pulled up to the park pavilion. Not to Tonya's surprise, it was a nice place to have a reunion. She wasn't surprised by anything her mother had planned. It was always guaranteed to be a success. There were several play areas for the kids and a big lake to paddle boats and swim in.

From out of nowhere appeared her uncle Roosevelt. "You must be the man keeping my niece too busy to call up her uncle and say hello," he said, extending his hand.

Tonya rolled her eyes to the top of her head. *As if we talk on a regular basis!*

"Yes, sir. I must say that I am." Dexter took his hand and gave it a firm grip.

"Good, good. Then we must have a long talk with each other," Roosevelt said, careening Dexter in a different direction. Tonya followed along like a puppy dog.

"Uncle Roosevelt, please behave yourself," Tonya begged.

"Why don't you go visit with your cousins, while I talk to what's his name here?"

"Not on your life," Tonya muttered under her breath.

"You know your favorite cousin Vince is here. He's been dying to see you."

"I'll just bet he has." Vince was the last person she wanted to see.

"So," Roosevelt said, turning to Dexter, "what kind of work you do?"

"I'm an attorney. Tonya and I work at the same firm."

"You're an attorney? That's nice, real nice." He turned and gave Tonya a thumbs up sign.

"Yes, I am."

"That's good. I take it, since you're an attorney, you don't have any felonies in your background. If you do, what was it concerning and about how long ago was it? See, I'm with the Houston Police Department and I can't have my niece running around with no criminal."

Dexter had to fight to hold back his laughter. He glanced at Tonya who looked like she would faint at any moment. "No, I can't say that I do."

"Then you won't object if I do a little background check on you? I'll be needing your social security number."

"Uncle Rose, no!" Tonya screeched. "You are not getting his social security number."

He pretended not to hear her. "About that social security number . . ." he continued.

Tonya gave up. She decided to visit some of her sane relatives if that were possible. Vince would have to be the first one she bumped into. She never could tell just who Vince was looking at, since he was cross-eyed.

"Hey, cousin! How's life been treating you?" he asked.

When Tonya realized that he was talking to her, she responded. "It's been treating me fair, I would say," she said smiling. She knew it wouldn't be long before he went off the deep end. He was about to start with the alien thing. She could tell by the wild-eyed look he'd get and his left eye would squint. That's when she was definitely sure he was about to launch into a "save the world" lecture.

"Well, cousin," he said, "on a serious note, I want to know if you've gotten yourself together—you know, spiritually?"

I knew it! For once can't I just be wrong? "Vinceton, I am very together spiritually. There is no need for you to get concerned about my spiritual well-being." If she were ever going to get away, this was the time to do it.

"You know, time is winding down. In the year two thousand, they'll be back." He pointed toward the sky. "And they are only taking the believers." He walked over to a park bench and sat down. Reluctantly, she followed behind him, otherwise, he would follow her.

"I know, Vince. I'm sure you'll be the only one going." There were children on the swings and seesawing happily in the sunshine. *Seesaws, I can't believe they still have seesaws! That's it! If I don't get away now, I'm going to have to be admitted into an insane asylum!*

"No. There are thousands of believers. You outta' come to one of our services one night. You know I've been ordained as a minister and if there's help for me, I'm sure we can save your soul as well."

"Thanks, Vince, but I've pretty much got all of that under control. I hate to think that you believe that I'm going to hell," she said in serious consideration. It was kind of sad to think that you and your family members would be heading in different directions in the afterlife.

"This is hell," he said, waiving his arms around him. "We are already in hell and it's going to get worse after the mother ship comes back for us. That will be the only ride out. Why not make your reservation now? Don't try buying a ticket when the ship comes in, because there will be no more room. It'll be too late, and the ship will have gone without you." He sat there gazing up into the sky, as if the mother ship itself was about to pop out any moment.

"Well, beam me up, Scottie," Tonya said, bursting into laughter. She must have rolled on that one. She laughed so hard that her side began to hurt. Vince looked at her stonily. Vince was quite handsome, but he would look even better if he wasn't so crazy.

"Laugh now and cry later," Vince warned. "There are

a lot of people who feel the same way you do, but just like you, they will all be left behind."

"Come on, Vince. Didn't you watch the news a couple of months ago? Remember when those people thought they were going to be picked up by a spaceship that they thought they saw through a telescope. They all killed themselves and that *supposed* spaceship turned out to be the Hale Bopp comet. Look what happened to them, learn from their mistakes."

Vince took offense to her pointing out that occurrence. "I'm not going to stay here and let you ridicule my beliefs. Hopefully, I'll see you in the afterlife." He stormed away.

"Hey, Vince. What did I say?" Tonya called after him laughing. "Vince, you are one weird character," she said to herself.

"See the reunion wasn't so bad," Dexter told her that night. "From the way you were talking, I thought maybe you had mutants in your family or something."

"Very funny." Tonya laughed. "As crazy as some of them are, they might as well be mutants."

"You know, I had to give your uncle a social security number before he would let me go." Dexter laughed.

Tonya's mouth dropped. "Are you serious?"

"No, I'm just kidding."

"Knowing Uncle Rose, he probably made you give him something. It doesn't matter anyway, seeing he's not a police officer. It's all in his imagination."

Dexter had been to two of her family functions. Tonya had yet to meet his family, well his mother anyway. Could it be that maybe he was ashamed of his family or that he was ashamed of her?

* * *

It had to have been a man who invented the Sony Play Station. Dexter had decided that since he was spending more time at Tonya's place, he would bring his *toy* with him. It never failed that when Tonya wanted to have a serious discussion, Dexter seemed to tune her out with that video game. What was with grown men and those things?

It was always, "In a minute" or "As soon as the Rockets beat Chicago." She could have walked around stark naked and Dexter would have never noticed. As soon as he got out of the shower, she was going to question him about him not inviting her to his family gatherings. He wasn't going to have an opportunity to hit the power switch on that video game and even if he did, she was unplugging it.

"Not tonight," Tonya said to herself as she reached behind the television and unplugged the game. *We are going to discuss this whether you want to or not.* She thought it was pitiful to have to resort to such silly measures in order to get his undivided attention, yet a woman had to do what a woman had to do—even if it meant unplugging a video game.

He could see it on her face as soon as he headed in the direction of the living room. She was patiently waiting for him. The determination in her eyes, the set of her mouth and shoulders was enough to warn him that she was in a *serious discussion* mood. Usually, the discussion was about something he wasn't ready to explain or reveal about himself.

He quickly detoured into the kitchen. He needed time to prepare himself. What could she possibly want to talk about now? What had he done? Better yet, what *hadn't* he done? It was always something. He listened carefully for the rumpling of the couch as she got up. That rumpling sound never came. Yeah, she was most definitely waiting. He opened the refrigerator and poured himself a tall glass of tea. He was going to need it. His mind rapidly ran down the list of possibilities for a topic of discussion. Each and every time, his mind drew a blank. There was nothing left for him to do but go into that living room. It was like going to war without weapons.

He downed the tea and placed the glass in the sink. Buying time was only going to put off the inevitable. Then it finally dawned on him that he had his Play Station. All he had to do was go into the living room and play a game. At least he could buy a couple of hours.

"Hey, you," Dexter said as he popped on the television, "what you know good?"

"Well, I was hoping you could enlighten me on something." Tonya watched as he reached for the Play Station. Just as she thought, he was going to try to put her off.

"How about after I finish this game?" Dexter said.

He switched on the power switch, blinking his eyes when nothing happened. He switched the power on and off again. It was a fine time for the thing to be going on the fritz. Why did it have to go out now?

"Don't worry, it isn't broken. I unplugged it." Tonya rescued him from his dilemma.

"I take it there's a reason it's unplugged." Dexter set the game on the floor.

"Yes, there is." Tonya slid over and patted the space next to her on the couch.

Now would have been the perfect time for his pager to go off. Better yet, why couldn't her pager go off? On second thought, he didn't want her pager to go off because he would have wanted to know who was paging her. Being the woman that she is, she would probably say it's just a friend calling. Thus, an argument would occur. But what difference would it make since they were headed in the direction of an argument anyway? It would make all the difference in the world because it would be *her* fault.

He finally moved over to the couch and sat next to her.

The last thing Dexter wanted to do was argue. At this point, he was willing to be as complacent as possible.

"Is there something you want to talk about?" he asked in a serious tone.

Maybe she was being petty, but it perturbed her that Dexter had never taken her around his family.

"You might think this is silly, but this is something that is important to me."

"If it's something that's important to you then it's not silly," Dexter said.

"Well, I was wondering why we never go to anything your family has. You've been to some of my family functions. I just get the feeling that you're ashamed to be with me."

"How could I be ashamed of you? You are a beautiful and intelligent woman. There's no way that I could ever be ashamed of you."

The determination that was in her eyes earlier was replaced by a certain urgency. An urgency that begged for the truth and reassurance that she could trust him.

"Then what is it?" Tonya asked.

Dexter unlaced his finger from Tonya's. He stood up from the couch and paced across the floor. This was a turn he didn't want the conversation to make. He could give her an explanation about his parents but it wouldn't be a total explanation. He would explain things to her as much as he could.

"As I've told you before, my parents and I don't have the best relationship in the world." He stopped pacing to watch her expression. "My parents and I just don't see eye to eye on a lot of things and I don't want you to have to witness that. Believe me, the tension would be so thick that you would be able to cut it with a knife. That's one experience I don't want you to have."

"Is that all?" Tonya noticed how nervous he started to act when she asked him about his parents.

"For the most part, yes. The rest you just wouldn't understand."

The last thing he ever wanted to do was hurt her. How could he keep that from happening? It was then that he thought of what the note in his fortune cookie at lunch had told him. *The source of your happiness will be your sorrow!* At the time he'd dismissed it, but something tugged at him to put the sliver of paper into his wallet. It was still there.

Twelve

Someone said that there is no such thing as the perfect man or the perfect relationship. Tonya would be the first to agree with this theory, but she wanted to get as close as possible to perfection. She and Dexter had been seeing one another for a while, yet she couldn't get used to the idea of having an undercover relationship. She couldn't help but think that Dexter not only wanted to conceal their relationship from those at work, but he wanted to hide it from *everyone* he socialized with.

Tonya felt like she was back in high school again having to sneak around. It reminded her of when she was fifteen. It brought to mind Jamie Jenkins, a boy who lived down the street from her. Jamie was the neighborhood nerd who happened to have a crush on her. He was the first boy she had ever kissed. It was the sloppiest kiss she ever had and his braces cut her bottom lip. Needless to say, her mother caught them kissing and Jamie was banned from the Locksley yard and Reggie and Kip gave him a bruising.

The time was out for sneaking. There comes a time in every relationship when everyone wants to know where they stand. It was all a matter of respect. If Tonya was Dexter's woman, she wanted to be respected as that. She decided to tell him what was on her mind at dinner. She knew he wouldn't like it, but she was going to bring it up anyway.

Dexter was over thirty minutes late. Tonya tore open two Sweet 'N Lows and briskly stirred them in her tea. What their relationship needed was definition.

Finally, she saw Dexter walking toward her. He seemed like he was stressed out. But it didn't matter, because she was discussing what was on her mind anyway. He planted a kiss on her cheek, which was to her surprise. *Ooh, a public display of affection!*

"Sorry I'm late. I was in a mediation that took a little longer than I expected. Have you ordered yet?"

"No, I haven't ordered. I was trying to be considerate and wait for you."

Dexter couldn't figure out what was wrong with her lately. She always seemed like she was in an agitated state. "What's on your mind? I know it's something you want to say so just put it on the table." He picked up the menu and scanned over it. He wasn't in the mood to get into a deep conversation with her.

"I know you probably don't want to discuss this, but I do. I want to know where I stand with you."

Dexter rolled his eyes to the top of his head. He knew it was coming. There was no way she would let them just have an enjoyable dinner without bringing up that subject. He didn't want to get pinned down in a situation he knew would blow up in his face. He put the menu down. "Is that what this is all about—a title?"

"That's exactly what it's all about." She didn't like having to ask where she stood with him. She wouldn't have had to ask him about her status if he would have just told her.

"I don't understand what the problem is. Do I not spend time with you? Do we not do the things that people in relationships do?"

"Anybody can go out to dinner or sleep together and

call themselves *friends*. I'm under the impression that we're more than friends. I just want to hear it from you." She couldn't believe that he was being so defensive and getting an attitude about it.

"Look, I don't want to argue with you . . ." Dexter would have finished his sentence but he caught a glimpse of his father walking their way.

"You two discussing business over dinner?" Mr. Freeman asked.

Tonya opened her mouth to answer, but Dexter quickly interjected. "Yes, we were discussing minor details of a case we're working on."

"I know it's a common thing for counsel to disagree, but you two seemed to be really at it." Mr. Freeman looked at Tonya who was as rigid as a board. "But that's a good thing. I love to see people who are as passionate about their work as I am."

Tonya decided to keep her mouth shut. There was no way she was going to be a party to Dexter's charade.

"What brings you to the Lancaster, Dad?" Dexter glared at Tonya for not commenting on anything Mr. Freeman had said.

"I'm supposed to be meeting your mother here. You haven't seen her yet, have you?"

Dexter was uneasy about his mother showing up. She would be all paranoid about him having dinner with Tonya. "No, I haven't seen her. Well, anyway, when she shows up tell her that I'll stop over and say hi before I leave."

Mr. Freeman said his good-byes and went to his table.

"What was all of that for?" Dexter asked Tonya.

"Why didn't you just tell your father the truth instead of saying it was a business dinner?"

"It was none of his business."

"That's a poor excuse." She pushed away from the table and picked up her purse.

"Where are you going?"

"I'm going home. You obviously need time to think about this."

"Yeah, maybe you're right."

Yeah, maybe you're right! That's it? "Good night, Dexter. I'll be talking to you." She couldn't believe it. No, I'm sorry. No nothing. A simple *Yeah, maybe you're right!*

Thirteen

"Tonya. Tonya Locksley!" A voice called to her as she put her key in the lock of her door. She turned to see Warren, her neighbor, walking to his apartment with an arm full of bags.

"Hi, Warren right?" She smiled.

"Right, how have you been? You sure are looking good."

"I've been fine, thanks. How have you been?"

"Good. I'm just coming from the store." He motioned toward the bags in his arms.

"I see. Here, let me help you with that." Tonya took a bag from him. What was she supposed to do, let the man stumble to his door?

"Great, now I can unlock the door." He took out his key and unlocked his door.

Tonya looked around his apartment. Warren seemed to be a big African art fan. He had paintings of tribes, African masks, as well as war shields and spears. Actually, it was a nice place. Tonya wasn't into African art all that much, but it suited Warren well.

"You have a nice place, Warren." Tonya moved from one painting to another examining each closely.

"Thanks. If you're referring to the art, I'm a collector. I've been to many different parts of Africa and I pick up pieces from here and there."

"Impressive. So, do you get to do a lot of traveling?"

"Not as much as I used to. I only get to travel about once a year. Sometimes I don't get to travel at all."

"Does your job require you to travel?"

"Never, I'm a number cruncher—an accountant. So what's your old ball and chain?"

"Oh, you mean my job?" It had been a while since she had heard that term. Actually, the last time she heard it, it was used to describe a spouse.

"Okay, I see you don't get out much." Warren laughed. "Yes, I mean your job."

"Oh, I'm an attorney. This is my first year practicing."

"Well, I guess it's my turn to say impressive. Hey, I was just about to cook up something Italian for dinner. I would love for you to be my guest. I can make enough for two."

Warren seemed nice and since she stormed out on Dexter, she didn't get to eat dinner. What could it hurt? "That sounds lovely. I just need to go change. Can I bring a bottle of wine?"

"Yes, that sounds perfect."

After changing she walked back over to Warren's. She handed the wine to him as she entered his apartment.

"Muscadine wine. That sounds good, I've never tried it."

"I've never tried it either, but I hear it's good. So, what's for dinner?"

Warren directed her to his small dining table. "I'll answer that in just a second. I've got to take the bread out of the oven." He ran into the kitchen and came out with a pan of garlic bread. "Oh, this is hot, hot, hot. Actually, we will be feasting on a Warren original meal. It's going to be good, trust me." He took the tops off several bowls.

If Warren didn't know what he was doing, he sure pretended to know his way around the kitchen. Tonya was getting hungry just from smelling the food. She wondered if Dexter had called—probably not.

"So, just what is Warren's original meal?" Tonya asked.

He put some of the food on her plate. "Well, I don't really know what the name of this dish is, so I just made up one. But it has fresh green beans, potatoes, whole tomatoes, grilled chicken, and some other good stuff."

"Well, I must say that it looks divine."

"What do you like to do in your spare time?" Warren asked.

"I like to read, but I don't get to do much leisurely reading anymore. The only thing I have been able to read is cases. What about you?" Tonya put a spoonful of food into her mouth and savored the taste of it.

Warren watched Tonya's expression change as she tasted the food. He took her expression as a good sign. "You're tasting what I like to do in my spare time. I like to cook."

"Wow, a man who loves to cook. That's a new one."

"This is the nineties. It seems like the roles have reversed. Women are more independent and less into the home, you know, the domestic thing." Warren took a sip of his wine. "Umm, this is good."

"It is good, isn't it. So, you're one of those men who believe that the woman's place is in the home." She didn't want to get into a debate about equality for women. People still had the tendency to be touchy about that topic and she was one of them.

"No, I didn't say that. But if you really look at it, women have gotten more into their careers and are putting off starting families until after they've reached their career goals." He hoped she wasn't one of those feminist who took everything a man said to the extreme.

"I will agree with that to a certain extent. But there are women who juggle careers and family at the same time. They take their careers seriously as well as taking care of their families. Not all women put off starting a family just for their careers."

"You have a point. As a whole, women have made dramatic changes as far as family life is concerned. Years ago, a lot of people's goals only went as far as graduating high school and getting married. Now, it's I have to get my bachelor's, as well as my master's and the marriage and the family—*if I want a family,* will come later."

"Well, I don't think too many educated men want a woman who has no intellect, running around barefoot and pregnant every time you turn around. I think men want something more challenging. They want women who can think for themselves and be an asset to them. I have to believe that the nineties man wants something more than just a baby-making machine. Besides, the woman's place is not just in the kitchen and the bedroom."

Warren could see that Tonya was a person who stood her ground and was passionate about her beliefs. "Again, you have a point. I see this could be the start of a debate, so I'm willing to change the subject." He laughed.

Tonya was embarrassed. Sometimes she could get so emotional when it came down to getting her point across. "I think that's a good idea. Well, from that conversation I can see that you are a man with strong family values."

"Yes, I am a strong believer in family. I believe that the man should be the head of the household. He should take care of his family and the wife shouldn't have to work, unless she wants to. Raising a family is a hard job and it takes full-time parents to run a household. I just haven't found anyone who shares my beliefs."

"You mean you don't have anyone special in your life?" Tonya asked. Since Warren mentioned it, she hadn't noticed any female traffic going to and from his apartment.

"I don't mean to be sarcastic, but you wouldn't be dining with me right now if I did. Too many people use the idea of dating to run around with this person and that person. Everybody is afraid of commitment."

Warren was one of a kind. If only *you know who* thought like that. "Yeah, you're right. Unfortunately, I know someone who is afraid of commitment."

"Ah, the boyfriend?" Warren smiled. He should have known that she was attached to someone.

Tonya sighed. She felt like talking to someone and Warren seemed like he had a listening ear. "Well, I don't know what to call him."

"Why is that?" He was getting interested now. Maybe there was trouble in paradise after all.

"I don't think he wants anyone to know we're dating. As a matter of fact, I *know* he doesn't want anyone to know about us. He uses this policy at work to keep our relationship a secret from those we work with, but he's also doing it outside of work. I think he's hiding something."

"I don't know what to say about that. As far as work is concerned, I think it may be somewhat appropriate. Now, what you do outside of work is a different story. Me personally, I wouldn't care who knew that I was dating a gorgeous woman."

She thought it was cute that he was flirting with her. "I guess the world needs more men like you." She was starting to feel sorry for herself. "What exactly are you looking for in a relationship?"

Warren tilted his head to one side in thought. "Humm, something good. Everybody is looking for something good."

"Something good. I think you're right, everybody is searching for something good. Well, dinner was lovely. But the time has come for me to head home. Thanks for inviting me."

"Anytime, I enjoyed having you. Look, anytime you

want to talk or just want to hang out, remember that I'm just a door away."

"I'll keep that in mind." She stepped out into the walkway.

"Let me see you to your door. I don't want anything happening to you on my account." He followed her to her apartment. "Remember, I'm only a door away," he said, pointing in the direction of his apartment.

Fourteen

He had done it now. Tonya was angry with him and it was all his fault. Things were getting too thick for him. As the old saying went, "If you can't stand the heat, get out of the kitchen." Something in the back of his mind told him to let go of Tonya and drop the whole situation.

Dexter found out that would be easier said than done. There was one little problem keeping him from leaving her, he cared deeply for her. In the beginning, getting his feelings involved wasn't part of the plan. He never anticipated the relationship taking off the way it did. The budding emotions for Tonya Locksley was the only thing keeping him there.

How could he wake up one day and find himself between a rock and a hard place? He wouldn't leave Tonya, and Melissa wouldn't leave him alone. Melissa was still very much a problem. He didn't want Tonya to get hurt with issues surrounding his ex-wife. But, if he didn't break it off with her, heartbreak would be impossible to avoid. *Damn! How did I get into this mess?*

If or when Tonya found out about Melissa, she wouldn't understand how complicated things were. He'd begged her to trust him. How could she trust him when he hadn't told her about his ex-wife? How could he tell Tonya that he could probably never get married again, if Melissa and his parents had anything to do with it?

Melissa. He didn't even want to deal with Melissa. Strangely enough, she had started calling even more. She didn't care how often or when she called. Apparently she believed he wasn't actively dating anyone. As far as he was concerned, he had nothing to say to her. He resorted to avoiding her.

The real confrontation with Melissa came when he went home to Atlanta for a couple of days on business. As usual, she caught him at home. It was funny how she always seemed to know when he was in town. He didn't mind being civil with her, but some people you just can't be civil with. She called and convinced him to have dinner with her. Instead of being downright rude, he agreed. She decided to pick him up and arrived before he had finished dressing. It never dawned on him that Melissa would want something other than dinner. He asked her to wait downstairs while he finished dressing. When he went back downstairs, Melissa greeted him wearing nothing but high heels. He was at a loss for words and really didn't know what to do. How could he tell her that he didn't want her? If she had the slightest idea that he was seeing someone, she would go off the deep end.

Stopping short of throwing her out, he finally convinced Melissa to leave. It wasn't that she wasn't desirable. At one point and time, he loved the ground that she walked on, but that was over. The feelings he had for Melissa didn't run deep enough anymore to make him want her. It was only then that he realized how he felt about Tonya. That was the first time that he faced the fact that he loved Tonya. Yes, love had reared its ugly head.

No matter what Melissa did, he could never love her again. Melissa called him after she left, wondering what was wrong. She wanted to know if the problem was with her. Dexter assured her the problem wasn't her, it was all him. He knew that explaining why they would never be together again would do little good. He hoped in time that she would find someone else and move on with her life. He was sure that his parents would see to it that it wouldn't happen. They had it set in their heads that Melissa would always be in the family.

Whenever Melissa called, their conversations had always been brief. She would often leave messages on his answering machine in Houston. She would tell him how much she missed him and how she couldn't wait to see him. Things of that nature prompted him to get an answering service so he could let his calls automatically roll over to the service. There was no way he was going to get caught with Tonya at his house and have Melissa call. That would have been too awkward for both him and Tonya.

He asked himself thousands of questions as he headed over to Tonya's place. He had wasted time trying to avoid going to see her. Heck, he even finished having dinner with his parents which was a rarity. After leaving the restaurant, he had planned on going straight home. But when he sat behind the wheel of his car, it did its own thing. Although he willed it not to, his mind seemed to focus on Tonya. She was angry with him, but he was willing to bet that she was sitting by the phone waiting for him to call. He'd do better than give her a phone call, he would go by to see her and straighten things out.

He walked up the flight of stairs to Tonya's apartment only to find her standing there thanking some guy for a lovely dinner. *Oh, so this is how it is!* He stood at the edge of the steps waiting for her to acknowledge his presence. The longer he had to wait, the angrier he became. *I should have known she wouldn't have been waiting for me to call!*

Tonya turned toward Dexter in surprise. She wondered how long he had been standing there. "Dexter, what are you doing here?"

How could he have been jealous? "You tell me," he said dryly. The guy she was talking to stood there as if he was waiting for an introduction.

She had almost forgotten Warren was standing there. "Warren, this is Dexter." They shook hands and went through the formalities.

"Thanks for the lovely evening," Warren said to Tonya. He seemed to be awkward with the situation. "It was nice meeting you, Dexter." He went to his apartment and closed the door.

"Did you want something?" Tonya snapped at Dexter. There was no way he was going to be forgiven that easily. He let her leave the restaurant without trying to stop her so it was obvious that he had nothing to say. If he cared anything about how she felt, he would have tried to make her understand where he was coming from.

"I would like to talk. I didn't know you and your neighbor were so friendly."

She didn't respond to the comment. She went inside the apartment and turned on the lights.

"So what did you want to talk about?"

He could see she was going to be difficult, but that was cool because he had it coming. "*Us.* I want to talk about us."

"What about *us?* From what I can tell, there is no *us?*" She turned away and went into the bathroom, barely closing the door behind her. Seeing him didn't make her feel any better about his behavior. As a matter of fact, she was tired of worrying about it.

Dexter could hear the sound of running water coming from the bathroom. He waited patiently for her to return so they could start their discussion. Five minutes turned into fifteen. *What is taking her so long?* It finally dawned on him that she had no intention of continuing their conversation, she was in the shower. Her silhouette could be seen in the mirror just outside of the bathroom. He couldn't help feeling like he was invading her privacy. He felt like a stalker, but justified his actions because he had seen her undressed many times before.

He stood staring at her outline in the mirror until she stepped out of the shower. There she was, naked. He kept forgetting how much she turned him on. He stood outside of the bathroom leaning against the wall. What would she say if he went in?

He gently pushed open the door. Her back was to him as she dried herself off. He walked behind her and slid his arms around her waist. She tensed up but didn't say anything. His hands massaged her breasts. He loved the way they fit into the palms of his hands, not too big or too small. He turned her around to face him. She looked so vulnerable as she stared up to him.

"So," he said as he planted kisses in the hollow of her neck. "Did you enjoy your dinner?"

Tonya's arms were strung across Dexter's shoulders and her fingers caressed the nape of his neck. "Mmmm-hum." She was sure Dexter thought he had her where he wanted her. But, was he in for a surprise. "Sorry." She pushed him away. "It's not that simple. You should explain why you're behaving the way you are. Don't give me any bull about some unwritten, unenforced, policy regarding dating in the workplace." She wrapped a towel around her and left the bathroom. She went to the kitchen and poured a glass of water. It was hard to stay mad at him. His very presence made every fiber in her body come alive.

Dexter followed her to the kitchen. Dexter didn't want to deal with what had happened at the restaurant. What concerned him most was her visiting the man next door and her resistance of his advances. "You never answered my question. Did you enjoy your dinner with your neighbor?"

Tonya could feel a headache coming on, so she decided to head it off before it got worse. She took two Advil and washed them down with the glass of water. "Why are you bringing that up? But, if it makes you feel any better, yes, I enjoyed dinner with Warren."

There was no way she was going to start another relationship right in his face. He wasn't going to be disrespected like that. "I guess that means we're free to see other people." He knew she wouldn't want that. A commitment was something she had been wanting from him for a while. He turned to walk away. "That's fine with me."

"I didn't say I wanted to see other people. I see dating other people is fine with you, so go ahead. It's probably what you wanted to do anyway. Go ahead and leave." There was no way she was going to let him use psychology on her. He was trying to use this as an excuse to do what he had been wanting to do all along.

That wasn't the reaction he was expecting. He thought she would seize the opportunity to solidify the relationship with a title. Obviously that was the wrong move. He didn't want to leave her because he pretty much knew that once he left, it would be over. He had to think quickly. "Why would I want anyone else, when it's you that I love?" He couldn't believe he'd told he her loved her.

Tonya couldn't believe her ears. Did he say he loved her? She nervously twisted the ring on her finger. "Don't say things you don't mean." Those were words she never thought she would hear falling from Dexter's mouth. She had always fantasized about how happy she would be when he told her he loved her. When he finally told her, what did she say? *Don't say things you don't mean! Way to go, Tonya!*

Dexter took Tonya's hands into his to cease their nervous movement. Now, he was happy to have told her how he really felt. "I wouldn't say something like that, if I didn't mean it. I love you and I hope you feel the same way about me."

Love was a scary word. Yet, she knew that love was what she felt for Dexter. She softly murmured the words he wanted to hear. "I love you, too."

Their lovemaking was like no other. It was more passionate and filled with emotion. It was an act of expressing how they felt for one another instead of fulfilling a need.

The next morning, Dexter decided to leave Tonya's place early since he hadn't brought any clothes for work. When he let himself out of her apartment, he saw Warren heading out at the same time. Dexter deliberately took his time leaving the apartment so that Warren could see him when he left. His jealously urged him to let the other man know Tonya was off limits.

"Good morning." Dexter smiled at Warren and fell in step beside him as he walked by Tonya's door.

Warren somehow got the feeling that Dexter was waiting on him. "Good morning. How's it going?"

"Pretty good." They headed down the steps to the parking lot.

"How's my neighbor doing this morning?" *It's obvious he spent the night.* Warren hoped Dexter wouldn't get offended by him inquiring about Tonya.

Why do you want to know? It's none of your business. Dexter took that as his cue to let Warren know he didn't have a chance with Tonya. "She's fine. I hope she's getting ready for work. I woke her before I left, but I think she went back to sleep. I'll give her a call when I get to the office." *Yes, homie, I spent the night!* Dexter turned toward his car. "See ya' around."

"Take care." Warren knew that Dexter wanted him to notice him leaving Tonya's apartment. So he took the bait, and asked about her. He decided it would be best to stay away from Tonya. But then again, if she continued to be friendly toward him, he would definitely continue to be friendly toward her. Either her boyfriend was the jealous type or he was insecure. He had received bad vibes from Dexter. He was all wrong for Tonya and Warren hoped that Dexter wouldn't hurt her.

Dexter took the scenic route to work. He needed time to think things through. He had crossed the line and there was no going back. He'd told Tonya he loved her and there was no way he could take those three words back. He didn't want to take those words back anyway, because he meant them. He had never told any woman that he loved her and actually felt the meaning behind the words. This time was different. Tonya Locksley was different. She was a much-needed change in his life. A welcome change, at that.

His heart wanted to be light, but there was a dark shadow looming overhead. How long was this happiness going to last? Tonya was something he wanted to be in his life always. Wasn't it true that true love could stand the test of time? Would love be enough to overcome the obstacles that Dexter knew would be waiting?

Dexter pulled into the drive-thru of a doughnut shop and ordered donuts and coffee. For some reason that he couldn't explain, he had to resist the urge to play hooky from work. He had the feeling that something was waiting for him and that *something* wasn't anything good. Whatever it was waiting couldn't have been anything that he was looking forward to.

He thought about Tonya standing outside of her apartment talking to her neighbor. Would he ever have told her how he felt about her had he not seen her talking to another man? How long would he have gone before he told her he loved her?

Dexter was vaguely aware that he was driving so slow

that even school buses were passing him. He thought maybe by taking the long way to work, his slight depression would lift. Instead of getting better, it had gotten worse by the time he pulled into his parking space at work. Maybe he was in no mood to go to work, or it could have been that something terrible was about to take place?

He removed his briefcase from the seat and closed the car door. He straightened his tie and mentally prepared himself to face whatever was coming.

Fifteen

Making up with Dexter was just what the doctor ordered. She had been daydreaming off and on all morning and was humming along with a tune that was playing on the radio when Rita popped her head in Tonya's office.

"What are you sitting there smiling and humming about?" Rita asked.

"Oh, I'm just in one of those happy moods." Tonya turned the radio off and leaned back in her chair, still softly humming the tune.

"And just *who* made this morning so wonderful?" Rita stood in the door lightly tapping her index finger on her temple.

"Why does it have to be a *who* to make me happy?" Tonya asked, still humming. "You should never let a *some-one* be the dictator of your happiness."

Rita eyed Tonya with an "I don't believe you" look. "I don't know about you, but my work doesn't make me all that happy. Don't get me wrong, I do love my work," she said as she sat down. "So, what is it?"

"Nothing," Tonya insisted. There was no way that she could tell Rita about her involvement with Dexter. Rita was nice and all of that, but she loved to gossip too much. As her grandmother always said, "A dog that brings a bone, will carry a bone."

"What's up? Is there a new love interest?" Rita pursed

her lips in deep thought. "I'd be willing to bet that's what it is."

"Okay, I'll admit that. There is someone involved."

"Who is it? Where'd you meet him? What's his name?" she asked rapidly.

"My, my, aren't we nosey. Let's just say he's someone we both know."

She looked thoughtfully. "There's nobody that we both know except . . . no, not him! Dexter, is it Dexter?" she asked, squealing in delight.

"Yes, girl. It's him." Tonya laughed.

Rita jumped up from the chair and closed the door. "Tell me every juicy detail. Don't leave anything out."

"There's nothing to tell. We had dinner one Friday, he came in to see my place, and the rest is history." She giggled as she said this. She knew it was killing Rita because she was only giving bits and pieces of information.

"Okay, you had dinner and he came inside. Then what?" she asked, hoping to drag out more information.

"We went out for dinner and he came inside to see my place."

"You can skip all of that. What happened after he got inside?"

"Nothing," she said, trying to suppress a smile.

"Aw, come on now, tell the truth," she begged.

"Okay, okay. You're right, *something* did happen."

Rita began squealing. "I knew it, I knew it. No wonder you're so happy."

"Yes, that's part of the reason why I'm in such a good mood."

"So, how was it?"

"Damn good. Each and every time was *damn good,"* she said, laughing.

"How long has this been going on?"

"Don't worry about it."

"Well, where is Mr. Wonderful today? I haven't seen him."

"I don't know. Maybe he hasn't made it in yet."

"So, what does this mean? Are you and he officially an item or what?" Rita asked.

"We talked about it. We decided to be friends first and if anything comes out of it, we'll deal with it at that time. You know, I thought about that woman you told me was with him at that party. I still don't know who she is."

"You didn't ask him?"

"No. I know it was stupid. What if she's his other woman or something? Where does that leave me?"

"You need to find out. I'm sure she was just a friend. Besides, why would he jump in the sack with you, when he could have been with her?" she asked.

"I don't know. Maybe he wants his cake and ice cream, too," she said with a hint of dread.

"It's probably nothing. Hey, let's go to lunch at Rico's. We can get some spaghetti."

She knew Rita was trying to change the subject to keep her from worrying about it.

"Okay."

They arrived at Rico's at one. There was a thirty-minute wait for a table. Rico's was well-known for it's Italian foods. They sat in the waiting area until a table was available.

Tonya was sipping on a coke and Rita casually thumbed through a magazine. Suddenly, she stopped turning the pages, as if her hand was glued to the page.

"What's wrong?" Tonya asked.

"Dexter's in this magazine." She closed the magazine in a hurry.

Tonya leaned over and read the cover of the magazine. "He's in Black Professionals? What's he in there for?" she asked with excitement.

"One of the most eligible bachelor's of '99. It's not all that interesting."

Rita was acting strange and this piqued Tonya's curiosity. "Oh really? What does it say about him?" The expression on her face was beginning to worry her.

"What law firm does Dexter work for in Atlanta?" she asked.

"Vince and Horton, why?" She didn't like the way Rita was acting. Something had to be wrong.

Rita figured Tonya would find out sooner or later. It may as well be sooner. She opened the magazine to the page she was reading. "Well, the article says that they are sad to announce that Dexter Freeman is no longer on the up for grabs list. Due to his recent engagement to his former wife, Melissa Ferguson, they aren't going to be featuring him in their most eligible bachelor's issue next year. It continues to say that his former wife is an associate attorney at Vince and Horton?"

"What? Give me that magazine." She snatched it away from Rita and began reading it. It was all true, every disgusting word was true. She was hoping that it was another Dexter Freeman. It was definitely him, plain and clear, in black and white and you know how the saying goes, "If it's printed in black and white, you can believe it."

"Wait, what issue is that? It could be an older issue. You know how these places have old magazines lying around." Rita didn't want to upset Tonya. It would be a drastic change from her higher than life mood earlier. "I didn't even know he had been married or did I?" Rita said thoughtfully.

Tonya's stomach was balling up in knots. There was no lying about it, it was true. "No. It's a current issue, February '99." Tonya examined the article closer.

"Maybe it was a misunderstanding or the engagement could have been called off," Rita said.

Tonya was close to tears. She could feel them welling

up under her eyes. Just when she thought she would be happy again. There was no use ordering any food because she no longer had an appetite.

"Rita, do you mind if we get out of here? I'm ready to leave. Maybe we could get something to go."

The hostess came over and said, "Your table is ready, ma'am."

"We won't be needing it," Rita said. "Okay, baby. We're leaving now."

On the way back to work she cursed herself. She shouldn't have fooled herself. It was just another time that she had been used. He was persistent, pretending like he was so interested in her. Men could be so cruel. Pretenders, that's what they were—great pretenders.

The rest of the day was terrible. She kept eyeing the clock and five o'clock wouldn't come. Rita stopped by at the day's end to check on her. Tonya assured her that everything was fine. Everything wasn't fine, she wasn't fine.

Sixteen

On the way home she kept telling herself that she wasn't hurt. She didn't care what Dexter did anymore. It wasn't as if he really loved her because if he did, she wouldn't feel the pain she was feeling right then.

To top it all off, there was bumper-to-bumper traffic on the freeway. There was always traffic on the freeways going south of Houston, but that day it was horrendous. People were tailgating and being very uncourteous, forget that they were being downright rude.

Tonya slowed down on the entrance to the freeway. She was already in a foul mood, and the attitudes of other drivers added to it. The car ahead of her dashed out in front of an eighteen wheeler and was almost hit. The angry truck driver blew his horn in aggravation.

It was now Tonya's turn to get into the traffic. She hated having to get on the freeway when it was that crowded. Sweat covered her brow as she waited for an opportunity to get on. No one would let her in. She tried to inch her Cirrus in front of a woman in a green Camaro. The woman was determined not to let her in and quickly closed her out of the flow of traffic. This just pissed her off. *So that's how you want to play?* Tonya sped up and swirved in front of the Camaro. *Take that!*

There, she was in. Through her rearview mirror, she

could see the woman's mouth moving, shouting obsceni-
ties. It was beneath Tonya to stoop to the other woman's
level. In today's society, one could easily become the victim of a drive by, and since Texas had made it legal to
carry a concealed weapon, Tonya was not about to get
into an argument with some stranger. She turned on her
radio to catch action traffic on 97.9 The Box. The DJ
mentioned construction on the freeway, which happened
to be in the direction she was going.

Finally, traffic began to move and Tonya was close to
her exit. She moved over into the exit-only lane and was
about to get off of the freeway, when she felt a jolt that
sent her car spinning. She could see the blur of a green
car whizzing by as her car careened into a guardrail,
bounced off, and hit a feeder wall.

Her head was resting on the steering wheel. She put
her hand to her forehead and could feel warm liquid on
her fingers. Her head was throbbing. There was the faint
sound of sirens in the distance. Someone was standing
outside of her car looking inside.

"Tonya, are you okay? Everything is going to be alright,
help is on the way."

Who knew her? She saw that it was Warren trying to
help her. "Warren?" Where did he come from?

He held her hand and gave it a light squeeze. "Yeah,
it's me. I was on my way home and saw the accident."

"What happened?" She tried to lie back in her seat,
but was dizzy. The sirens were upon them.

"Don't try to move, the ambulance is already here. Let
them move you."

"The ambulance? I don't want to go to the hospital."
The car door was pried open by the fire department.

"Don't worry, I'll go with you. I'll follow the ambulance
to the hospital."

She had a slight concussion, a few bruises, and a totaled out car. The doctor loaded her down with pain medication and was directing all instructions to Warren, as if she was his responsibility.

"Make sure she takes this medication twice a day," the doctor said to Warren. "The pain pills can be taken every four to six hours. She will experience some dizziness from time to time but if this lasts over two days, you need to bring her in for further examination."

"Okay, doctor. I think I can handle it from here. Twice a day." Warren held up each pill bottle. "Every four to six hours and if dizziness persists, back in two days."

Warren helped Tonya into the car. She didn't want Warren to feel like he had to see after her. She could go to her parents house to stay. "Warren, you don't have to look after me. I'll be alright. Maybe I could have my mother pick me up."

Warren looked sideways at her and started the engine. "You heard what the doctor said. I'm supposed to make sure you take your medication. Besides, I don't mind." There she was in his car and vulnerable. She needed someone to be there for her and he wanted to be that someone. She never asked him to call anyone for her or to get in touch with that boyfriend of hers.

"I just don't want you to feel like I'm your responsibility."

"Is there anyone you need me to call for you? What about your friend, Dexter?"

The very mention of his name added to the pain in her head. "No, I don't want you to call him and he's no friend of mine. I need to call my mother when I get home and that's it."

He had to suppress the surge of happiness that threatened to overflow. He was almost elated with the idea of her misery with the boyfriend. This was a window of opportunity, but he couldn't rush her.

"Okay, you can call her when you get home. Since I'm going to be keeping an eye on you, why don't you crash over at my place. I'm harmless, so you don't have to worry about me trying to take advantage of you."

"Is that right?" Tonya eyed him warily. "No taking advantage, huh?"

Warren smiled and put his hand to his chest. "Cross my heart. Besides, you'll be all doped up on pain pills and I prefer my victims to be well aware of what's going on."

Tonya attempted a smile that was cut short by a wince. "Since I can't convince you otherwise, why don't you stay over at my apartment. It will be easier for you to go back and forth if you need anything. Since I'll probably be sleeping, you might want to take a spare key to let yourself in."

"Yeah, you're right. At least we know your brain is still functioning okay, that's a good idea."

Warren escorted her inside of her apartment, but said he would return shortly after he gathered up some of his work from home and picked up some clothes.

After Warren left, she gazed at the closed door. There she was inviting a stranger into her house. Not only did she invite him in, she gave him a spare key. Dexter never had a spare key to her place. She knew little, if anything, about her assumed caregiver. It was nice of him to take on that responsibility, but, she preferred to have family to take care of her. Tonya knew that as soon as she called her mother, she would get all in a fluster, fly over to her apartment and insist of staying with her until she decided that Tonya was all better. *Nah, I don't need that. What I need is space and some time to think.*

She convinced herself that Warren was no sadistic killer. He worked every day, had a great outlook on life, and truly seemed like a nice person. For God's sake, he lived right next door! There was no way that there could be a psycho living next door to her and she not know it—right? Right.

Her ordeal had almost overshadowed her depression over Dexter. That is—almost! Then she remembered her bad mood that eventually resulted in her having a wreck. The man was more trouble than he was worth.

She closed her eyes, trying to blot out the impending misery. One eye opened and the phone stared her in the face. She closed her eye again, only to open both of them and the phone stared her down. She wasn't calling him. As much as she wanted to give him a piece of her mind, she couldn't.

With one ragged movement, she picked up the phone and slammed it back on the receiver. What would she say? Dexter, I thought we were starting out with a trusting relationship. How are we supposed to start a relationship when you failed to mention that you are engaged?

It was plain and clear that she had been used, *again*. It was true that they talked about starting a relationship, but settled for being friends first. Of course, he said he loved her, but now that she thought about it, it was when he thought she was breaking up with him.

She had no idea what his intentions were for her. She knew that if she picked up the phone and called him she would make herself look stupid. She was mature enough to handle it. Like most men, he would think she was over-reacting if she jumped on his case about it. Maybe it was like Rita said, maybe the engagement was off.

Although her mind kept trying to convince her to do otherwise, she made up her mind, she wasn't calling him. If he wanted to talk, he would have to call her. The wait was killing her. She sat on the couch staring at the phone, hoping it would ring. *Ring! Ring!* Where was Warren when she could use the distraction? What was taking him so long?

Thoughts of her and Dexter making love flashed in her mind. *How could I be so naive?* What did she mean how could she be so naive? She was bred into naivete. There she was once again, blaming her parents for her sheltered life. How could she blame them, when she was the one making the decisions?

The phone would never ring if she kept watching it. Walking slowly to the bathroom, she turned on the shower. She ached in places she didn't know she had and then there was the fatigue. She was almost exhausted just from walking to the bathroom. She put the phone close by so she could hear it ring. Still, there was no sign of Warren.

She undressed and became disgusted with herself. She could feel Dexter's hands touching her and caressing her all over. She stood with her face under the streams of water. The hot beads pelted her body, numbing her all over. She could have sworn she heard the phone ringing. She peeped her head from behind the curtain. It was only her imagination. After she got out of the shower, she picked up the phone just to make sure it was plugged in. There was a dial tone, he just hadn't called.

She set the phone on the bed and waited, as she put on her nightgown. It was after nine o'clock, he wasn't calling. There was the faint sound of someone turning the knob on the front door and at the same time, the phone rang and her heart started racing. She didn't know whether to see who was at the door or to answer the phone. Catching a glimpse of Warren coming through the door, she opted to answer the phone.

"Hello," she answered, short of breath. Every fiber in her body told her that it was Dexter on the other end of the line. Warren was moving around noisily in the kitchen.

"How are you feeling?" It was Rita.

Tonya couldn't hide her disappointment. "Oh, I'm fine." She didn't mean to sound like she didn't want to talk to her. Why is it that when you are waiting on a particular phone call, everybody calls but that right person? Isn't that the most irritating thing? Tonya stopped short of smacking her lips in agitation.

"Jeez, I'm happy to hear from you, too." Rita pretended to be hurt.

"You won't believe what the end of my day was like. It was a nightmare." Her voice cracked slightly.

"What happened? Did you confront Dexter?"

"No, that's the last thing I feel like doing right now. I had an accident on the way home."

Rite sucked her teeth. She figured that Tonya had gone out and darn near killed herself because she was upset with Dexter. "An accident? What—how did it happen?"

Tonya went into the details of how she and the driver of the Camaro got into a curse match and how the car hit her from behind.

"That is unbelievable." Rita was shocked that Tonya would actually get into a bout like that with someone. Was Tonya reduced to this? It was so unlike her to stoop to that level.

"I know. This all stemmed from me being angry with him!" Warren stood at the door and mouthed out *time to eat!* She nodded her head and mouthed *okay!* That was Warren's cue to leave, but he stood planted where he was. What was that supposed to mean? Was he going to patrol the area until she hung up the phone?

"I know you were hoping it was Dexter calling. Have you talked to him yet?"

Tonya lowered her voice. Although she had no intimate ties to Warren, she didn't want to blab to the whole world that she had been treated like a doormat and stepped on—*once again!* "No. I'm not sure I want to. I don't know what to say or how to bring the subject up."

Rita, being her usual sharp self, noticed her voice going soft. "What are you whispering for? You're acting like this is a secret conversation. Just ask him if what they said in the magazine is true. The only thing he can do, is say yes or no."

"You're right. I'm just afraid of what that answer might be. Why would he do this if he was engaged to someone?" Warren remained at the door, glancing irritably at his watch. *What?* She wasn't forcing him to wait for her to end her conversation. "Excuse me a moment, Rita." She put her hand over the phone. "Warren, I'll be off soon. Can you give me a couple of minutes?"

"Okay, a couple of minutes and then you *must* eat. You know you have to take your medications." He went back to the kitchen and resumed doing whatever he was doing in there.

"Girl, I'm back. Sorry about that." She should have gone ahead and explained because the inevitable was about to come. Rita was going to ask her what that was all about.

"Who were you talking to? Did I hear the sound of a male voice in the background?" There she was feeling sorry for Tonya because she was upset about Dexter and she has some brother over there.

"That's my neighbor, Warren. He saw the accident and followed me to the hospital. Needless to say, that he has declared himself as my caretaker until I get better."

"I've seen him a couple of times when I was going over to your place. Seems like he might be a nice guy. What is he going to do—spend the night?" Rita was laughing. Surely that wasn't the case. He was going to make sure she was okay and then go home—right?

"Actually, he's going to stay over for a few days and go back and forth to his place as he needs to."

Obviously, that accident damaged more than just her car. It apparently wrecked part of her brain too. "Tonya, you don't know that much about him, except that he lives next door."

"You don't have to remind me. It seems like it means a lot to him to do this. Besides, he wouldn't take no for an answer."

"Why don't you give Dexter a call, you might feel better about the situation."

"No, I'm just going to forget it all happened. Well, maybe I will call him and give him a piece of my mind."

She told Rita that she would talk to her later and her hand began to shake as she dialed his number. *What if she's there, how would he treat me?* She was so afraid. It began to ring.

"Hello." He answered half asleep.

"Dexter, it's Tonya." She felt faint.

"Hey," he said. "So what's up?" Her timing couldn't have been worse. Melissa decided to surprise him by coming to visit. It was a good thing she was asleep, at least he hoped so.

"Why didn't you tell me you were engaged?" she asked, trying to keep her composure. Why was he sounding so guarded? Was he trying to pretend it was a business call. "How could something so important slip your mind? I saw the article on you in the magazine. All I want to know is why me?"

"Tonya . . ." he began. He knew it was only a matter of time before something happened to ruin his life.

"No, no, don't Tonya me. I don't ever want to see you again. Don't bother calling me, because I won't be here." She slammed down the phone.

Warren stepped in her door. "Is something wrong?" He didn't want to get in her business, but she seemed to be terribly upset. When she didn't answer him he walked over to her and sat next to her on the bed. "I'm not trying to pry, I just want to help, if I can."

Tonya let out a groan. "There's nothing you can do to help. I'm not trying to be rude, but I want to be alone."

"Do you want to talk about it?"

"No, I just want to be by myself and think about some things." She rested her head on her knees.

Warren could feel the pain she was going through without her ever saying a word. He took her hand and caressed it. "I know you're upset, possibly hurting but, I can't leave you alone."

Tonya gave Warren a crossed look. "What do you mean?"

"You have to eat and take your medication. Then and only then, will I leave you alone. We had an agreement, remember?"

"Oh, I forgot about that. I'm not hungry right now."

"You can't take your medicine on an empty stomach. If you eat just a little and take your medicine, I'll leave you alone."

"Okay, just a little." If she didn't agree, she knew she would never have any moment of peace. Warren went to the kitchen and brought back a bowl of soup.

The phone rang, but she didn't answer it. She already knew it was Dexter. He kept calling and calling.

"Why won't you answer the phone?"

"It's just someone that I don't want to be bothered with." There was nothing she had to say to Dexter. She was hurt, but she would get over it.

"Would you like for me to answer it? I can take a message."

Tonya shrugged her shoulders, it didn't matter anymore. Warren took her indifference as an okay to answer the phone.

"Hello," Warren answered. There was a pause on the other end of the line.

"Is anyone there?" Warren asked the silent end of the line. Warren got the feeling that it was Tonya's boyfriend refusing to say anything.

"I'm sorry, I must have the wrong number," Dexter said.

"Who did you want to speak to?"

"I wanted to speak to Tonya Locksley, apparently I have the wrong number."

"No, you have the correct number." Warren looked at Tonya, who kept her head to her knees. "She's here, but she's indisposed at the moment. May I take a message?"

Indisposed? What does he mean indisposed? "Who am I speaking with?" There was a touch of anger in Dexter's tone.

"This is her neighbor, Warren." Warren was happy to announce himself. Now, who was on the other side of the door?

"Just tell her to call Dexter," he snapped.

"I sure will." Warren smiled to himself. Warren was sure this ticked Dexter off by the way he slammed down the phone.

"I'm sure you know who that was," Warren said.

"Dexter, right?"

"Right. He said to tell you he called."

"And so you did. You're keeping up your end of the bargain and so am I. I'm going to eat and call it a night."

"That's fine with me."

She was determined to get herself better and get Warren back to his own apartment. His mothering was getting on her nerves. She ate what she was supposed to when she was supposed to and took her medications on time.

Three days had gone by and her phone continued to ring off the hook. She had finally convinced Warren that he could go back home. He was a little reluctant, but he gave in.

Tonya had decided to go back to work on the next day. Her insurance company provided her with a loaner car until they decided whether her car could be fixed or if it was beyond repair.

She looked at the clock. It was three o'clock, time for Jerry Springer! A lot of people at the firm watched Jerry Springer. They would tape it while at work and watch it later. The next day, that would be the morning topic. On that afternoon, Jerry's subject was *My Husband's in Love with My Sister!* Tonya never got off into Jerry because it wasn't all that much to her. She didn't understand what excited people the most about his show. She was going to find out just what was so hot about his show that day.

About fifteen minutes into the show, one lady's husband was beating down his wife's sister's husband. There were nothing but fights on the show. It was annoying that the bodyguards would only let the people who were fighting get one or two punches in before breaking them up. *Hey, this show's kind of exciting!*

Two women were sitting on the stage talking to Jerry. Both were from a small town in Mississippi. One of the women, who was in disguise, went by the name of Angel. The other woman who didn't bother hiding her identity, was Cheryl. Cheryl brought Angel on the show to tell her what her husband refused to admit.

"I don't know why you bothered with a disguise," Cheryl told her sister.

"Usually when people are brought on this show, it's because of something that is shocking. I'm not going to be embarrassed on national television," Angel replied, pushing her shades farther up on her face.

Tonya thought Angel was smart. She went to the show expecting the worst and planned to save face at the same time. It was obvious to Tonya that there was some animosity between the two women.

"Well," Cheryl began, "everybody back home is going to know who you are."

"That doesn't bother me. At least all of America won't know who I am. What was so important that you had to bring me on this show to tell me?"

Tonya could not blame the woman for concealing her identity.

"I brought you here to tell you that Harold has been making a fool out of you." Cheryl watched her sister's expression remain passive. "He's been having an affair."

"How do you know so much about what Harold is or isn't doing?" Angel asked.

"Telling you that Harold is having an affair is not as important as *who* he's having an affair with."

Cheryl seemed to take pride in telling her sister that her husband was having an affair. Some people could be so tacky. Tonya sank deeper into the couch, wrapping her blanket around her tighter.

Angel didn't respond to Cheryl's statement. She was moving her head from side to side, as if she was trying to control her temper.

Cheryl said Angel's real name, which was bleeped out. "Harold's been having an affair with me for several months now. I wanted to tell you because Harold swore he would never tell you."

Things got out of control when Jerry brought Harold on stage. Cheryl and Angel had to be broken up twice. When Cheryl's husband and Harold went blow for blow, the audience started chanting Jerry's name. It was pitiful that family would do such treacherous things to one another.

Tonya was so involved in the show that the person knocking on her door must have knocked five times before she heard it. She looked through the peep hole.

There was Dexter standing in front of her door as if he expected her to open the door. She ignored him and turned up the television to drown out his knocking. *That's what I think of you, Dexter Freeman!*

Seventeen

"Guess who just walked into the building," Rita was on the lookout with concern written in her features.

"I don't want to know." Tonya was busy and she didn't care what Dexter did or didn't do. At least this is what she told herself.

"You can drop the act, you know you're anxious. Maybe there is a good reason why he didn't mention this *Melissa* woman to you."

"I can only guess why." Tonya sneered. "He wanted a woman in Houston and a woman in Atlanta, how convenient." She was sick of talking about him. Everything was on instant replay in her mind, every smile, every touch. *Player, player!* She had gotten played by a player.

"I think I'd better make myself scarce. You will probably be the first person he'll come to see."

"That's where I think you're wrong. He'll probably take the attitude that he didn't need me anyway. You know how some men think." She was once again mad at the world, and it was all because of the actions or inactions of one man.

Dexter barged in with much attitude. There was no way he was going to let a woman dismiss him. He wasn't about getting dismissed. Nah, that wasn't with his program. She was going to listen and if anybody did any dismissing, it would be him. At least that was his plan. A brother had to be hard, even if it was just a front.

He ignored Rita's presence and said, "We need to talk."

Rita headed out the door. "I'll see you later. Nice seeing you again, Dexter."

Dexter nodded. "I've been constantly calling you and you won't pick up the phone. I even went to your front door and you wouldn't open it. I guess this is the only way to get you to hear me out . . . and what was your neighbor doing at your house that time of the night?"

"I don't want to hear any of it," she said, trying to keep her voice down. She didn't want to be the one to initiate the screaming.

"Well, it's not about what you want, is it?" he asked angrily.

"Look . . ." Tonya looked at Dexter with an *I don't have time* expression.

"No, you look." He leaned over her desk, pointing his finger at her. "How are you going to ask for an explanation and not wait to hear it?" It was beginning to be important to him that she listened to his explanation—whatever explanation that may be.

"I have work to do. After all, that's what I'm here for. This is a job, and I can't do my job if you're here interrupting me."

"Your work can wait. If it's that important, I'll get someone else to work on it until we've discussed this matter."

"Not only is it important to me, it's important to you, too. It's the Tanzent case." He was starting to intimidate her as he stood staring down his nose at her. She was determined not to be dissuaded from her objective of being angry.

"Okay, I'm listening," she snapped. If she listened to him right then, it would get him out of her office sooner. He seemed to be caught off guard.

Now that he had her undivided attention, he didn't know what he was going to say. He was so busy trying to get her to hear him out that he hadn't thought about how he would begin to explain. He sat down and gathered his thoughts. "What you read in the magazine isn't true. I am not engaged to Melissa. She made it up," he explained. He could tell by her expression that she wasn't buying it.

"How can you sit there and accuse this woman of lying? Either you are or you aren't. Let's call a spade, a spade. Which is it?" She could feel herself about to nut-up on him. Men think women should believe everything they say. If they say the sky is orange, you're supposed to believe the sky is orange. If he had told her that a year ago, she would have believed him and been outside waiting for Skittles to fall from the sky.

"Lisa . . . ah, Melissa," he corrected himself, "and I were college sweethearts. She was there with me through my struggle in college and we dated on and off while I went to law school. As the years went on, the love I had for her started to fade. I started to realize that we were just two totally different people. I loved her, but not the way a man should love a woman when he wants to spend the rest of his life with her. I caused her a lot of pain and still, she was there. I didn't *love* her, but I felt as if I owed her.

"She couldn't deal with the way other women reacted to me. Everywhere we went there were women who knew me or wanted to get to know me and she couldn't deal with it. Obviously, marriage was something she wanted desperately and she felt that if we were engaged, our relationship would be secure. Maybe the only way for her to feel secure was for me to marry her. Anyway, my parents convinced me that I should marry her and I did. As far as I'm concerned, it was a mistake," he finished. He wanted to play the hard role with her. Somehow he found that he wanted to tell her the truth and that was the truth. He couldn't tell her the real reason he never brought up Melissa. No one wants to go into a relationship with the idea of competition waiting in the wings, especially persistent competition. How could he tell her that his parents planned for him to remarry Melissa? How could he tell her that his father would never accept her as a member of their family? He wanted to spare someone as nice as she the heartbreak.

"I can't believe you would marry someone you didn't love." *Pl-lease, I know he doesn't think I'm going to believe that lie.*

"That's the truth, I swear."

"I guess your ex-wife is so desperate to have you back that she deliberately lied about getting remarried to you. Apparently you haven't told her any different, so obviously you agreed. I'm happy you took the time to explain this to me, but I'm not buying it. You can go back to *Lisa* or whoever she is."

"I thought we were working on something here. I'm not ready for something that's barely begun to end." He was being greedy and he knew it.

"How can we be working on something when you never told me you had an ex-wife? Are there any kids I should know about? What am I supposed to do? You can't expect me to wait around for you while you pretend that this engagement will go away. I can't—I won't do it." This was tearing her heart out. She wanted so much to say let's just put all of this behind us. He was adding salt to an open wound just by being in her presence.

He stood up with what appeared to be sadness on his face. "Is that it? It that your final word?" He knew it would all end soon.

She couldn't look him in the eyes so she focused on her desk.

"Yes," she answered with finality. He was about to say

something else, when his father walked in. He stood in the door and looked at the both of them. She was unaware of the tears welling up in her eyes.

"Is something going on here?" Mr. Freeman asked looking from Dexter to Tonya.

"No," Dexter said coolly, looking directly at her. "We were just ending a discussion."

Mr. Freeman looked intently at her and asked, "If nothing's going on, why are there tears in her eyes?"

Dexter looked surprised when he saw her face. She picked an awkward time to be embarrassed.

"Ms. Locksley, what's wrong?" Mr. Freeman asked.

"Oh, it's just problems at home. It's nothing I can't deal with," she said, avoiding his gaze. He looked at Dexter and said, "I want to see you in my office—right now."

Mr. Freeman left her office with Dexter in close pursuit.

Tonya was a mess and didn't want anyone to see her in such a sappy condition. She headed down the hall to the restroom to check her face. She had to pass Mr. Freeman's office to get there and overheard them engage in an intense conversation.

"Dexter, what's going on between you and Ms. Locksley?" Mr. Freeman asked.

"There's nothing going on," Dexter answered.

"Don't lie to me. Anybody can see *something's* going on. What have you done to her?"

"What do you mean, *what have I done to her*? If I did do *something* to her, it would be *my* business."

"When *your* personal business enters *my* workplace, it becomes *my* business, too. You should stay away from her. You seem to have caused her enough misery already. How can she work proficiently if her mind is occupied on other things—on you? Besides, you know Melissa wants to reconcile."

"Melissa had no right to tell that magazine that we

were engaged. That could be nothing further from the truth."

"Melissa didn't tell Black Professionals you were engaged. I told them," Mr. Freeman said. "It may as well be publicly known."

Tonya didn't want to get caught eavesdropping, so she went on to the restroom. How could she face Mr. Freeman, knowing that he knew what happened between them? She really knew how to complicate her life.

She dried her eyes, determined to keep her composure. Leaning over the bathroom sink, she fought to keep her composure. Although she cared deeply for Dexter, she would not be his fool. Yet, that's the role she played. How could she not see what was coming? How could she have fallen into his trap so willingly? Beating herself over her mistakes would never change the way things were.

He had met her family for God's sake! Now her family would think she couldn't keep a relationship without something going wrong. *Who cares what they think? They don't know the reason we broke up and they never will.* She gazed at her puffy eyes in the mirror. For all the brains she had, she was dumb in the man department. Once again, she wanted to blame it on her parents, but they couldn't be held accountable for her failed relationships.

She could hear Reggie now, *I told you to stay away from him! You never listen.* Maybe she would avoid Reggie for a while. Tonya wouldn't have to tell him she and Dexter had broken up. All he had to do was take one look at her and he would know. Oh yeah, she could see Reggie now, sucking on those gold teeth before launching into his lecture. *Didn't I teach you anything? You've been in school all this time and still haven't learned a thing. I tell you, my work is never done.*

Yes, that was Reggie alright. For someone who was always down on himself, he had the tendency to be right. God she hated when he was right!

* * *

Dexter knew something was coming, he just didn't know what. More than anything, he didn't want to admit he was wrong. But, he knew he was. No matter how he switched the scenario, it all boiled down to him not being totally open with Tonya. Had he been up-front with her, perhaps he wouldn't be in this predicament. He would have preferred for her to be angry with him and she was, but more than being angry, she was hurt. He would have given anything to keep those tears from falling from her eyes.

"But that's just it. I could have done something about it," Dexter said to himself.

He stared at the closed office door. His father was overstepping his boundary. How dare his father just assume that he had the right to invite himself into his personal business? Angrily, he picked up a dart from his desk and flung it at the board attached to the back of the door. How could his father continue to try to control him? He flung another dart, barely hitting the edge of the board. How dare his father tell him to stay away from Tonya? Another dart hit the board with a *whack*. Didn't his father realize that he wasn't a kid anymore? *Whack!* He was angry with Melissa for ever walking into his life. *Whack!* He was angry with his father. *Whack!* He was angry with himself for falling in love with Tonya Locksley. On that final *whack*, he hit the bull's-eye.

That's what irked him the most. He loved her and she dumped him. *He had been dumped!* He had never been dumped before. It was always the woman who had messed up any of the previous relationships he had been involved in. *Well, there is a first time for everything!*

Why didn't he think his explanation through a little further? He walked over to the board and removed the darts. He returned the darts to his desk tray and sat on the edge of his desk. He could have come up with a more elaborate reason for not telling Tonya about his *hypothetical* engagement to Melissa. Was Melissa always going to be a dark cloud hanging over his head? Just when he had found his silver lining, she came along and destroyed it. Was he ever going to be in complete control of his life? He had to think of a way to get Tonya back and that was all it was to it. Dexter was determined not to let her get away from him.

Would a more elaborate excuse have been a lie? There is only so much truth to be told before the truth ends and the lying begins. Lie, lie, lie, lie, lie! That's what he was—a liar by default. But if he got down to it, he didn't lie about anything. His personality was befitting to his profession. He was a liar and lawyers lied—right?

Dexter shrugged off the thought. No. Not all lawyers were liars. His job was to find justice—the truth. The truth is what he loved the most. Why was he so down on himself? He had told her the truth and she couldn't handle it. *She couldn't handle the truth!* His lips curled into a wry smile. He really had a way of consoling himself. He found himself back at square one. He simply lied to Tonya.

"Forget her. That's what I'll do." Now he was lying to himself. He studied the dartboard before picking up a dart.

"If I make the bull's-eye, I'm going to get her back. If I don't, I won't get her back." He aimed the dart carefully before releasing it.

Dexter frowned when the dart missed the board altogether, lodging into the door.

"Damn! That's a stupid game to play anyway. Stupid childhood games!" He removed the dart from the door.

"I'm going to use this same dart. This time, I'll change the rules. If I hit the bull's-eye, I'll get her back. If I

miss . . ." He paused before laughing. "I'll get her back."
He aimed carefully and released the dart.

Bulls-eye! Just as he thought. He was determined to
make this a no-lose situation.

Eighteen

Tonya found herself evaluating her life more often than she wanted to. What could she say? It was a complete mess. The more she thought about it, the more distraught she became. She had become so wrapped up in her own life that she barely talked to her mother. This was rare since, she and her mother were so close. Reggie had called her and she hadn't bothered to return any of his calls.

Sometimes, there's no company like male company. You can hang out with your girlfriends, but it's not the same. At some point and time, the male perspective can be enlightening to your own problems. Warren was this source of enlightenment. Anytime she needed someone to talk to, he was there. At first, Tonya was reluctant to share her problems with him. Since her accident, she felt a special closeness with him. Some guys you want to date and some guys you want only as friends. Warren was this friend for her. Although he was wrapped in a nice package, Tonya only felt a need for friendship. When Warren realized that Tonya was having problems with Dexter, he didn't press the issue. He let her tell him in her own time. The only thing he did tell her was if she needed a friend and a listening ear, he was there. The first time she told him what was really going on between her and Dexter, she was close to tears. Not only was he sympathetic, he took her in his arms and held her close. Not a passionate close, but a comforting close. Warren was a blessing in disguise.

For the first time in weeks, she noticed that her plants were starving for water. The leaves were beginning to whither and about to take on that brownish color. She busied herself at plucking the dead leaves from the plants. It was ironic that her life, like her plants, needed pruning. In order for the plant to stay healthy and continue to grow, the dead leaves had to be removed. It was a hard fact that she had to get rid of the dead leaves in her life or be destined to stunted growth. There was a familiar knock at the door. It was funny how someone who visits a lot has a distinct knock. Tonya knew that she was long overdue for a visit from Reggie. Reggie stood in front of Tonya smiling two new gold teeth at her.

"What's up, sis?" There were two suitcases resting near his feet. He picked up the luggage and marched past Tonya.

"Nothing much. Long time no see, where have you been?"

"Down at the county?"

"The county?" Tonya asked. "What were you doing in jail?"

"Ah, you know, I had about fourteen hundred dollars in tickets. There was no way I was going to give up that kind of money to the county, so I laid it out."

"Reggie, how do you get that much in tickets? I just don't understand it. I haven't had a ticket in over four years."

"Well, I missed a couple of court dates and they issued warrants and all of that. My license was about to expire, so I had to clear up those tickets to get it renewed." Reggie explained. "Don't worry, I don't plan on getting any more tickets anytime soon."

Tonya clicked her tongue, eyeing his bags. "What time

This fall, BET Arabesque Films will create 10 original African American themed, made-for-TV movies based on the Arabesque Romance book series.

The list includes some of the best-loved Arabesque romances including Francis Ray's *Incognito*, Donna Hill's *Intimate Betray* Bridget Anderson's *Rendezvous*, Lynn Emery's *After All*, Felic Mason's *Rhapsody*, Monica Jackson's *Midnight Blue*, Dianne Mayhew's *Playing with Fire*, Donna Hill's *A Private Affair*, Jacquelin Thomas' *Hidden Blessings*, and Donna Hill's *Masquerade*.

And now BET is offering you the chance to win a cameo appearance in one of these upcoming productions! Just think, you can join some of today's hottest African-American movie stars—like Richard T. Jones, Loretta Devine, and Holly Robinson—in the creation of a movie written by, and for, African-American romantics like yourself! All you have to do is complete the attached entry form and mail it in. Just think, if you act now, you could be in one of these exciting new movies! Mail your entry today!

PRIZES

The **GRAND PRIZE WINNER** will receive:

- A trip for two to Los Angeles.
  Think about it—3 days and 2 nights in L.A., round-trip airfare, hotel accommodations.

- $500 spending money, and round-trip transportation to and from the airport and movie set...sounds pretty good, right?

- And the winner's clip will be featured on the Arabesque website!

- As if that's not enough, you'll also get a one-year membership in the Arabesque Book Club and a BET Arabesque Romance gift-pack.

5 RUNNERS-UP will receive:

- One-year memberships in the Arabesque Book Club and BET Arabesque Romance gift-packs.

WIN A CHANCE TO BE IN A
BET ARABESQUE FILM!

Yes! Enter me in the BET Arabesque Film Sweepstakes!

NAME

ADDRESS

CITY _____ STATE _____ ZIP

TELEPHONE _____ AGE

SIGNATURE

(MUST BE 21 OR OLDER TO ENTER)

ARABESQUE FILM SWEEPSTAKES
P.O. BOX 8060
GRAND RAPIDS, MN 55745-8060

AFFIX
STAMP
HERE

This fall, BET Arabesque Films will create 10 original African American themed, made-for-TV movies based on the Arabesque Romance book series.

The list includes some of the best-loved Arabesque romances including Francis Ray's *Incognito*, Donna Hill's *Intimate Betray* Bridget Anderson's *Rendezvous*, Lynn Emery's *After All*, Felici Mason's *Rhapsody*, Monica Jackson's *Midnight Blue*, Dianne Mayhew's *Playing with Fire*, Donna Hill's *A Private Affair*, Jacquelin Thomas' *Hidden Blessings,* and Donna Hill's *Masquerade*.

And now BET is offering you the chance to win a cameo appearance in one of these upcoming productions! Just think, you can join some of today's hottest African-American movie stars—like Richard T. Jones, Loretta Devine, and Holly Robinson—in the creation of a movie written by, and for, African-American romantics like yourself! All you have to do is complete the attached entry form and mail it in. Just think, if you act now, you could be in one of these exciting new movies! Mail your entry today!

PRIZES
The **GRAND PRIZE WINNER** will receive:
- A trip for two to Los Angeles.

  Think about it—3 days and 2 nights in L.A., round-trip airfare, hotel accommodations.

- $500 spending money, and round-trip transportation to and from the airport and movie set...sounds pretty good, right?

- And the winner's clip will be featured on the Arabesque website!

- As if that's not enough, you'll also get a one-year membership in the Arabesque Book Club and a BET Arabesque Romance gift-pack.

5 RUNNERS-UP will receive:
- One-year memberships in the Arabesque Book Club and BET Arabesque Romance gift-packs.

WIN A CHANCE TO BE IN A BET ARABESQUE FILM!

Yes! Enter me in the BET Arabesque Film Sweepstakes!

NAME _____

ADDRESS _____

CITY _____ STATE _____ ZIP _____

TELEPHONE _____ AGE _____

SIGNATURE _____

(MUST BE 21 OR OLDER TO ENTER)

ARABESQUE FILM SWEEPSTAKES
P.O. BOX 8060
GRAND RAPIDS, MN 55745-8060

AFFIX
STAMP
HERE

is it, beauty shop time?" She knew that Reggie would
want to crash at her place for a few days.

"Ha, ha, very funny." He put his luggage away in
Tonya's room and returned with a strange expression on
his face. "Nah, this time it's a little more than that." It
wasn't very often that she saw her brother in the strange
mood that he was in.

Tonya continued pulling away the dead leaves from her
plants as she talked. "Sounds serious. What's up?"

Reggie stretched his medium-size frame out on the
floor. "There're two things of importance on my mind.
The first, of course, is Ramona, and the second, is Kip."

Tonya glanced up from her plant for a moment. "Kip?
What about Kip?"

Reggie laced his fingers together before continuing.
"Can I give you the information based on priority? I really
need to talk about the Ramona situation first."

A chill went up her spine. Her brother, the happy-go-
lucky one, was dead serious. Tonya threw away the dead
leaves she had collected and stretched out alongside her
brother and stared blankly at the ceiling. She folded her
arms across her chest. "If that's more important right
now, then shoot."

"I guess it has a lot to do with Ramona, in a way. She's
a big part of it." Reggie was stalling.

"Will you quit procrastinating and just spill it out." She
could feel her brother staring at her profile.

"You know, Moms and Pops don't think I'm about anything. Sometimes I look at you, my little sister, and realize
that I was never the big brother you deserved. I feel like
such a failure." He took a deep breath then laced and
unlaced his fingers, while Tonya continued to stare at the
ceiling.

Tonya could hear the hurt in her brother's voice. She
knew this was hard for Reggie to admit. "Reggie, you're

anything but a failure. I think you've done well for yourself."

"Don't you see? It's not about what you think right now, it's about what our parents think. Why don't they ever give me any credit?"

This time, she faced her brother, who was wearing the pain he felt on the inside on his face. "Reggie, you know how our parents are, they are proud of you, they just don't know how to tell you. What brought all of this on anyway?"

Reggie rolled onto his back. "I heard them talking to some of their friends the other day. Their whole conversation was about all of the things you have accomplished. Not once, not once, did they mention anything that Kip or I have done. It was almost as if we don't exist. You know, I pretend like it's nothing, but it is something. I'm somebody, too."

"It doesn't matter what they say or don't say, Reggie, you're still their child. Whether you know it or not, you have been a great inspiration to me." Reggie's slight smile revealed the gold teeth.

"Don't try to make me feel better by making up stuff."

"No, I'm not kidding." Tonya looked Reggie directly in his eyes to confirm her point.

"How could I have been an inspiration to you? I dropped out of high school. I turned out to be everything that our parents wanted me not to."

"You dropped out of high school, but you got your GED. You still have the opportunity to go to college if you want to. Having a GED is better than having nothing at all. For Pete's sake, you have your own business. You're an entrepreneur. I don't think you're doing too bad at all. Cutting hair is something that you were talented to do. It's something that you love, and I figured to myself, if you could be successful doing something you loved, so could I."

"You're just trying to make me feel better."

"No, I kid you not."

"No bullshittin'?"

"No BS'ing."

Reggie cracked a smile. "Why couldn't you just say the word—no bullshittin'? You had to be all proper and say the acronym. Always a goodie-two-shoes. Go ahead, say it. You know I'm not going to leave you alone until you do."

Tonya smiled to herself. If only he knew half of the things she knew, he'd change his mind about the goodie-two-shoes thing. "Okay. No bullshitting."

"Damn, Tonya. You can't even cuss right. How are you going to cuss all proper? It's not *bullshitting*, it's bullshit-tin'."

Tonya rolled her eyes toward the ceiling. "Thank you, Reggie, for your curse 101 class."

"See, you were in the wrong class—again! My course was *Cuss* 101."

She couldn't believe her brother. At least he was beginning to sound more like himself.

"Have I ever told you that you were kind of on the off side?"

"Ah, maybe once or twice. Have I ever mentioned to you that Ramona is pregnant?"

Tonya closed her eyes. Now, they would never get rid of her. Ramona would be a permanent blemish in their family.

"Is it yours?"

"What do you mean, is it mine? Yeah, it's mine. At least I think so. Why? You think Ramona's been stepping out on me?"

She wished she hadn't asked the question. "You know I don't know anything about you and Ramona. It was just a question, that's all. You know Mom and Dad are going to flip on this one. Is that what brought all of this on, Ramona being pregnant? You've heard Mom and Dad talk about me to other people before and it never affected you like this."

"Maybe. I was just thinking, how am I going to be a father to a kid and I'm a failure? I wouldn't want my kid to turn out to be a failure, too."

"You know, I think you'll be a wonderful father. So, what about Kip?"

"Man, Kip is out there bad. Somebody came into the barbershop and told me they saw Kip the other week, lying in a ditch, passed out drunk. Kip's drinking is out of control. It's getting so bad that he comes around the shop begging people for money so he can buy a drink. I'm starting to think he'll run off my customers."

Tonya chewed her bottom lip. "I didn't think it would have gotten this bad. We've got to get Kip some help."

"I think you're right, but Kip don't want to be helped. He's happy doing just what he's doing. I saw him hanging in front of the liquor store and I told him that he needed help because he was an alcoholic. You know what he told me? He said that he wasn't no alcoholic, he was a drunk, alcoholics go to meetings, drunks don't. I said, man, look at you, you're staggering and all. He said that he wasn't staggering, he just took a couple of steps backward. He is in complete denial."

"Did you tell Kip that he was in denial?"

"Yeah, I told him. He said that he wasn't in denial, the Nile is a river and he ain't in it. He's sad, I tell you."

"We'll think of something. We can't let our brother waste his life away like this."

Getting Kip help turned out to be more than a notion. Every time Tonya went looking for Kip, he turned out to be drunk. She felt sorry for her brother and there was no one to put the blame on, except him. Since they were kids, Kip planned to be an alcoholic. Whenever an adult would ask him what he wanted to be when he grew up, he would say he wanted to be an alcoholic. Sure enough, when Kip was old enough to legally drink, every day was a holiday for him. He even refused to get a driver's license because he knew that he was going to drive drunk. Instead of driving, he rode a bicycle. A bicycle was his transportation. Talk about being pathetic. The odd thing about the situation was, while riding his bicycle one night, he was hit by a drunk driver. He wasn't hurt or anything, but he did give the intoxicated driver some advice. He told the driver that he should turn in his license and get a bicycle. Now, they were the best of friends and hang around the liquor stores together.

How can someone be changed when they don't want to? Tonya was starting to believe that there was no hope of changing Kip. This particular day, Kip was at a popular hangout located near Reggie's shop. This hangout was on a vacant lot where there were makeshift stools set up under a tree. These drunks would sit under that tree from sun up to sundown.

It was easy to spot Kip. He was the one with the loudest laugh. Apparently, it had been several days since he'd had a bath or change clothes for that matter. His clothes had oil stains on them, like he had been working on cars. He kept on laughing and turned up a beer can as he did so.

Tonya touched him on the arm. She was afraid that dirt would smudge her fingertips. "Kip, can I speak to you for a moment please."

He turned around in surprise. "Well, if it isn't Miss High and Mighty. What are you doing in this part of town, slumming?" There was an air of hostility in his words. He took another swig of his beer.

"No, I'm not slumming. I came to see you. We need to talk." Tonya walked a little ways away from the tree, hoping Kip would follow suit. When he stood rooted in his spot, she knew she would have to convince him to visit with her away from his friends. "Do you mind coming over here so I can speak with you privately?"

Kip looked around at his friends. "Anything you have to say in private, can be said in front of my friends." He waved his arms in the direction of his friends. "This is my family away from my family. You can say what you have to say in front of them."

She hadn't come prepared to discuss something so private in front of his friends. "What I have to talk to you about doesn't concern your friends."

"Like I said, say it in front of them or don't say it at all."

"Okay, Kip. It's about your drinking."

Kip hung his mouth open in disbelief. His voice rose an octave. "My drinking? What about my drinking?"

"You don't think there's a problem with your drinking, Kip? Don't you think you drink too much?"

Kip laughed a hard laugh. The laughter rippled through his friends. "You hear that guys? You think I drink too much?" His friends laughed in chorus and testified to him not drinking too much. "Drink too much? I don't think I drink enough."

"Of course, your friends don't think you drink too much. Misery loves company. They want you to be down and out like they are." At first, she was leery of voicing her opinion. Since they all thought it was so funny, she didn't care. Kip was making her rescue effort difficult, but he would be saved yet.

Nineteen

It had been almost a month since she and Dexter broke it off. She hated to admit that she was miserable. He made it a point to let her know that he wasn't happy with her decision. What was she supposed to do—get with him on the down-low? That wasn't her cup of tea. Sneaking was something she wasn't capable of doing.

She often found him watching her when she was looking in another direction. Sometimes he'd look away when she caught him, most of the time he would continue staring and she would look away. She never thought she would resort to such childish behavior. When it was necessary for him to communicate with her, he would be strictly business. Sometimes, she would get phone calls at home and no one would say anything. She assumed it was him, but she could have been wrong. She couldn't take working under all of the stress. The whole situation was getting to her physically, she started getting sick every morning when she got to work. She couldn't keep anything on her stomach.

One morning Dexter went to her with some ideas on the Tanzent case. They were going to submit the original petition to the court and he wanted to make sure all of the addresses were correct in their name search.

"Here are some documents I want you to look over. I'm going to need you to talk with Mr. Tanzent for me this afternoon. I have an appointment with another client."

The more he talked the sicker she got. Her head was swimming and she could feel her breakfast on it's way up.

"Excuse me," she said as she ran to the restroom.

When she got back to the office, he was gone. The day was so long. It dragged on slowly. At four o'clock, Dexter went back to her office, only to find that she had dozed off.

"What's wrong with you?" he asked. He didn't like the looks of her. She was sick all of the time and now he found her sleeping. He knew they were careful when they made love except for that one time when it was just a spur of the moment thing. Anything was possible.

"What do you mean what's wrong with me?" she asked sharply.

"I've noticed you running to the restroom every morning for the last week. What's wrong?"

"I must have some kind of stomach flu. I just haven't been feeling well." What was he jumping down her throat for?

"Go to the doctor tomorrow. It doesn't make sense for you to be at work like this. Don't come in here tomorrow. Just to make sure you go, bring a doctor's permit when you come back."

"Don't worry about me, your concern is *Melissa.*"

"This isn't about *Melissa.* Get that doctor's permit," he said as he walked out.

Maybe he was right. She did need to go to the doctor. She called her doctor and scheduled an appointment for the next morning. She couldn't shake that tired feeling. It seemed like she couldn't get enough sleep. She hurried through her meeting with Jimmy. Any other time she would have been happy to be in his company, but today wasn't one of those days. She was exhausted.

Twenty

Dexter wasn't pleased with the idea that she didn't want him around anymore. He knew from the beginning that if he got involved with her, it would be the means to an end. Melissa would see to that. He didn't regret getting to know her or what happened between them. *How could my own father spread such a lie about me being engaged to Melissa?* If there was anyone he should be engaged to, it would have to be Tonya.

He picked up the phone to call Melissa's answering service. He was going to tell her that there was no way they would ever reconcile and she should get over it. He was sick of this stupid notion his parents and Melissa had that they would get back together. As far as his parents were concerned, it boiled down to monetary issues. He dialed her number.

"I have to talk to you." It was Mr. Freeman. He sat down in front of his son's desk. This matter with Dexter and Ms. Locksley had to stop.

"Can't it wait, Dad?" Dexter didn't have time for his father's lectures. His father could be domineering at times and now wasn't one of the times he wanted to be the star pupil.

"No, as a matter of fact it can't."

Dexter put the phone down. It was just like his father

to come in at the opportune moment to deter him from doing something that *he* wanted to do.

"What is it?" He knew it was a grave subject, because his father looked at him over the rim of his glasses. This was something he often did to Dexter when he was in chastising mode.

"I'm only going to say this once and once only. You and Ms. Locksley are not going to happen. I know you've been seeing her and I've noticed the way you watch her whenever she's around. You are going to remarry Melissa so, whatever is going on between the two of you must stop *right now.*"

He couldn't believe he was thirty years old and his father was telling him who he could and couldn't date.

"My personal life, and who I choose to put in it, is none of your business. I happen to care a lot about her." It was because of his father that he wasn't with her anymore.

"Now, son, I only want what's best for you."

"And what is that supposed to mean?"

"Just what I said—the best. Ms. Locksley is a nice young lady, but she's not what your mother and I had in mind for you."

"What did you and mother have in mind for me—Melissa?"

"Exactly. Her father and I go back ages and we've always told you that you and Melissa patching things up would be perfect. You also know that her father agreed to send some clients my way as soon as this little *marriage* issue is resolved."

"Damnit, father. I don't care about your potential clients." He slammed his fists against the hard wood of his desk and papers scattered. "You have no idea what's best for me. You only *think* you know what's best for me. You don't even know why I divorced her."

"And I don't want to know why you divorced her. Don't

say you don't care about our potential clients. This is our family's bread and butter we're talking about. Having clients is the way we make our living. Listen, Dexter, I will do everything in my power to keep you from hurting Melissa—*everything*. Now, you think about that and the future that Ms. Locksley has here with us."

Was his father trying to blackmail him? If he didn't know him better, he would think that was exactly what he was trying to do.

"What is that supposed to mean?"

Mr. Freeman walked to the door and opened it. "You just think about what I said. No Melissa—*no Ms. Locksley*. Don't make any hasty decisions, son. The future of our firm rests in your hands." He closed the door behind him. There was no way he was going to let his son make the biggest mistake of his life.

Twenty-one

She hated being in the doctor's office. There were nothing but sick people there. There was one obese woman there who coughed and hacked the entire time she was there, without so much as lifting a hand to her mouth. Another woman sniffed mercilessly. Germs were milling all around. After a forty-five-minute wait, she was called. She sat in the examining room waiting for the doctor to come in.

"Good morning, Ms. Locksley," Dr. Beverly said as he came in.

"Good morning, doctor." *Let's just get this over with, Doc?*

"So what seems to be the problem?" he asked.

"I think I must have some kind of virus, because nothing stays on my stomach. I stay tired all the time, and sometimes I feel dizzy."

"I see," he said as he wrote notes in a folder with her chart in it.

"And when was your last menstrual cycle?"

"The twentieth of last month."

"Well, how about we get a urine sample and rule out pregnancy."

"Oh, I don't need a pregnancy test. I'm not but a day or so late and that's usual for me."

"After we rule out pregnancy, we'll do other tests to see if there is a virus that's causing you to be sick."

She hated those little plastic cups. How were you supposed to use something that small? She gave the sample to the nurse and went back to the examining room and waited for the doctor to return.

A few minutes later the doctor walked back in. "Ms. Locksley your test results came out positive. You're about five weeks pregnant."

She couldn't be hearing right. "There must be some mistake. I can't be pregnant," she said in shock.

"You are very much pregnant. I'll need to do some blood work and get you started in prenatal care as soon as possible."

Prenatal care!! Everything from that moment on was a blur. He started rambling on and on about vitamins and iron and getting plenty of rest. This couldn't be happening! How could she tell Dexter?

Somehow the thought of falling from grace danced in her head. This one would kill her parents. How would she say it? *Mom and Dad, I'm pregnant by someone I'm not involved with anymore.* No, that won't work. *How about, Mom and Dad, you know I would never do anything to disappoint or embarrass you but . . .*

She worried more about what her parents thought than what Dexter would think of the situation. She had decided that he wasn't a factor in the situation, because he would never know about it.

Dexter entered her office bright and early the next day. He was the last person she wanted to see. "Since you're here, I assume that you've gone to the doctor," he said crisply.

"Yes, I did go." Tonya was vaguely aware of his presence. Her mind was on everything the doctor had told her. *I want a second opinion!*

"So, what did he have to say? Is there anything wrong?" he asked.

"I'm fine." She stared out the window. There was no way she could look him in the face and not tell him what was going on with her.

"Well, why have you been sick?"

"I don't have to discuss my medical conditions with you."

"If everything's fine, why not discuss it? Everything is supposed to be fine—right?"

Her mind was running wild. Little voices in her head kept telling her to tell him about the baby. She couldn't tell him, he's engaged, it would ruin all of his plans and hurt his fiancée terribly. *But, what about me? Do I keep this baby? I just don't know what to do.*

"Are you listening to me?" Dexter asked.

"What? Oh, yeah everything's fine. Could we discuss this another time? I have a lot I need to catch up on."

"I guess so, you're right, it's not any of my business. I was just concerned," he said, looking out the window.

He would never know how much she wanted to share this with him. In actuality, it was his right to be told, but she couldn't tell him. He turned toward the door and started to walk out.

"Dexter . . ." she called after him.

"Yes," he answered.

"Thanks for your concern, I didn't mean to be rude." It was on the tip of her tongue to tell him, but she changed her mind at the last minute.

He smiled. "Anytime."

After he left, she couldn't help thinking that this had been her opportunity and she had let is slip away. Shortly after Dexter left, Rita walked in.

"Hey, girl. How are you feeling?" Rita asked.

"I'm exhausted, I'm sick, and I am so confused."

"I can understand being sick and tired, but where does confused come in?" she asked.

"Girl, I just don't know." Her eyes brimmed over with tears. She turned her back to Rita so she couldn't see.

"What's wrong? Is it anything you want to talk about?" She hugged Tonya lightly on the shoulder.

"I went to the doctor yesterday."

"What—is anything wrong?" she asked, coming around to face Tonya. "Girl, you're crying, what's wrong?"

"I, I'm pregnant."

"Pregnant! By who?" she asked in disbelief.

"Dexter."

"Oh, girl, it's just a baby. Have you told him yet?"

"Told him! I can't tell him, he's engaged. Do you know what that would do to his fiancée? She would be devastated. I know I would. It's not that I'm so concerned about her feelings, I just don't want to be the cause of all of the problems," she said through sobs.

"That is his little red wagon. When do you plan on telling him? You do plan on telling him—right?" She pulled a couple of Kleenex out of the box on the desk and stuffed them in Tonya's hand.

"Rita, I can't tell him. Please don't say anything about this to anyone." She patted her eyes and the tears kept falling.

"Tonya, I don't think you're doing the right thing. He's going to have to know this is his child. You can't keep this man away from his own flesh and blood."

"I'm not keeping it." She had thought about it. There was no way she was going to be the source of confusion nor was she going to disappoint her parents.

Suddenly, Rita stopped hugging Tonya and looked at her in disgust. "You mean you're going to kill it?"

"Don't say it like that. I mean, it's not even a baby yet. I can't bring a baby here just to be fatherless."

"Fatherless! Do you know how many single parents

there are in this world? I'm the product of a single parent. My mother raised three of us by herself. Let me tell you, there isn't anything I wouldn't do for that woman. Besides, I don't think your child would be fatherless."

"Rita, I'm not going to ruin his marriage like that."

"That's just it, he's not married. Don't use that as an excuse to do what you want to do. You need to get it in gear and start planning to take care of that child."

She had never seen Rita so adamant about anything since she had known her. Her usual happy-go-lucky demeanor had disappeared.

"I just don't know if I can do it. I want this baby, Rita, but the circumstances just aren't right."

"Tonya, my husband and I want kids and we can't have any. You're blessed with the ability to bring a child into this world and don't know if you want it. I fail to understand. Do you know what I would give to be in your shoes? If you don't want that baby, have it and let us adopt it, but don't get rid of it. Please, don't do this."

"I don't know. I don't know."

"Well, whatever your decision, just know that I'll still be your friend."

Tonya spent the whole weekend thinking about the situation and about what Rita said. She finally reached a decision and decided to call the doctor on Monday. She kept hoping that she was making the right decision.

Twenty-two

As soon as the opportunity presented itself to make that phone call, she took it. She picked up the phone and dialed the number.

"Dr. Beverly's office," a woman answered.

"This is Tonya Locksley. I'd like to make an appointment please."

"For the obstetrician or termination?" she asked.

"Termination," Tonya answered.

"Can you come in this morning at eleven?" she asked. "We don't have any other appointments available for the next two weeks, but we had a cancellation for this morning."

Tonya was surprised by the woman's answer. She hadn't expected to have to go in so soon. "This morning's fine," she answered.

"Okay, we'll see you at eleven o'clock."

She hung up the phone and sat there feeling numb at the decision she'd made for the life of the child she was carrying. She couldn't bring this child into the world amid such a ball of confusion.

She went to Rita's office to tell her that she would be leaving early. Rita was on the phone when she walked in. Rita held up her hand, motioning that she would be with Tonya in a minute.

Tonya sat there looking around Rita's office. She had

never noticed how nice it was. There was this huge picture of an African woman with long, jet-black hair, riding an elephant across the desert with pyramids in the background, hanging on the wall behind her desk. Her desk was very contemporary, it had a glass top that rested on two blocks of black marble. She had a magnificent view of downtown from her window. The sun was shining brightly, as if it was going to be a beautiful day.

"Hey, girl. It's nice of you to drop in." Rita smiled.

"Well, unfortunately this isn't a social visit. I just wanted to let you know that I'll be leaving for the day. I already let Mr. Freeman know."

"What's wrong?" she asked.

"Nothing, I just have an appointment this morning at eleven," she said, looking down at the floor.

"I see," Rita said slowly. "So, that's your decision?"

"I'll talk to you tomorrow. I'll be back by then."

"I guess you'd better be going, it's already nine. I hope you're making the right choice."

After Tonya left Rita's office, heading to the doctor's office, Rita went looking for Dexter.

"Has anyone seen Dexter?" Rita asked Dexter's secretary.

"He should be back in his office. He had a meeting with his father and Mr. Reynolds this morning, but I think it's over," Simone answered.

Rita knocked on Dexter's door.

"Come in," he answered.

"Good morning, Dexter," Rita said.

"Good morning, Rita. What can I do for you?"

"Nothing really. I need to talk to you about something, but I don't think I would be in proper protocol if I do."

"We won't know that until you do," Dexter said.

"Actually, it's a personal issue and it's not any of my business at all, I just think you should know."

He looked up from his paperwork, not totally understanding what she was talking about. "Tell me—what's this all about?"

She hesitated and thought about backing out before betraying her friend. "Maybe this was a mistake, I'm sorry. I think I'll just go back to my office," she said, walking toward the door.

"No, wait. What's going on?" he asked with concern, pushing his papers aside.

"There's no other way I can put this except straight. I'm her friend, but I don't agree with what she's about to do." *She'll be angry at first, but she'll thank me later.*

"With what who's about to do?" Dexter asked, frowning.

"Tonya."

"Tonya—what about Tonya?" he asked with rising interest. His heart started to accelerate.

"Dexter, I promised her I wouldn't tell anyone, but I think she's making a mistake. She's pregnant."

"Pregnant!" he said breathlessly, absorbing it all in.

"Yes," Rita answered. "It's yours."

"I knew it was something, but she wouldn't tell me what it was. A baby, my baby. Where is she? What's this about a mistake?"

"She's going to have it aborted."

He could have been knocked over with a feather. The blood drained from his face. "What? No, she can't. I'm going over and talk to her right now."

"That's just it, you can't. She left early for her appointment at eleven."

"No, no. Where did she go? Who is her doctor?" he asked frantically.

"Dexter, I'm sorry, I don't know," Rita answered.

"Maybe she wrote the number down somewhere in her office. She can't do this."

He ran over to her office and began shuffling through all of her paperwork. There wasn't anything that wasn't pulled out of the desk. Her office was a total mess after the last piece of paper had been turned over. When Rita walked into Tonya's office, Dexter was sitting at her desk watching the clock. It was five minutes to eleven.

"She won't do it. I know her better than that, she won't do it," he kept saying as if he were trying to convince himself.

"I hope you're right," Rita said.

I don't know if I can go through with this. There she was lying on the table, thinking she didn't know if she could go through with it. She had been through a thirty-minute counseling session and she'd pretended that it was what she wanted. She'd shed no tears, but that wasn't how she felt deep down inside. Yet, she lay in the sterile white room with her legs in chrome stirrups.

"I'm going to put this mask on your face and I want you to count to twenty," instructed Dr. Beverly.

She thought of Dexter, how she was saving him a lot of heartache by not bringing this into his future marriage. She also thought about how sad she was going to be when it was over. She couldn't do it!! *What am I thinking? I'm not about to make the biggest mistake of my life.*

Twenty-three

"Dexter, it's after one o'clock. You've been in this office for nearly two hours. Why don't you get something to eat?" Rita couldn't help feeling that it was all her fault.

"I, I gotta go," he said, standing up in a daze. "She didn't do it, I know she didn't."

Words couldn't express the relief Tonya felt after she walked out of the doctor's office. It was already after two, she desperately needed to get some rest. It seemed like it took forever for her to get home. She parked her car and started up the walkway that led to her apartment. The heat had drained her of all of her energy.

She rounded the corner of her building and headed toward the last set of stairs. There was someone standing outside of her door. Maybe he was visiting Warren. As she got closer, that person started to look familiar. *Oh, my God!! It's Dexter!* Automatically her pace began to slow down, click-clack . . . click-clack . . . click . . . clack . . . click . . .

What was he doing there? He hadn't been there since they broke up, and what a mess he looked. His tie was undone and his shirt was unbuttoned. Why was his jacket lying on the stairs? He waited at the top of the stairs for her. She held the rail tightly as she made her way up. His eyes were bloodshot, was he sick?

"God, Tonya. Please don't tell me you did it," he said in a broken voice.

"What are you talking about?" she asked, pretending not to know. There was no way he could have found out, unless . . .

"Why didn't you tell me? Don't you think I had the right to know."

"Who told you?"

"That doesn't matter. What matters is that you didn't come to me. What made you think I wouldn't want it? Regardless of the circumstances, that was still my baby."

What could she say? Who knew he would ever find out? She wasn't going to let him know that she was still pregnant. *Rita told him. I trusted her!*

"Dexter I . . ." she started to explain. The words wouldn't leave her lips.

"There are so many women who wish their children had a father. I've always wanted children, and you just took one away from me, without letting me have any say in the matter." Her grabbed her by the arm sinking his fingers into her skin.

She wriggled under his grasp. "You're hurting my arm. I don't know what to say. I'm sorry doesn't seem like it's enough. I just didn't want to stand in the way of your reconciliation."

"You weren't thinking about me, you were thinking about yourself. Besides, you missed the whole point. I'm not getting married."

He was a total mess, he kind of wavered when he spoke. It looked like the slightest breeze would blow him over. He smelled of liquor. She knew he was an occasional drinker, but this was not like him.

She opened the door and he followed behind her. She was afraid he was going to do something to her. She didn't know what he would do because he was just that upset.

"What on earth were you thinking?" he asked.

She sat on the couch and began picking at imaginary lint on her blouse. "I don't know. What was I supposed to do? I couldn't just walk up to you and drop this on you after we fell out with each other. Besides, I was sure you'd set a wedding date by now."

"You didn't make any effort to discuss this with me. You make it seem like I would have rejected my responsibility or something. I don't know what kind of guys you're used to dating, but obviously they weren't real men. I don't know how *David* would have handled the situation, but I'm Dexter and I'm a man. I take care of mine, don't forget that," he said, pointing his finger at her.

"I didn't want us to get together because of a baby. I didn't want to trap you into anything."

"Actually, I'm tired of this conversation. I'm only going to make myself even more upset talking about this. I've gotta go, I can't stay here," he said, pacing around the living room.

She touched him on the shoulder. "You don't need to leave like this."

He snatched himself away from her. "Don't touch me. Just stay the hell away from me. You didn't have to get rid of that baby. I can never forgive you for what you've done. Then again, God is the one you'll have to answer to. I'm through with it." He flung open the door and was down the steps in seconds.

"Dexter wait! I'm sorry, I didn't know what else to do," she shouted after him.

It was too late, he wasn't listening. He jumped in his car and she watched as he sped away. There it was, all of her business was in the streets. Rosie, one of Tonya's nosy neighbors, watched the whole scenario. She always seemed to be around when anything happened. She heard Rosie saying, "You should have told him, girl!"

Tonya wanted to tell her to mind her own business, but didn't bother wasting her breath.

Her heart ached to tell him the truth. How was she going to explain as she got later into her pregnancy?

Twenty-four

Tonya didn't see Dexter for the rest of the week. He took off for Atlanta the day of their big argument. She didn't know whether he was running from their situation or if he actually had business in Atlanta. Of course, he had business, he had Melissa to tend to. Kiera had called and left a message on Tonya's voicemail at work and she never thought about returning her call. She wasn't up to getting into all of that drama. She had enough theatrics in her life without digging up old news. Nope, there weren't going to be any sequels to the Tonya and Kiera situation.

She was in turmoil because of her bad decision making and she had lost out on a good man. If she knew her as well as she thought she did, Kiera would be calling her back soon and she couldn't avoid her forever. She needed help with the mess she had made of her life. She thought about going to church. Why was it that people didn't turn to God until they were faced with adversity? As long as things were going their way, they thought nothing about him except as a last resort. She wasn't going to lie, she was guilty of that.

They say when you don't give God enough of your time, he has ways of bringing you back to the church. Maybe this was his way of getting her back in church. On that day, she was going to give God some of her time. She heard an advertisement on the Christian station that morning about a church on the south side called New Life Baptist Church. She planned to visit there that morning. If she went to her church and her parents saw her, with one look, they would know something was wrong.

Feeling holy, she had the Christian station blasting as she dressed for service and thought all pure and heavenly thoughts. As the old folks would say, she could feel a blessing coming on. The clock read twenty minutes after ten.

She would have to leave right then if she was going to be on time for eleven o'clock service. After running out to her car, she realized she didn't have her Bible, so she had to run back up stairs to get it. *I tell you, the devil is really trying to keep me home today.* She wasn't going to let him stop her.

She got to the church at five minutes to eleven. The parking lot was packed. The church was huge and it was crowded as well. She'd never seen so many handsome men in one church in her life. She had to keep focused, Satan was trying to dissuade her with fine, gorgeous men.

The choir was excellent and had the crowd standing on its feet singing praises to God. Shortly after the third song by the choir, Pastor Otis began to speak.

"Let me hear you say amen if you love the Lord. God sho' is good. He woke us up this morning, started us on our way, and got us all safely to New Life today. You ought to want to thank him, this morning." There were frequent *amens* and *let the Lord use yous*.

Pastor Otis was a very dark skinned, robust man, about fifty-something years old with graying hair. He had a thunderous voice that kept your attention. She wondered if his preaching was as good as their pastor's at Smyrna Baptist.

"If you would just bear with me this morning while I talk from the subject of 'Oh, What a Friend We Have.'" The congregation said amen.

As Pastor Otis went on, it seemed as if his message was especially for her. She was convinced that someone had told her life story to this man. His message was so accurate, it scared her out of her mind.

He continued with his sermon. "I'm tempted to sing a little of that song when I think of Jesus. Oh, what a friend we have in Jesus, all our sins and griefs to bear. I . . . I can't think of a single friend who would lay down their life for me. How many friends do you know you can call on every day and every night, anytime? See, our so-called friends would say, why you calling me this late? Or, I would love to help you out, but you know I have other obligations. See, Jesus would never put you on hold or say some other time. As I close, I want to say that if you have someone you can honestly call your friend, you need to hold on to them."

Just then, Tonya spotted Kiera on the other side of the church seated between two large women wearing hats that resembled big, red birds, sitting in nests. Kiera must have noticed her, too, because she was looking directly at her when Tonya saw her. Tonya turned back to the pastor.

"You mothers and fathers need to know how to be a best friend to your children. If you would teach them things at home, you wouldn't have to worry about the world teaching them something they don't know. I don't know what the world is coming to. Some of you mothers don't even bother keeping up with your kids. You let 'em run wild and act like they ain't got no home training. Some of you women get pregnant and decide you don't want the child, so what do you do? You give 'em up for adoption, put 'em in trash cans, or even worse, you end their lives before they even begin. I'm so sick of these people running around here talking about I'm pro-choice. Yeah, well I'm here to tell you that God didn't make it that way. The only choice you got is God's choice and he ain't say nothing about it's alright for you to do away with no baby. Now how are you to be a best friend to someone else, when you can't even be a friend to yourselves, damaging your bodies like that? Men, don't think you're off the hook 'cause I'm getting to you in a minute."

Tonya felt like Pastor Otis was looking directly at her, she thought he knew what was going on in her life. She could feel tears falling onto her cheeks. *It's so hot in here.* There was a wave of heat from her head to her feet and she began crying uncontrollably. She didn't know what was wrong with her. This was something she hadn't experienced before. Her body began to shake as she got up to leave the pew. She walked halfway down the aisle and went limp into darkness. Kiera noticed Tonya fall down and rushed outside after she was carried out. Tonya seemed to have started a trend because several other people had to be escorted out, too.

"Are you her sister?" one of the lady ushers asked Kiera.

"No, I'm a . . . a friend." Kiera wasn't sure she could call herself a friend because she had behaved like less than one.

"That Pastor Otis know he preached till the spirit came down, didn't he?" the woman asked Kiera.

"Yes, the sermon was quite inspirational," Kiera responded.

"Your friend will be alright, she's comin' round now." The usher lightly tapped Tonya on the face.

"I think I can handle her from here. I'm sure you all are needed inside," Kiera said, smiling at the ushers.

Tonya sat up and Kiera gave her a glass of water, which Tonya took graciously.

"That was some sermon, huh?" Kiera said, trying to make conversation.

"Yeah, that it was."

"I bet you didn't expect my face to be the first one

you would see." Kiera said, looking everywhere but at her.

"It's not all that surprising," she said with a small smile on her face.

"Really? Why's that?"

"I guess we've been through so much together that I'm just used to you being somewhere around."

"That's kind of true. Why didn't you ever call me back?" Kiera asked. "I was going to give you another call today."

"I don't know. I was just stalling. I wanted to call just as much as you wanted me to. I've just been going through a lot lately."

"Tell me about it. You'll never believe what I've been through these last few weeks."

"I can only imagine."

"Why don't we put the past behind us and start all over? I kind of miss my best friend."

"Yeah, me, too," Tonya said.

"You know, they say the Lord works in mysterious ways."

"Ain't that the truth. I never expected to see you at church," Tonya said, laughing to herself.

"What's that supposed to mean?" Kiera asked with a puzzled expression.

"What do you mean, 'what's that supposed to mean'? It means that you never go to church."

"I do go to church."

"Okay, not counting today, when's the last time you went to church?" Tonya asked as they walked toward the parking lot.

"I went to church last . . . last . . . the other . . ."

"Uh-huh, just like I thought. You haven't been to church since last Easter, when you bought that Versace suit. You know you only went to church to let people know you had on a new suit."

"That's low! How shallow do you think I am?" Kiera laughed.

It felt good to laugh. That was something she hadn't done in such a long time. She laughed till she cried. They both did.

Twenty-five

Although Tonya and Kiera had patched up their friendship, Tonya hadn't confided in her about the Dexter situation. In a way, she couldn't help but think that she wasn't opening up as she should. Kiera meant well, but how could Tonya trust her? She also had to wonder if she was really her best friend anymore. She found herself confiding more in Rita. Even though Rita had betrayed her by telling Dexter about the baby, she still considered her a friend. They often had lunch together and visited on the weekends. She decided not to mention that she was still pregnant, she would be the first to tell Dexter.

She wanted things to get back to normal. She wanted things to be the way they were before the fight with Kiera and before Dexter walked into her life. She hadn't heard from or seen him since he walked out on her.

When she got to work Monday morning, there was a pile of work to do. On top of all of that work, Mr. Freeman called a meeting of the litigation support staff and the associate attorneys.

She sat at her desk looking over the list of clients she needed to contact, when Rita walked in. "Hey, it's meeting time. I thought we could catch the elevator up together."

"Oh, it's that time already? Time has been merciless to me this morning." Tonya put away her work.

"I know what you mean," Rita said. "I've been down to the crunch myself. Did you know Dexter was here?"

The blood began to drain from her face. She should have been expecting it. "No, I didn't know," she said, looking at the burgundy carpet. Her stomach began to lurch and she had to make a break for the bathroom. Rita followed her into the bathroom.

"Girl, are you feeling okay? I wanted to tell you, because I didn't want it to be a total shock, in case you didn't know. It'll be okay, just listen to whatever Mr. Freeman has to say and we'll be outta' there in no time. Don't let Dexter upset you."

Little did she know that it wasn't Dexter who was making her upset, it was his baby.

"I'll keep that in mind," she said as she wiped her mouth. "What's the meeting about anyway?" Tonya was relieved to change the subject.

"I think it's about us winning the Chrisman case," Rita said.

They walked out of the bathroom to the elevators. While they stood there waiting for the up elevator, Dexter, clad in tan baggy slacks and a crème shirt, emerged from his office. She hoped he wasn't going to take the same elevator they were. She tried to be casual as she glanced his way. He was looking straight at her. *What is he trying to do, intimidate me?*

The elevator came and he held the door open for them. He didn't crack a smile or speak when they got on. The only thing he did do was stare her down.

They finally reached the conference room and met with Mr. Freeman and the other staff members. There was a long oval table that sat twenty. There was coffee and doughnuts at every seat with a glass of orange juice. There were four seats reserved at the front of the table. That must have been a mistake because there were only supposed to be three reserved seats. There should have been one each for Dexter, Mr. Freeman, and Mr. Reynolds. She and Rita sat on the right side of the long oval table, close to the front. Dexter sat at the front on the opposite side. Rita noticed the fourth seat, too.

"I called this meeting this morning to congratulate you all on a job well done on the Chrisman case. I know a lot of you didn't actually work on this case, but this was a winner for us all. I want to let you all know that your diligence has been appreciated and has not gone unnoticed. To show our gratitude, we are giving you a little token of our appreciation. Vivian . . ." He motioned for his personal secretary, who began handing out envelopes with their names written on the fronts.

"I would appreciate it if you would refrain from opening your envelopes until after our meeting. I also have an announcement to make . . ." Mr. Freeman continued.

She couldn't tear her eyes off Dexter. She had to admit that she had been stupid, she wanted him back in her life. Their eyes met for a moment, but he looked away. She had to let him know about the baby, it wasn't fair to him.

"As you all know, my son works here from time to time. He's decided to work with us on a permanent basis. He's now a partner in our firm."

Everyone began clapping. She was shocked and was the only one who wasn't clapping. He gave her a long look and she mechanically began to clap. That was the softest look he had given her in a long time.

"I hope you all approve of the newest addition to our family, although, that's not the announcement I had to make. I don't know if many of you know that my son was once married to a wonderful woman by the name of Melissa Ferguson. To make a long story short, they have decided to give marriage another try. In order for them to make a smooth transition into marriage, I have made her an associate attorney for our firm. It makes no sense

for two lovebirds to have to be in two different cities."
Mr. Freeman beamed with pride.

Dexter's head shot up from his note pad. There was a
frown on his face. Tonya didn't know if it was a look of
surprise or anger. Mr. Freeman gestured for Vivian to
open the door and in walked Melissa. She was exactly
what everyone thought he deserved. She was average
height with long, jet black hair that reached the middle
of her back, green eyes, and a shape that would make
any woman jealous. She wore a short emerald green suit
with gold buttons and a fuschia blouse. *She must be a Skee-
wee,* Tonya thought to herself with a twisted lip.

Mr. Freeman made introductions and everyone seemed
to be caught up in the excitement. Dexter stole an uncomfortable glance at her and pretended to be caught
up in the moment. Tonya didn't like this woman already.
Melissa had an air of superiority about her. She tried to
pretend to be down-to-earth, but it wasn't cuttin' it. She
latched her arm around Dexter's, making sure every
woman in the room knew she was the queen bee and
everyone else were worker bees. Tonya couldn't stand it.

She didn't want to be introduced to the competition,
and whether she liked it or not that is exactly what she
was—competition. She spoke to Keith Lexington before
making a beeline for the door. It was too much for her
to handle, she was sick with jealousy. She made a quiet
exit and waited by the elevators. No one seemed to have
missed her from the *celebration,* until about twenty minutes
later.

"Girl, are you okay?" Rita had been looking all over
for her. She checked the bathroom and asked several people if they had seen her leave. She finally decided to
check Tonya's office. In spite of how she tried to pretend
that everything was fine, Rita knew facing the new woman
had upset her.

"Yeah, I'm okay. It was getting a little too crowded for

me and I have a thing about crowded rooms." She tried in vain to mask the pain she was feeling.

"I know this is hard for you, and I wanted to make sure you were okay."

"I don't know if I can work under these circumstances. It's getting harder every day. First, he leads me on and I find out he's engaged to his ex-wife, then she comes here permanently. I can't win."

"Look, whatever happened between you and Dexter is behind you now. You shouldn't have any problems with her. Besides, what she doesn't know, won't hurt her."

Little did Rita know, Tonya's problems were just beginning.

"I haven't had time to get over my feelings for him. What if we could have worked it out?" she asked in despair.

"I understand that. Like you said, you did what you had to do so that he could be happy with her," Rita said.

"Yeah, I thought I did it for their happiness."

"Have you opened your envelope yet?" asked Rita.

"No, I forgot about it." She picked up the envelope and tore it open. She glanced at the check for two thousand dollars.

"I wonder if Dexter knew about the announcement. I couldn't read his face. I don't know whether his expression was one of excitement or surprise."

"I doubt it, he looked pretty surprised to me. He left shortly after Mr. Freeman dropped the bomb on everybody. Melissa was too busy trying to latch on to him and he was looking for an escape route."

"I was happy that he wasn't the one making the introductions," Tonya said bitterly.

"I hear my phone ringing. That's my cue to get back to work."

It wasn't long after Rita gave up trying to cheer her up that Mr. Freeman brought Melissa in to be introduced.

She almost thought he did it on purpose—to make a point.

"Excuse me, Ms. Locksley, I don't think you've met Melissa, have you?" It was clear that there was an underlying message to his bringing Melissa by Tonya's office.

"No, I had to get back to work. You know the Tanzent case is being presented to the court soon," she said, with little interest in Melissa.

"Well, Melissa, this is Tonya Locksley. She's also an associate with our firm. Tonya, this is Melissa," he said, smiling the broadest grin that she'd ever seen him wear. She would have sworn that he was showing off a prized possession.

I got the point!! "It's nice to meet you." She smiled.

"Charmed," Melissa drawled. Tonya was sure that at any moment she would extend her hand as if she wanted *her* to kiss it.

After they left, Tonya dove into her work. It was lunchtime before she knew it. As much as she liked Rita's company, she wanted to be alone. She grabbed her purse and made a quick exit from the office. She went to the underground mall. She wasn't looking for anything in particular, she just wanted to walk. She came across an art store before she reached the food courts. It was called Expressions of You. They had all kinds of wall pictures and statuettes. She hadn't made any efforts to personalize her office, so she decided to buy a picture. She browsed around, but nothing caught her eye. She was determined to find something, and then she saw it. It was a picture of the silhouette of a woman lying on a dark beach under the moonlight. The moonlight spilled across the ocean. The woman appeared to be extremely sad because of the way she was lying on the sand. She seemed to have been lying face down on the sand and had raised herself up looking at the moon. It was as if she were looking to the heavens, begging for answers. This picture was her.

She was a little late returning to the office. When she walked inside, Dexter was there waiting for her. "Dexter, I mean Mr. Freeman, I didn't expect you to be here when I got back. I was running a little late." She wondered why he was there. She knew it was probably to smooth over things from the morning's meeting, but nothing he could say could make her feel better.

"Tonya, I wanted to let you know that I knew nothing about this morning. It was as much a surprise to me as it was to you, and I'm sorry. I can't imagine how you must feel," he said, looking out of the window.

"No, I don't think you can. There's nothing to apologize for. It was Mr. Freeman's doing not yours, right?" she asked with a hint of sarcasm.

"Right." He ignored her sarcasm. "I also think it might be best if you went to another firm. I'll see to it that you get an offer from a bigger and better firm."

"What do you mean? Am I going to be fired?" Her heart started to speed up.

"No, quite the contrary. I'm just sure you won't be very comfortable working here under these circumstances."

"I see. Are you doing this for me, or are you doing this for you? Maybe *you* won't be comfortable under these circumstances," she said coldly. *Now that he's gotten the draws and gone, he wants to make things easy for him to be with Melissa.*

"Tonya, the circumstances aren't perfect for either of us and you know this. I thought you'd welcome the opportunity for something stress-free."

"I appreciate your concern, but I think I'll find my own job opportunities. Whatever decision I make, I don't want you to have anything to do with it."

Dexter was starting to get worked up. "Is there a problem with having someone to open a door for you? Most people would take the opportunity with open arms. You have to question everything, except the things you should. I swear I'll never get you figured out," he said as he walked away from the window.

It was her turn to get pissed off. She couldn't take his attitude anymore. "What are you trying to do, compensate me for bringing her here? Why don't you explain this sudden interest in my career."

"Look, I don't know what you're talking about and I don't have time to get into this with you. All of my obligations to explain were thrown away when you went to that appointment. My obligations to you *ended* when you forgot to tell me that you were pregnant."

"The moment *you forgot* to tell me you were planning on remarrying your ex-wife is the moment your obligations ended." She couldn't believe him.

He paced around the office, as if he was trying to calm down. "I explained that situation to you. I never lied to you."

"That's right, you didn't lie, you just forgot to tell the truth," she bit out with pain written on her face. "I saw a ring on her finger today. Did you give it to her?"

He let out a deep breath. "No. Why can't you get it through your head that I don't want her? I just can't . . ." He didn't finish his sentence. He felt there was no reason to.

"What am I supposed to think? If you will excuse me, I'd like to finish the rest of this work before the day is over."

She wasn't sure when he left, she never looked at him after picking up her paperwork. *Sex in the workplace is not good. Damn him!*

Dexter didn't like the way things were going. He was starting to have to visit his father a little too often about issues that didn't concern him. When he entered his father's office, he and Melissa were heavily engrossed in conversation.

Melissa's eyes lit up when she saw him. "Darling, where did you run off to? I've been waiting for you. Father just finished giving me a tour of the firm. I must say that it has changed a lot since the last time I visited."

"I'm sure it has," Dexter responded, looking directly at his father. "Father, can I speak with you for a moment—privately?"

"Son, can't it wait? I was just catching Melissa up to speed on things. How about we discuss whatever it is later?" Mr. Freeman said in a dismissing tone.

"I think now would be the perfect time. It can't wait until later." Dexter waited by the door for Melissa to catch a clue and leave.

"Honey, what's wrong?" Melissa asked.

"Nothing out of the ordinary," Dexter said through clenched teeth. *Why is she continuing to delude herself? She can't go on pretending that everything is fine between us. Things haven't been fine between us in a long time.* The constant twitching above his left eye let Dexter know that he was about at the end of his rope.

Mr. Freeman turned to Melissa. "Melissa, we will pick up our discussion later."

"Dexter, how can you be so rude to your wife?" Mr. Freeman asked after Melissa had gone. "I'm sure you made her feel insignificant."

"She is *not* my wife. How could you bring her here without discussing it with me first? I'm sure that Melissa could have moved on with her life if had you not been instigating this remarriage issue."

"This situation is more than just you and Melissa. This situation involves the growth potential of our firm. Melissa's father has referred one of Houston's top attorneys to our firm. I'm sure you've heard of Jaleel Gregory." Mr. Freeman waited for Dexter's response.

"Yes." A scowl crossed Dexter's face and his eyes rolled to the ceiling. "That's one name I will never forget."

"I see his reputation precedes him," Mr. Freeman said.

"That's an understatement." *First Melissa, now Jaleel.* "You don't plan on making him an offer do you?"

"Why not? Think of the clients he would bring with him if he came to our firm. Freeman and Reynolds is a well-known firm now, but we could be number one with a man like Jaleel on our side. There will be other opportunities like this one if you handle your business with Melissa."

"Is that all you can think of? Do you always have to be number one at everything? You want this firm to rise to the top at my expense. Why am I the one who has to make sacrifices?"

"Don't think of this as a sacrifice." Mr. Freeman chewed on the arm of his eyeglasses thoughtfully. "Sometimes you have to make choices that are beneficial to more than just yourself. You love Melissa, you just don't think you do. Jaleel will be in the office tomorrow. I want you to join me in making him feel welcome."

What's the use? It's just another dead end conversation. What could he do to convince his father that Melissa was out of his life for good? He could never forgive her for what she'd done and Jaleel's presence only added to his bitterness.

Jaleel Gregory was the name on everyone's lips. Apparently the firm had made him an offer he couldn't refuse. After wrapping up another late night at work, Tonya watched as building services moved in Jaleel's furniture. His office was diagonal to hers. She glanced warily at the modest furniture in her office. Jaleel's furniture was by no means modest. His furniture made the statement I'm the best and I deserve the best!

Mr. Freeman was ecstatic about Jaleel joining the firm. He kept going on and on about how the firm was going places no other firm had gone before. You'd think this man was offering salvation for the firm. The question was salvation from what?

The elevator doors opened and out stepped a tall man with gentle features. Tonya smiled at him as she moved toward the open elevator.

"Excuse me," the man said. "I'm kind of embarrassed to say this, but I'm looking for my office."

"You must be Mr. Gregory." Tonya couldn't help smiling. The man seemed a little flustered.

"Please, Jaleel," he said.

"Alright, Jaleel. I'm Tonya Locksley and I know exactly where your office is."

They shook hands and Tonya led him to his office. He could be in his late thirties or early forties.

"I tried using my parking card to enter the garage and it wasn't activated. Then, I attempted to get into the building and that card wasn't working either. When I finally got to our offices, I couldn't remember which floor the litigation section was on."

Jaleel seemed to be a little out of breath. Beads of sweat broke out across his forehead.

"This is it." Tonya gestured toward the open office. "That is, unless we've made offers to other attorneys."

"Great, this is it. Where are you located?" Jaleel moved around the office inspecting the work building services had done. He straightened a picture that wasn't hanging perfectly.

Just as I thought, he's a perfectionist! "I'm just across the hall—diagonally. Well, I'm going to call it a night. It was nice meeting you."

"Thanks so much for your help and it was nice meeting you, too," Jaleel said.

So that is our deliverer. Wonderful!

* * *

It was déjà vu. The same thing was starting to happen to him all over again and right under the tip of his nose. As hard as he tried to leave his problems behind, they had a way of catching up with him. One of his problems had literally followed him from another state. Placing Jaleel and Melissa together would only have a negative synergistic affect. His father didn't know what he was doing. Melissa wasn't the angel he thought her to be. If anything, she was the devil in disguise.

Dexter made it a point to be out of the office most of the day. He wanted to put off welcoming Jaleel to Freeman and Reynolds for as long as he could. There was no way he was going to wholeheartedly welcome Jaleel into his family's firm. As a matter of fact, he had no intention of attending the dinner his father had planned for Jaleel.

His plan was to drop by the office and pick up his papers for court the next morning. Unfortunately, he met his father on his way out.

"Dexter, we're just about to leave for the restaurant. Try to hurry and get there so we can order." Mr. Freeman turned to walk away.

"I'm not going. I've made other plans," Dexter called out to his father's back.

Mr. Freeman pivoted and stood in front of Dexter.

"We've already discussed this. Son, I don't know what your problem is. Whatever it is, you've got to get over it. Let bygones be bygones."

"You don't know what it is that I have to get over. It's not as simple as you think." Why wasn't his father ever on his side?

"I'm sure it's not as complex as you would have me think. I'll see you at dinner." Mr. Freeman turned and walked away.

* * *

"Dexter, you remember Jaleel." Melissa cooed.

"Of course. How could I forget?" Dexter ignored Jaleel's extended hand and pulled up a chair. There was no need to pretend that he and Jaleel were on a friendly basis.

The atmosphere immediately became tense from Dexter's gesture. Mr. Freeman gazed condescendingly at his son.

"You'll have to excuse my son, apparently he's had a hard day," Mr. Freeman interjected. "I wasn't aware that you two were acquainted." He looked from Jaleel to Dexter.

"There are a lot of things you aren't aware of," Dexter said cooly before ordering a glass of wine.

A strained silence followed Dexter's statement. Keith, Rita, and Mr. Freeman were baffled by the tension between the other three attorneys. Even more than being baffled, surprise was on Keith and Rita's faces.

"Yes, we worked at Vince and Horton together," Jaleel said after clearing his throat.

Dexter checked his watch. Time seemed to be dragging. *Where was Tonya?*

"Is Ms. Locksley not joining us?" Dexter asked no one in particular.

"Apparently not," Mr. Freeman answered with a dismissing wave.

"I'm not sure if she's coming. I didn't think to remind her about dinner tonight," Rita said. She noticed Mr. Freeman's flippant demeanor toward Tonya and didn't like it.

Dinner remained uncomfortable for everyone except Melissa and Jaleel. They spent the rest of dinner reminiscing about old times.

Twenty-six

Just when she thought things could get no worse, they did. In large law firms most sections are divided into groups. If the attorney was a litigation attorney, depending on what kind of litigator he or she was, he or she worked with other attorneys who practiced in the same field. Tonya, Rita, and Dexter were all in planning and probate of estates. It was just her luck that Melissa was also in that field. They were group partners. She knew she was going to like that just great—in another lifetime.

"In case you didn't know, we are going to be in the same section—group partners," Melissa said when she stopped by Tonya's office that morning. She blew in wearing an overpowering perfume. She hadn't bothered to knock. She burst in with this announcement as if Tonya was supposed to be thrilled. Tonya gave her an annoyed look. *Wonderful!*

"Yes, I heard." Tonya didn't want to be bothered with the competition at that moment. As a matter of fact, Melissa was no longer the *competition*—she was the *winner!*

Melissa closed the door and helped herself to a seat, crossing her legs as she did so. Her demeanor turned cool. "I'm not going to procrastinate. I'll get straight to the point. I'm not here to talk about our group arrangements. There's something else I want to discuss."

Tonya shifted uncomfortably in her chair. There was

only one thing she knew Melissa had in mind. "Okay, I'm listening."

"It has become painfully obvious that something has been going on between you and Dexter. I've noticed the secret glances you give him whenever he's in the room. I recognized it instantly when I first arrived here. I'll even admit that he may also initiate these secret meetings. However, I will not be made a fool of. Dexter and I were fine before you entered the picture and we'll be fine after you leave the picture. He's my husband and I will not have someone who could never be more than a mere fling tear down what has taken me years to build," she said sweetly. "I'm sure you understand."

Tonya could not believe Melissa had strolled into her office to put her in her place. However, she was not going to get angry about it. She put on her professional attitude and answered just as sweetly as Melissa had. "Of course, I understand."

"Good," Melissa snapped. "I shouldn't have to worry about you trying to take my place with Dexter."

Was Melissa waiting to exhale or what? Tonya didn't take too well to Melissa's icy attitude. Maybe some heat would melt her cold disposition. "Melissa, as I'm sure you know, there is no such thing as job security in the 90s. So, if it's reassurance you're looking for, I can't give it to you. Let me correct you on one thing—he's not your husband, he's your *ex-husband.*"

Obviously Melissa didn't like Tonya's counter. She rose from the chair and headed for the door. She turned to Tonya before heading out the door. "In case you haven't noticed"—she held her hand out for Tonya to see—"I'm the one wearing the ring, and right now, that's security enough for me." She sneered. "Would you prefer that I leave the door open or closed?" When Tonya didn't respond, she made a decision for her. "I guess you need time to think, so I'll close it." She closed the door behind her.

Tonya came to the conclusion that Melissa was materialistic. How could someone base their relationship on a ring? Sure, you can have the ring, but that doesn't necessarily mean you have the man. She knew that for a fact. Being involved with David was a testimony to the fact that sometimes what you *think* is yours isn't always yours. Not only was Melissa materialistic, she was a fool!

That little visit from Melissa was only the beginning of a terrible relationship. Melissa's move from Vince and Horton was a lateral move, meaning she kept the same status she had at that firm when she moved to Freeman and Reynolds. This wasn't good for Tonya, since she was a beginning associate.

Melissa began dumping work she was supposed to be responsible for on Tonya. Tonya started working late hours just to keep up with the work she had to do. Even when Tonya did a wonderful job on her assignments, Melissa would find problems with everything she had done. Therefore, she would have to start all over again. Tonya was sure this was a ploy on Melissa's part to get her to resign. Little did Melissa know, her faux displeasure with Tonya's work was a driving force behind Tonya's determination to succeed.

Sometimes Tonya would do such a good job, that Melissa would take credit for all of Tonya's hours of hard work—work that she had stayed up mulling over until the wee hours of the morning. She was beginning to resent Melissa's vainglory for her hard work.

Melissa would even go so far as having Tonya's billable time written off because, according to Melissa, Tonya's work was inadequate and the clients couldn't be billed for her inaccuracies. This was beginning to mess with Tonya's livelihood. She would be fired if the management committee thought she was doing fruitless labor and that's just what Melissa wanted them to think. If Tonya wasn't going to quit, Melissa would just get her fired.

It finally dawned on Tonya that Melissa had been setting her up. Melissa wove her web so intricately that Tonya almost didn't realize what had happened. It was then that Tonya began keeping a log of all of the work she had done and the hours spent on each. Whenever Tonya did research on cases, she used the Westlaw system because it was the only system the firm had given her a password for. Her password gave an identity to the user and kept track of the time billed to a particular client for research, but Melissa soon put a stop to that. Melissa had come to her telling her she had to use another service for all of her research.

"Could you use Lexis instead of Westlaw?" Melissa had asked nicely. "I guess I'm just used to their format and sometimes they give a little more information."

Tonya should have known right then that something was wrong for Melissa to be so nice. "I don't have access to Lexis. I only have a password for Westlaw."

This information seemed to please Melissa. "Oh, you can use my password for Lexis. From now on, do all of my research on Lexis. Feel free to use my password until the firm authorizes one for you. Really, you'll see that it's more useful."

"When do you need the memorandum?" Tonya asked.

"By the end of the week, if possible," Melissa replied.

"The end of the week is fine."

"Good."

Tonya wrote down Melissa's password on a notepad. She worked over four hours pulling cases to use in her memorandum. It took another four hours to draft the memorandum. She spent the next day cleaning up minor glitches.

Tonya submitted the memorandum to Melissa on the next afternoon, which, she took eagerly, too eagerly. Tonya had submitted it early because she knew Melissa would have a lot changes to make. Tonya was waiting for her to complain, but the complaint never came. She could smell a rat and it had light skin with long hair.

Twenty-seven

Tonya sat around her apartment pondering all of the chaos that had unfolded in her life. Some of these things were good and some were bad. The good didn't outweigh the bad and the bad didn't weigh more than the good. However, the confusion in her life seemed to dominate everything. In an effort to keep her mind occupied, she began to clean out her closet and pulled out the clothes that she had bought too large. It was a good thing she had bought them because she would need those more than anything.

Although the closet was a walk in, clothes were piled up on the side and shoes cluttered the walkway. There were so many clothes she hadn't bothered wearing. She'd either bought them too large or she'd realized she had no place to wear them. She grabbed handfuls of clothes and threw them across the bed. She caught her reflection in the full-size mirror. She raised up her oversize T-shirt and turned sideways to see if her belly had grown any bigger. The bulge in her abdomen had expanded, and she was reaching the point that zipping her pants would be a thing of the past. Even though she was four months pregnant, it was hard to tell that she was pregnant at all, yet she could tell and so could anyone who knew her well. This meant that she had to think of something soon.

She stood absently, rubbing her belly and the knock at

the door startled her. *Who could that be? Why don't people bother to use the doorbell?*

A look through the peephole revealed Rita, standing there with an armful of things. She opened the door. "What do we have here?" Tonya asked in surprise.

"Hey, thought you'd like to watch some movies and have popcorn and cokes," she said, smiling, as she put the cokes on the counter and flopped down on the couch. She didn't know how much Tonya needed the company.

"That sounds great to me." Tonya grabbed some glasses from the cabinet. Rita never failed to come through for her just when she needed her the most. After she popped the popcorn and poured the cokes, she walked into the living room and sat on the floor next to her. She had already put *Enemy of the State* in the VCR and the previews were showing.

"You know," Rita said through her smacking. "This could really use some butter."

"I think you're right." As Tonya attempted to get up from the floor, the T-shirt caught on the edge of the coffee table. Just as it did that, it clung to her more than average belly size. Rita's eyes quickly darted to it, yet she said nothing.

I hope she didn't notice it. The whole world will know it if she did. She walked into the kitchen, took out the butter, and melted it in the microwave. "Here's some freshly melted butter." Tonya smiled as she put the melted butter on the table.

"Thanks. You're a pal."

"Sho' you right." Tonya laughed nervously.

"Well, if you haven't heard . . . word through the grapevine is, Dexter's getting married on the twenty-first."

Great, just when things were going fine. She would mention him. I can't believe he's really going to marry her. "The twenty-first? You mean of this month?" Tonya asked, recovering from shock.

"Yep. I guess the old girl is tired of waiting around, especially since she's now in the same city with him."

"She thinks I'm a threat. Maybe that's why things are moving so fast."

"Hey, why didn't you meet us at the restaurant the other night? After all, it was a welcome dinner for Jaleel."

"What dinner?" Tonya frowned. "I didn't know anything about a dinner for Jaleel."

"Do you ever read your E-mails? We *only* received about three reminders about the dinner." Rita dug into the bowl of popcorn and looked at Tonya in disbelief.

"That explains it." Tonya tapped herself on the forehead. "I've been so busy trying to stay on top of everything. You're right. I haven't been reading my E-mail. How was it?"

"I shouldn't tell you anything since it was your *own* fault that you didn't go." Rita smiled. "But since I'm a true friend, I'll go ahead and tell you that it turned out nice."

"Just *nice?*" Tonya asked. "I'm getting the impression that I didn't miss too much of anything."

"It turns out that Melissa's father is the reason Jaleel is here. I don't know what the connection is there, but I think Melissa and Jaleel have a history."

"What? You think they've dated?" Tonya asked.

"I don't know. Maybe. Melissa is nothing but a southern flirt. From the way they were acting, one would think they were *special* friends."

"You think?"

"I don't know. All I know is there was a lot of hostility between the three of them."

Tonya frowned. "Between the three of whom?"

"Between lover boy, Jaleel, and Melissa. That's who. You really missed it. You could cut the hostility with a knife." She made a cutting motion in the air. "It was just that thick. You could have sliced it like a loaf of bread and served everybody some. You always manage to miss the good stuff."

"Nah, I'm glad I missed it. I didn't want to be stared down by Dexter anyway. What makes you think there is some tension between those three?"

"For one thing"—Rita chuckled—"Dexter refused to shake Jaleel's hand when he got to the restaurant. That was bad enough. The killing part is when Dexter almost told Mr. Freeman to shut up because he didn't know what he was talking about. Keith and I looked at one another, trying not to laugh."

Tonya laughed. "You are too silly. I know you're exaggerating."

"I kid you not," she laughed. "I nearly choked when Dexter said that. I had to take a sip of water. Keith got to coughing and had to excuse himself from the table. It was pathetic."

"That's so sad. I did miss it."

"Girl, you sure did. Melissa was like, 'Dexter, you remember Jaleel?' Dexter said, 'How could I forget?' It was so sarcastic. Girl, Mr. Freeman had no idea that they all knew each other. Check this out." Rita wiped the tears of laughter from her eyes. "They all worked at Vince and Horton together. I'm telling you, something must have gone down at the law firm. Keith and I died laughing when we got to the parking lot. I think it's safe to say that Dexter has a strong disliking for Melissa and an equally as strong disliking for Jaleel."

"You're probably reading too much into it. So the wedding is on the twenty-first. That's just two weeks away." Men were so wishy-washy. She knew that Melissa was the one putting on the pressure. She probably gave him the old ultimatum—either you do it my way or no way at all. Why would he marry her?

"What are you going to do?" Rita asked.

"What do you mean what am I going to do?" What in the world was she talking about?

"Oh, come off it, Tonya. You know very well what I'm talking about," she said as she grabbed a handful of popcorn. Will Smith was acting his butt off, but no one paid him any attention.

"No, come on, I don't know what you're talking about." Tonya could feel a sticky perspiration over her brow and spilled coke on the carpet in her anxiety.

"Be careful," Rita warned. They both began sopping up the mess.

"Really, I am in the dark about what you're talking about." Tonya had to convince her that everything was okay or else it would be all over.

"Yeah, right. Tonya, you're pregnant and everybody knows it. Look, it's Rita you're talking to. You can be honest with me." Rita put her hands on Tonya's shoulders and sat on the couch beside her "I'm not trying to be nosy or to get in your business, but everybody who doesn't know now, will know later. Why try to hide it?"

Who was she trying to fool? She may as well get it over with. "You're right. I don't know why I didn't tell you." She looked her straight in the eyes. "I guess I was still upset from when you told Dexter I was pregnant in the first place. I know you were only trying to help, but I couldn't risk that again."

"I know it wasn't my place to do that. I was wrong, but I believed in my heart that it was for the best for you. I didn't do it to hurt you, only to help."

Tonya got up and walked over to the window. Cars were passing up and down the street. A woman was pushing a baby in a stroller on the sidewalk. Life was so complicated. Rita was rambling on and on in the background.

"Are you listening to me?" she asked.

"What? Oh, yeah. I'm listening," Tonya lied.

"You don't have much time. You need to tell him before it's too late."

"You're right. I'll think of something."

A silent tension covered the room that was only interrupted when the phone rang.

"Hello," Tonya answered. It was Kiera on the other end of the line. She was talking so fast that Tonya could hardly understand what she was saying. Something about her father and Hermann Hospital was all she understood.

"I'm on my way," Tonya said. "I'm sorry, Rita. I hate to cut our visit short, but something's happened to Kiera's father and they're at the hospital."

"Oh, she finally calls you after something drastic happens. Do you need me to go with you?" Rita asked.

"I know. Isn't that what friends are for? I'll be fine, thanks anyway. I'll give you a call later." She grabbed her purse and keys and shot out the door.

When she reached the hospital, she had no idea where Kiera's father would be. "Do you have a Brice Winters listed?" Tonya asked the nurse.

The nurse looked him up on the computer. "Yes, he's in ICU. That's straight down the hall to your left."

"Thanks." She walked quickly down the hall and saw Kiera, Anthony, and Mrs. Winters in the waiting area.

"How is he?" Tonya asked after she hugged Kiera's mother.

"We don't know. He's in critical condition. He suffered a massive heart attack. All we can do is pray," Mrs. Winters sobbed.

"I know we haven't talked and it isn't because I haven't wanted to call. I feel so ashamed for everything I've done," Kiera said.

"That's not what is important right now, okay? Besides, we decided to let bygones be bygones. Let's try and get your dad all better and then we can talk about us. What happened?"

"We were at our family reunion earlier and he decided he wanted to play basketball. I knew he shouldn't have been on that court. Why didn't I try to stop him?" Kiera said. "I keep thinking that I could have done something."

"Don't blame yourself. It was going to happen regardless. If not today, then it would have been another day. We can't blame ourselves for something that was in God's will," Tonya said, trying to offer some sort of comfort. What could she say? She could never say, "I know how you feel," because she didn't. There was nothing that could be said or done to calm their anxiety.

"Would you all like some refreshments?" Anthony offered. Kiera and Mrs. Winters both refused, as did Tonya. "Well, I could use something," he said, excusing himself.

"This can't be happening. I don't know if he's going to make it," Kiera said sadly.

"Don't think that way and don't let your mother hear you say that. You've got to be strong and think positive. You've got to be there for your mother." Mrs. Winters had gone into ICU.

"I called Janice and Kelly. They'll be in from California in about five hours." Tonya hadn't thought about Kiera's two sisters and where was her brother?

"Where's Mark?" Tonya asked.

"You know, he's been working in Alaska and he won't be here until sometime later on in the week. We had to leave a message for him since he works out on the oil platform, but he's on his way."

"Good."

Anthony returned and sat next to Kiera. She turned to Tonya and looked into her eyes. "I really want to thank you for coming. I just had to call you. You're like another daughter to Dad. I thought you would want to know. You don't have to stay, Anthony will be here. I'll call you if there are any changes."

"Are you sure? If you need me here, I'll stay."

"No. You go ahead and do what you need to do. I'll keep you posted, I promise." She smiled feebly.

Twenty-eight

What started off to be a good morning turned bad as soon as she walked into the office. Tracie Margo, chair of the management committee, asked Tonya to meet with the committee in the conference room. Tonya had been going through enough problems without having her job in jeopardy, too. The office was buzzing about the fine job Melissa had done on her memorandum. According to everyone, the memorandum would boost the Tanzent case in a positive direction. Tonya wanted to scream *that's my work!*

She opened the door to the conference room and sat in the only empty seat available. It seemed that all of the management committee had showed up to the meeting. There were ten members on the committee. Mr. Freeman and Dexter both were there. Tonya could look at neither one of them.

Tonya decided to initiate the conversation. "May I ask what this meeting is about?"

Tracie Margo, was a stocky woman with a round face, answered for the group. She looked over the rim of her black-framed, out-of-fashion glasses. "It has come to our attention that most, if not all, of your hours billed to several clients have been written off. In essence, what this means, is the cost of your work product has been paid for by the firm. The purpose of billing the client is to generate money for the firm, not to give the firm a deficit. We"—she paused—"were wondering if there was a problem."

Mr. Freeman sat with a smug expression on his face. His piercing gaze was intimidating, yet she wasn't going to falter. To her own surprise, her voice came out clear and crisp. "No, Tracie, there is no problem, at least, not with me."

"Then, what exactly is the problem?" Tracie asked. The other members of the committee sat stony faced without saying a word.

It was long overdue to get the tension between herself and Melissa out into the open. Her fingers idly drummed the table. "The problem is Melissa Ferguson." Mr. Freeman's smug expression washed away and Dexter's brows shot up.

"What does this have to do with Ms. Ferguson? Ms. Ferguson's work product is excellent," Mr. Freeman said.

"The problem with Ms. Ferguson is, the work she claims to have done is actually my work. She seems to have a problem with everything I do. After revising perfect documents over and over again, I give her the final work product, which she accepts and claim as her own. After all of the revisions are done, she writes off my time and claims my work is worthless."

"Such accusations are serious. If these accusations are found to be unwarranted, there could be grounds for punishment, including termination," Tracie said.

"I know the consequences. I wouldn't make such accusations if they weren't true. She has . . ."

Mr. Freeman interrupted. "I just happen to have Melissa's billable time right here in front of me." He opened the manilla folder on the table in front of him. "I was afraid something like this would happen. Therefore, I came prepared." Mr. Freeman passed around copies of Melissa's hours for the month to Tonya and the committee. "Look at all of those hours of research Melissa's done. There is no way Ms. Locksley can say Melissa doesn't do any work."

Tonya examined all of the hours, which happened to correspond with the work hours she had done on the same cases listed on the bills. "These hours are all mine."

"Don't be absurd. Anyone can say these hours are theirs, but Melissa's name is on all of them, along with details of what was done," Mr. Freeman said.

"Melissa came to me and told me to use her password because she preferred Lexis over Westlaw. I didn't have a Lexis password, so she said I could use hers until the firm issued me one. This seemed strange to me because Westlaw and Lexis basically offer the same features. I didn't see what the big deal was. It was then that I started keeping a log of everything I did for her, including the memorandum for the Tanzent case. I also have details of the work I've done and they correspond with Melissa's time."

"Is it possible to see this so-called log?" Tracie asked.

Tonya looked in Mr. Freeman's direction and smiled. "I happen to have a copy of my log right here." She passed the log to Tracie, who examined it thoroughly. After reviewing the log for a moment, she passed it around to other members of the committee.

"It's strange. These hours are exactly the same as the hours Melissa billed. It appears that we're going to have to conduct an investigation of these allegations," Tracie said. Several other members nodded in agreement.

"I don't think there is a need for an investigation." Mr. Freeman rapped his hand against the table trying to get his point across. "We have concrete evidence right here in front of us."

Dexter, who had been quietly observing the whole scene, finally spoke. To Tonya's surprise, it was on her behalf. "I think an investigation is necessary. It's obvious that there is a problem with these billing hours. Ms. Locksley is a fine attorney and I have never had to write off anything she's done for me. All of her research has been right on point." Everyone in the committee agreed to an investigation, except Mr. Freeman.

"From the way Ms. Ferguson has been behaving toward Ms. Locksley, I would think there was some sort of personal problem between the two of them. It's awfully funny that no one else has had any problems with anything Ms. Locksley has done, until Ms. Ferguson arrived," Keith Lexington told the committee with a wink in Tonya's direction.

"I see." Tracie continued writing on her notepad. "it's settled. We're going to conduct an investigation. Until then, Ms. Locksley will do no work for Ms. Ferguson. Does everyone agree?" A majority of the committee agreed with Tracie. Jaleel sat quietly observing the scene taking place. Why hadn't he made any decisions?

After the meeting had adjourned, Tonya lagged around in the conference room waiting to speak with Keith. She thanked him for sticking up for her in the meeting. She knew she had to thank Dexter. But it was hard to face him after all that had transpired between them. Instead of having to face him, she decided to send him a nice thank you card. Talk about taking the chicken way out. The plan to buy him a card was kicked to the curb because he was waiting for her outside of the conference room. She didn't want to have a long, drawn out conversation with him. Besides, what did she have to say to him? She knew they had unfinished business, but his plans were final and so were hers.

She stood next to Dexter outside of the conference room. "I must thank you for speaking up for me in the meeting. I don't know what would have happened if nobody was on my side."

"I did what was right. You've been working hard and you should get the credit you deserve."

"Good luck. I hope all turns out well," Jaleel said in passing.

"Thanks." She headed down the hall to her office.

"Tonya," Dexter called after her.

"Yes?" Tonya waited for Dexter to walk close to her.

"I wish you would reconsider my offer to help you get into another firm. I feel like everything that's happening to you is my fault."

"I can't spend my life running away from problems. If there are problems here, there will be problems there— whereever there may be." Tonya noticed that his necktie was crooked. She resisted the impulse to reach out and straighten his tie. Instead, she twisted the ring on her finger. "When you really think about it, a majority of the things that have happened to me are your fault." If he only knew the actual meaning behind those words.

Tonya was saved from her discussion with Dexter when the receptionist interrupted them and told her there was a gentleman waiting in the lobby to see her. She wondered who that gentleman could be. There was no one scheduled for an appointment that morning.

She excused herself from Dexter and followed the receptionist down the hall to the lobby. Dexter's curiosity as to who the gentleman was compelled him to trail behind her.

Impeccably clad in a navy suit, David stood with his back to her. He was checking out Freeman and Reynolds fortieth floor view of the downtown skyline.

He turned to face her when she walked into the lobby. "You have a wonderful view from up here," he said, returning his gaze to the window.

The nightmare continued—how much could happen to her in one day? "David, what are you doing here? As a matter of fact, how do you know where I work?"

"A business card. The last time I was at your apartment I helped myself to one of your cards."

"What do you want?"

"I told you I was giving you time to think about us. I think you've had enough time. I was thinking that maybe we could discuss everything over lunch."

His first error had been coming to her job unannounced, his second was thinking they had something to discuss. As bad as things were going in her life at that time, she wasn't desperate enough to try to convert a bisexual. "David, you have some serious issues. As I've told you before, we have nothing to talk about. I don't appreciate you dropping by my job and I most definitely don't appreciate you taking things from my apartment without my permission."

With a smooth flick of his wrist, he held out her business card. Tonya took the business card from him.

"Have lunch with me. If a relationship with me is totally out of the question, I'll leave you alone for good. That's the deal."

Tonya cocked her head to one side. "If I refuse lunch, then what?"

David smiled. "Then I'll be forced to keep trying. You know how persistent I can be."

Tonya knew there would never be anything else between herself and David. But with the day she was having, she didn't see what one last outing with David could hurt. "Okay, let me get my purse. I'll be right back."

"So, where do you want to go?" asked David when she returned with her purse.

"I thought maybe we could go to the deli downstairs and sit on the patio. I didn't want to go too far away, I have a lot of work to do."

For a minute, it felt like old times when David would take her out to lunch. If only David hadn't deceived her. She wondered what her life would be like if things hadn't ended the way they had. Maybe they would have eventually married and had a couple of kids—who knows?

Tonya noticed Melissa and Jaleel on the opposite end of the patio. Melissa was too busy tossing her head back in laughter and batting her lashes to notice her. *What's the deal with that?* Just then, Jaleel spotted Tonya and waved in her direction. Melissa's eyes landed on Tonya and the smile on her lips faded. Tonya waved back to Jaleel and returned to David.

"Let's get this discussion started. What do you want to talk about?" Tonya asked between bites of her club sandwich.

"Well, I want to know what's up with us. I must admit that I still love you. After all of this time, the love I have for you never died. So, I know what I feel for you is real."

"David, you don't love me," Tonya said with disbelief.

"Then, what is it?"

"I don't know what it is, but it isn't love. Love is such a strong word."

"I know love is a strong word, but I mean it. Can you find it in your heart to forgive me? Do you think it's possible to wipe the slate clean and start over?" David smiled at a woman sitting alone at a table across from them.

"It's too late for us now. My life has changed so much since the last time I saw you."

"How has your life changed? What, besides my one mistake, could keep us from starting over?" David seemed so sincere. But there was no way she could forget what happened. Every time she was in his presence, she felt like a fool. How could she not know that he and his best friend were lovers? She had to dash all hope of rekindling a relationship. "I must tell you that I'm expecting a baby."

David shook his head as if he were hearing wrong.

"You're expecting what?" He hesitated. "I must have misunderstood you."

"No, you heard correct. I'm expecting."

"From who? Oh, wait, let me guess. It's that guy you were with at your apartment."

"That's correct. As you can see, I've pretty much moved on with my life. The most we can be is friends."

David couldn't absorb anything she said after confirming she was pregnant. He was still in shock at her being pregnant and over who the father was. "I guess that's why he was hanging around at the receptionist desk like he was busy. He wasn't busy at all, he was watching us."

"What are you talking about? Who was watching us?"

"Your boyfriend, that's who. He kept looking over in our direction like he was expecting someone." David tried to shake off the shock he was in. Suddenly, he became serious. "So are you happy?"

How could she tell David the truth? If there was one thing she didn't want from David, it was his pity. "Yes, I'm happy."

David thought she would resist when he took her hands into his, but she didn't. "Tonya, I never meant to hurt you. Hurting you was one of the last things I ever wanted to do. I'm not trying to bring up old water under the bridge, but I never had the chance to tell you I'm sorry. I hope what I did in the past doesn't have a lasting effect on your life. After all that I've put you through, you deserve to have something good happen to you."

"Thank you, David. Your apology means a lot to me." She wasn't just saying those words just to be saying them, she actually meant it. Tonya wanted to ask him about his relationship with Ken. She wanted to know if he had been with any other men after they broke up. But what good would knowing do her? The truth would possibly bring her more pain, so she didn't bother asking.

"I guess we've gone as far as we can go, huh?" David asked.

"I guess so." Tonya glanced at her watch. "I've got to be getting back." She stood up to leave.

"Can I get one last hug for old times' sake?"

"Sure." Tonya hugged David. For a split second, it felt good to be back in David's arms. "Good-bye, David."

"Good-bye, Tonya" David seemed reluctant to let her go, for he knew he would be letting her go forever.

Saying good-bye to David was closure to a chapter in her life and the opening of another. It was like going to a bookstore to buy a new book. If the first couple of pages didn't grab her attention, she didn't buy the book. So far, the first couple of pages in the new chapter of her life almost made her want to return the book to the shelf.

Twenty-nine

Why was it that when you wanted a relationship, you could never find one, and when you didn't need one, potential relationships were falling from the sky?

"I consider you a friend, but I think you know that my feelings run deeper than a mere friendship," Warren professed to Tonya.

"I know, but it wouldn't be fair to either of us if I attempted to start a relationship with you. Honestly, I'm not over Dexter."

Warren's lips twisted in frustration. "Why are you chasing after something that was never meant for you? Why go for the single tree upon the hill when you can have your pick of the trees right here in the forest?"

"I can't help the way I feel. Sometimes we have no control over our emotions, they kind of do their own thing." She didn't want Warren to get the impression that she didn't want him around. She wanted him around, but only as a friend.

"It's obvious he doesn't want you. If he did, he wouldn't have run back to his ex-wife as soon as he did."

Why did everyone seem to have an opinion about something they knew little or nothing about? As a matter of fact, the only thing these people did know, was what she told them. "Warren, I'm not trying to be funny, but don't speak on things you know nothing about. I never told you what *I* may have done to drive Dexter back to her."

Warren positioned himself next to Tonya as if he were about to counsel a teen runaway. "Don't blame yourself for his mistakes. If he would have been up front about his situation, you wouldn't be having this problem. He should be the one taking the blame."

"Okay, I'll tell you the part of the story I failed to mention, and you can draw your own conclusions then. Is that fair?"

"That's fair." Warren agreed.

"After I broke up with Dexter, I found out I was pregnant. In my panic and confusion, I decided keeping it wasn't a good idea. I made an appointment to—you know—but I couldn't do it. When I got home he thought I had gone through with it. I wanted to tell him that I didn't do it, that I kept our baby, but I couldn't. I felt like I would be forcing him to make a choice between me and his fiancée. I couldn't let him make a decision for us because I was pregnant. I wanted him to be with me because he cared, not out of necessity."

Warren's eyes immediately focused on her stomach. "You're pregnant?"

"Yes."

"I see. I don't know what to say. I want to be happy for you, but I know the circumstances aren't all good. I think you should tell him the truth."

"It's too late. His wedding date has already been set."

"It's not too late until he says, *I do.*"

"Well, he's darn near there."

"If it's any consolation," Warren said. "I think it's his loss. Anyone who would miss out on you is on the losing end."

"Thanks for making me feel better." Tonya smiled.

"I'm not just saying it to make you feel better, it's the truth. How does your family feel about it?"

"I don't know how they feel about it. I haven't told them yet." Warren took a deep breath. From the way he was acting, you would think it was his problem. "When do you plan on telling them? I know you don't think you can keep this a secret forever. Not to mention that eventually, your boyfriend is going to find out."

Tonya held up an open palm. "Correction, he's not my boyfriend and I'll just have to deal with it when he finds out. As far as my family goes, all I have to do is tell my brother, Reggie, and he'll do the rest."

"I want you to know that your being pregnant doesn't change the way I feel about you. In all honesty, I hope Dexter makes the right decisions when it comes to you and the baby you're carrying."

Warren was too sweet for his own good. Tonya hoped with all of her heart he would find someone to make him happy. Usually, good guys like him wound up with someone who didn't know how to appreciate them.

Was it too much to ask to have a traditional nuclear family? Was the traditional family becoming extinct? Tonya was starting to believe this was the case. She wanted a family like the one she grew up in. A family with a loving mother and father was what she wanted for her baby. This wasn't to say that her family was the epitome of the functional family, because it wasn't.

Thirty

There was still no change in Mr. Winters's condition. He was still unconscious and on a respirator. Kiera and her family continued to hope and pray for a full recovery.

That Monday was definitely manic. For some odd reason, work mode eluded her. There were stacks of papers on her desk and she moved them from one spot to the other, getting nothing done. Thoughts of Dexter continued to flood her mind. With less than two weeks until the day of Dexter's wedding, Tonya resolved to believe that she didn't care.

Her first case on her own dealt with a grown woman who had been molested by her father. The woman was nine when the molesting began and it continued until her mid-teens. Now she was twenty-five and was suing her mother for doing nothing to help her. Her mother, of course, claimed that she had no knowledge of the alleged molestations. It was a case of liabilities. Was her mother at fault? She could really like this case. She sat for what seemed like hours, mulling over relevant cases and other research. The distraction from her chaotic life was welcome. Until . . . he came in. She hadn't planned on a visit from him.

"Good morning," Dexter said silkily. Morning was it still morning?

He was like a fine wine, the more she drank him in,

the more intoxicated she became. She hadn't expected to see him after the date had been set for the wedding. He probably didn't think she knew about it. Dexter seemed somewhat fidgety as he stood in front of her desk putting his hands in and out of his pockets.

"Good morning. What can I do for you?" Tonya asked lightly. *God! If only my attitude was the same.* She was packing a heavy load on her shoulders.

"How are things going on your case?"

"Fine," she answered.

"That's good. I'm glad." It was the first time that she had ever seen him at a loss of words. There was something wrong with him.

"Dexter, is there anything you want to talk to me about?" she asked frankly. His gaze shifted away from her and out the window.

He sat in one of the chairs in front of her desk and stretched out his long, muscular legs.

"Tonya, I want to be the first to tell you about my upcoming wedding plans. I'm getting married on the twenty-first of this month." He paused to let his words sink in. "I didn't want you to hear it from someone else."

Why are you telling me? What difference does it make whether I know or not? "Congratulations." That was all she could muster up to say. She tried to be as indifferent as possible.

"You don't mean that. Why say things you don't mean?" he said dangerously low.

"I mean it with all sincerity. I'm happy for you and Melissa," she said with synthetic happiness. *I will never be happy for you and her. It should be me!*

He leaned over her desk and looked her deeply in the eyes. "You mean you don't mind the idea of me spending the rest of my life with someone else?"

Was this a trick question? "Dexter, I have no control over your life. You are free to do whatever you please," she said quickly, avoiding the question. She knew he was too sharp for that.

"You didn't answer the question," he said sternly.

She quickly turned the question around. "Do *you* like the idea of spending your life with someone else? I think you will be the one with the problem, not me." He wasn't prepared for that and for a fleeting moment she saw what she believed to be vulnerability, but he quickly recovered.

"That, my dear, is out of the question," he said as he kissed her roughly on the lips. She didn't protest. His face hovered much too close to hers. "Why do I like you so much? Every time I'm around you I seem to lose it." The question was more to himself than to her.

"Dexter, I . . ." she started. He put a long finger to her lips and kissed her for what seemed like eons. She found her hands intertwining in his dark mass of hair.

"I have to do something about you before . . ." his voice trailed off. He marveled at the significant differences between Tonya and Melissa. Melissa was raised with southern hospitality and learned that being dependent on a man was the thing to do. On the other hand Tonya, had just the right amount of independence and never bit her tongue on what she had to say. She was too candid to be polite. Then he returned to normal, as if nothing ever happened. He stood up, stretching his lean frame. "Well, anyway, I wanted to be the one to tell you."

The man was crazy. *He stands here and tells me he's getting married to someone else. Then kisses me and lets me know that I drive him senseless only to remind me that he's getting married in a few days.* All she knew was that he drove *her* crazy.

"Why was it so important that you be the one to tell me?" She might as well take advantage of a good situation.

"Well, you know how rumors are." That was all that he said before opening the door and closing it after him. So much for taking advantage of a good thing.

Thirty-one

His intentions were to make her uncomfortable and to watch her squirm under pressure. He was the one who couldn't take the heat. He knew deep down inside that he was in love with her, but what could he do? She didn't want him and he definitely wasn't about to chase after her. She was just so pretty to him. Today as she sat behind her desk in her oversized chair, she was extraordinarily beautiful. No, she was radiant. Yes, she was a striking contrast to his light-skinned ex, but her silky brown skin and mysteriously gorgeous smile intrigued him.

He hated himself for being so taken with her. It wasn't fair. Not to him and certainly not to Tonya. This had to stop. He pretended to be busy as he sat on the edge of his desk. Holding some papers idly in his hands he let his mind drift. *What would our baby have looked like?* He kicked himself for letting his mind touch the subject. That was something he fought hard not to think about. It angered him that she did not include him in the decision making. Yes, he loved her and the thought of her being his wife and having his children wasn't bad at all. He quickly banished the thought. *Get a grip man!* That's over and done with. Maybe that was his reason for telling her about his wedding plans, maybe he wanted to see what her reaction would be.

He realized that he wanted to upset her, he needed to

know if she loved him even the slightest bit. She revealed nothing, until she kissed him. Her response said it all, but he didn't want to confuse her physical longing for something more. If only she knew why he was going to go through with the wedding. He loved Tonya so much that he would sacrifice his own happiness just to make sure her career didn't go down the drain. His father would keep his word about ruining her and he couldn't let that happen. His father could be ruthless, but it was all going to come to an end one day soon. He decided to let it go . . . for now.

"Pardon my interruption." Jaleel walked into Dexter's office, closing the door behind him.

Dexter's head started throbbing. What did he want now? He immediately put on his professional mask. "Is there something I can help you with?"

"We're long overdue for a talk. We can't continue tipping around one another." Jaleel took a seat.

"Have a seat," Dexter said sarcastically. "You're right. We can't continue tipping around one another. So, why don't you go back where you came from?"

"I can't do that." Jaleel stared at his laced fingers. "I had no idea that you were at this firm. Had I known, I wouldn't have come here. Given all that has transpired between us, I would think distance is the safest thing."

"I couldn't have put it any better," Dexter agreed.

"Why do you harbor these ill feelings? You never loved her." His eyes met Dexter's fierce gaze.

"Whatever the case may have been, she was my wife. You should have respected that."

"Don't place all of the blame on me. It takes two to tango. Besides, I respect the institution of marriage. Had you not been so into your career, I wouldn't have had to take care of things at home for you."

"Be glad that I'm not the same person I was a few years ago. If I was the same person, you would be lying on the floor right about now. I'm only going to say this once. I've moved on with my life and I don't care what you or Melissa choose to do with your lives. Have a nice day and get out of my office."

Jaleel rose from the chair, straightening his suit. "Dexter Freeman, you try so hard not to be like your father, yet you are. You hate to lose to anybody. Why don't you try being a good loser sometimes? If you remarry Melissa, the same thing is going to happen. She's just too much woman for you and you don't know what to do with her." He made a hasty departure from Dexter's office.

Thirty-two

Tracie Margo was the first person she bumped into on the way to the office. For someone who made as much money as she did, Tonya couldn't understand why Tracie continued to wear such outdated clothes. She would be so much more attractive if she just put a little effort into it. "I was just on my way to see you," Tracie said.

Tonya tried to read Tracie's expression, but it revealed nothing. The investigation was more than likely what Tracie wanted to discuss with her. If only Tracie would give a clue as to how things were going, Tonya would feel better. She told herself to stay calm, even if it meant she would be unemployed at the end of the day. "Is that good or bad?" Tonya laughed nervously.

Apparently, Tracie didn't find any humor in Tonya's statement. "Will it be okay if I close the door?" Tracie asked after they entered Tonya's office.

Tonya leaned on her desk. There was no need to take a seat if she was going to be packing up her things because she was fired. "That will be fine."

Tracie pushed her styleless frames up on her nose. "As you probably know, I'm here to discuss the results of our investigation. As I've told you before, your accusations may have serious consequences."

Tonya knew what was coming next. She didn't know if she could listen to Tracie tell her to pack her bags and get out. "I understand, Tracie. I knew what I was up against when I mentioned my situation to the committee. Since the committee didn't find favor in my allegations, I am prepared to suffer the consequences."

Tracie seemed surprised. "Who said anything about the committee not finding favor in your allegations? As a matter of fact, we agree with you."

Tonya exhaled the breath that had been constricted in her chest. "You do? I can't believe it. I don't know what to say, except, thank you."

"You don't have to thank me. The kind of things Ms. Ferguson did were wrong and shouldn't take place in our firm."

Tonya was beaming. Finally, there was something positive happening in her life. "What does this mean for Melissa? I know she's not going to be fired."

"No, she didn't get fired, but she was reduced to a staff attorney. Does that seem appropriate?"

A staff attorney! Good. "Yes, that seems appropriate." At least as a staff attorney, there was no chance of Melissa becoming a partner until she was reinstated as an associate.

"Is there a reason why Ms. Ferguson would do something like this to you?" Tracie seemed hesitant to ask what was on her mind, maybe it was out of fear of what the answer might be.

Tonya didn't want to explain the situation to Tracie. Explaining would only reveal the love triangle they had been involved in. "I'm sure she has her reasons. Maybe you should ask Melissa what the problem is when you have a chance."

"It's not that important. Whatever her reason, she shouldn't have reacted the way she did. At any rate, hopefully this situation has been resolved. If you have any further problems, don't hesitate to come to me."

"Thanks, Tracie. I won't."

It felt good to have someone on her side. She knew that if it were up to Mr. Freeman, she would be without a job. She couldn't understand why he seemed to dislike her so much. She had an overwhelming desire to know why he wanted to make things difficult for her. The tension between them would surely affect their on-the-job relationship in a negative fashion. There was only one way to resolve their problem and that was to have a talk with him. Her first impulse was to call Vivian, Mr. Freeman's secretary, to let him know she wanted to schedule an appointment with him. She decided against that idea because she knew he would avoid any confrontation with her.

Tonya had to pump herself up to make that lonely trek down the hall to Mr. Freeman's office. Her heart pounded louder and louder with each step that brought her closer to Mr. Freeman's door. Luckily, Vivian was away from her desk. She knocked on the door and heard a muffled, "Come in."

She entered the office to face the back of his leather chair. A steady stream of smoke poured from his cigar, adding to the already thick smoke screen. "Mr. Freeman, I was wondering if now is a good time to have a discussion with you."

Mr. Freeman spun around as if he were caught off guard. "Where's Vivian? I told her I didn't want to be disturbed."

Tonya walked closer to his desk. "Is now not a good time?"

"Well, I . . . have a lot of work to do. Can this wait?" He fumbled around on his neatly arranged desk, searching for the so-called *work* he had to do.

She was determined to speak her mind and to clear the air between them. "This won't take but a minute."

"Well, if you insist. I figured you would be making your way to see me soon. What's on your mind?"

As if he didn't already know. "I was wondering if it's just me or do you think there's some tension between us, too?" *Yes, Mr. Freeman, you are being confronted.*

"Yes, you're correct, there is tension between us." He took a puff of his cigar and deliberately blew it in her direction.

"May I ask why you have a problem with me? I've done nothing wrong and I don't deserve this kind of treatment from you."

"Okay, Ms. Locksley." Mr. Freeman put down his cigar. "You want an answer, I'll give you an answer. I have no problem with you as an attorney. As a matter of fact, I think you're a pretty good one. My concern with you is on a personal level."

Tonya shook her head in disbelief. "I know this doesn't have anything to do with Dexter."

"As a matter of fact, it does. I like you as a person, but my son is already spoken for. I have always planned for my son to have the best of everything and I'm not about to let anyone take that away from him."

"In other words, I'm not good enough for him. Is that it?"

Mr. Freeman cleared his throat, the same way Dexter did when he was under pressure. "I didn't say that. I'm sure you would have been fine for him *if* Melissa weren't in the picture."

She couldn't believe Mr. Freeman was telling her she wasn't good enough for Dexter. What was so wrong with her? She was just as nice as Melissa. "I don't think that will be a problem anymore. You don't have to worry about me messing up your plans." She didn't wait for a response before storming out of his office and slamming the door behind her.

Mr. Freeman took a long drag from his cigar. He had to admire her tenacity. There was no way she was going to let anyone run over her. She was a little too self-confident for her own good and people like that had to be taken down a notch or two. He was just the person to do it. Tonya Locksley had no idea who she was messing with.

Thirty-three

On her way home, she had almost forgotten she was supposed to meet Reggie at the barbershop. She was so angry with Mr. Freeman that she had pushed Reggie to the back of her mind. As she drove to the shop, her eyes were automatically drawn to every liquor store she passed. There was someone loitering in front of every one of them. A police officer had someone jacked up against the police car. She slowed down and strained her eyes to make sure it wasn't Kip. After being assured it wasn't Kip, she sped up. Kip loved to drink, but he wasn't a trouble-maker.

When she pulled into the parking lot of Reggie's shop, she had to find a place to park. The place was packed. She didn't like meeting Reggie at the shop when it was packed like that. That meant more than likely, he was still cutting hair and she would have to wait a while before they could leave. She glanced in the cutting area and gave a wave to Reggie to let him know she was there. He held up one finger, telling her that the client in the chair was his last one for the evening. Tonya gave a thumbs up and pointed to her right, saying she was going to grab a burger. He gave a nod of his head and resumed cutting the client's hair. Talk about using sign language.

Reggie's shop had a burger bar inside, a game room, a patio out back, an open bar, and pool tables. All of these things made Reggie's a happening place. Sometimes people went to the barbershop just to hang out. There was always a domino game going on and people loved the burgers. Mrs. Zellermyle Anthony was Reggie's cook and man, could she throw down in the kitchen. Her burgers were the best. Tonya ordered a burger and watched a domino game until her order was ready.

"Big ten!" An older man yelled out as he slammed his domino on the table.

Tonya picked up her burger and sat at one of the empty tables close to the domino game. She couldn't play dominoes, but enjoyed watching the game. She didn't play because people said she took all day counting.

"Big six, old man!" A younger guy said to the older gentleman, slamming down his domino.

"And I got fifteen on yo' young butt!" The old man said.

Tonya could hardly eat for laughing at how grown people behaved during a domino game.

"I don't know why you're always around a domino game when you know you can't play." Reggie sat at the table with Tonya.

"Whatever, Reggie." Tonya wiped away some mustard from her mouth.

"What's up, Reggie?" A guy over at the pool tables called.

"You man," Reggie answered. They both laughed.

"What's up this time?" Tonya asked.

"Nothing. I'm coming over to your house." He took one of her fries and dipped it in ketchup before it disappeared in his mouth. "You need some hot sauce, black pepper, and salt on those fries."

"Don't tell *me* how to eat *my* fries and how are you going to just invite yourself over to my house?"

Reggie dropped his mouth like he was trying to say, *as if!* "Since when do I ask to stay at your place? I didn't ask when you first moved, so why should I start asking now?"

"I hope you have your bags because I'm not going over to Ramona's."

"Have you ever known me to be unprepared? My bags are in the other room, thank you." Reggie smiled, knowing he had won her over.

"Wipe that smirk off your face. You think you're slick, but I know what you're doing."

Reggie placed both hands on his chest, laughing. "Girl, what are you talking about? What am I doing?"

"You come over to my house just to escape your problems at home. I got news for you, my house is not a resort."

"Ah, man, it's not? I guess I have to take my flowered shirt and Bermuda shorts back, huh?" He laughed.

Tonya laughed in chorus with him. "I guess so and take your leis back, too. Where's your truck? I didn't see it outside."

"My friend dropped me off at work this morning. My truck is at home." Reggie looked toward the domino game, as if he were really interested.

Tonya did a double take. "Wait a minute. Did you say your friend? What friend dropped you off?" Things were starting to get interesting. Reggie had her undivided attention then.

"Don't worry about things you ain't got nothing to do with," Reggie said slyly. "Let's go get my bags and get out of here."

"I take it you're not going to tell me who this mysterious friend is."

"Bingo."

Tonya followed Reggie to get his bags. He said goodnight to a few of the other barbers who were still working or about to leave. She put his bags in the trunk of her car.

Reggie got in on the passenger side. "When are you going to get out of this rental car and into your own?"

Tonya looked sideways at her brother. "I know you're not complaining. You should just be happy that you're riding."

Reggie snapped his seatbelt. "I'm not complaining. I'm just ready to see what you're going to buy next. If I were you, I would get a BMW. But knowing you, with your conservative butt, you'll probably go get a Saturn or a Taurus."

"What's wrong with those cars? I happen to like the Saturn." Tonya steered the car into the busy street.

"Darn, Tonya. Don't go out there, buying a car just to have a car. You need to buy a car that fits you. You should take me car shopping with you. I'll pick out a nice car for you."

"I'm sure you will. It will probably have jet black tint, hydraulics, and a loud stereo."

"You damn skippy." ·

There was very little traffic on the freeway as they passed downtown and the convention center. The glimmer of the lights from the International Festival could vaguely be seen in front of city hall.

"So, Reggie." Tonya was trying to figure out how she could launch into her interrogation of Reggie's whereabouts from the previous evening.

Reggie pulled down the sun visor and looked in the mirror. "So, Tonya."

"Where were you last night and who were you with?"

Reggie closed the visor and smiled to himself. "What's up with the interrogation?"

"I know you weren't out with Ramona. Who was it? You know you can't keep water to yourself so you might as well tell me." Was Reggie cheating on Ramona? Tonya had never known Reggie to step out on her. If what she was thinking was true, that was a good sign. Her heart leapt at the idea of having no Ramona around.

"Alright already. I was out with someone new—a teacher."

Tonya darn near had a wreck at Reggie's confession. "What? You're cutting out on Ramona?" she asked, smiling. "I can't believe it. What brought this on?"

"Forget Ramona. I'm not worried about her conniving butt. Regina is so much different from Ramona. Instead of paging me to find out where I am and what I'm doing, she calls to say 'hi' or just to see how my day is."

"She sounds like a wonderful lady." Tonya was starting to get scared. Her brother seemed like he was falling in love for the first time. What he had with Ramona wasn't love, he only thought it was. Tonya smiled. Reggie was long overdue for something good to happen to him, too.

His face was beaming as he talked about Regina. "Man, is she wonderful. She's not all loud and rude. She's cool and calm, but demands her respect."

"How long have you known her?"

"For about a month. I met her at the grocery store, but last night was the first time we, you know—got together."

"Does she know about Ramona?" She hoped her brother wasn't trying to pull a Dexter move on his new friend.

"Does she know about Ramona? No, she doesn't know about Ramona."

"I know you don't plan on playing both of them." Tonya frowned at Reggie, who had lowered the seat as if he were hiding from someone.

"Nah, I'm letting Ramona go."

This was music to her ears. She and their parents had been waiting for the day to come when Ramona would be a thing of the past. "That's why you aren't going home, huh?"

"That's right. Besides, I saw her getting in the car with some brother the other night."

She pulled her car into her reserved parking space in front of her apartment. "So what about the baby?"

"That's just it. She's not pregnant, she lied because she thought I was going to leave her."

"That's good because I am." She couldn't believe the words came out of her mouth and to her big mouthed brother. What had compelled her to do such a thing?

Reggie raised up his seat. "Excuse me? What was that?" He stuck a finger in his ear, pretending to clean it so he could hear better. "You are what?"

"I didn't say anything." Tonya opened her door and hopped out quickly.

Reggie hopped out of the passenger side. "Yes, you did. You said you're pregnant. Pregnant by who?"

She ignored Reggie and unlocked the trunk. "I'll meet you inside," Tonya muffled.

Reggie quickly lugged his bags from the trunk. "Damn straight you'll meet me inside."

Tonya turned on the lights and went into the kitchen and took out a frozen dinner. Reggie walked into the kitchen with a wild-eyed expression on his face.

"Who's baby is it?" He leaned on the counter, waiting for a response. "It better not be for the person I think it is. Moms and Pops are going to kill you."

Why was everyone treating her like a kid? "I'm not a child, Reggie. In case you've forgotten, I'm the responsible one." She put her dinner in the microwave and slammed the door.

"Yeah, look what your being responsible has gotten you. Who did you say the father is?"

"I didn't say."

Reggie's voice was getting louder and louder. "Well, don't you think you need to say?"

"It's Dexter's, okay. That's what you wanted to know, now you know."

"Tonya! Didn't I warn you about him? I told you to stay away from him. Where is he now? He probably took off and left you to deal with this by yourself. I guess you just think I'm stupid. I don't know anything because I didn't go to college. You should have listened because I could have saved you from what you're going through right now."

She turned her back to him. He was right. If she had listened to him, she wouldn't be in the situation she was in. The truth hurt. "I know." She sobbed. "You told me and I didn't listen. It's all my fault."

Reggie cursed to himself. If there was one thing he couldn't stand, it was to see his baby sister cry. He turned her to face him and hugged her tight. "I'm sorry. I didn't mean to upset you. It's just that I don't expect anything like this from you and neither do our parents. Now, you're making me an uncle at a young age." He smiled. He tore off a paper towel and wiped her face.

"I know you're going to tell Mom and Dad," she sniffed.

"No, I'm not going to tell them this time. I promise. How does he feel about the baby?"

"He doesn't know."

"Aren't you going to tell him?"

Tonya wriggled out of his embrace. "It's a long story. Promise you won't tell Mom and Dad."

"Okay, I promise."

"Yeah, right. I've heard that before. You promised not to tell anyone about David but you did and had me looking like a fool in front of our friends."

"Yeah, but I didn't tell Moms and Pops. Besides, you didn't look like a fool, he did."

"You're not telling Mom and Dad about David is not

the point. You promised not to tell anyone. I trusted you, and you let me down."

"Look, sis, I know I let you down before. This time is different because I've changed and I want this situation to turn out for the best. I want you to be happy 'cause if you're not happy then I'm not happy. You're my little sister and I love you."

Stop the press! This was truly a Kodak moment. Reggie had used the "L" word for the first time. "Reggie, that's so sweet of you to say. You've never told me you loved me."

Reggie laughed. "How can I not love my family? I may not say it, but you know I do. You should have recorded that 'cause you might not hear those words fall from my lips anytime soon."

She planted a kiss on his cheek. "I love you, too, Reggie, and don't you ever forget it."

"Okay, that's enough. I might get an allergic reaction from all of this mushy stuff." Reggie retreated to the living room. "I have to start looking for an apartment."

Tonya followed Reggie with her entree. "You're serious about leaving Ramona, huh?"

"I am serious about leaving her. I'm not getting any younger and I don't want to spend the rest of my life on the wild side. I can't see Ramona being the mother of my children. She won't even cook for me so I know our kids would starve. Speaking of starving"— Reggie looked at Tonya's dinner—"you need to lay off of the frozen dinners and cook. I know you know how to cook 'cause Moms taught you. Besides, didn't you just eat before we got here?"

Tonya smiled. "Remember, I'm not just eating for myself anymore. I don't have time to cook. When I get home, all I want to do is sleep."

"I just can't believe you're pregnant. I'm ready for a

positive change in my life and I think Regina is the key. Next week, I'll have a surprise for you."

"What's the surprise?"

"If I tell you then it won't be a surprise. You'll see next week."

"So when are we going to meet Regina?"

"I don't know, sometime soon."

"Oh, man, am I glad to see the end of another work day," Reggie said to himself as he hung the closed sign on the door.

He took the push broom from the closet and began sweeping up hair from the floor. His mind was focused on his baby sister. How could she allow herself to get pregnant by the same guy he told her to stay away from? If she wouldn't have broken down crying and all that, he would have chewed her out something terrible.

He stopped his sweeping motion and rested on the broomstick. "What was she thinking? Doesn't she realize her having this baby is affecting a lot more people than just her and that loser? I'm going to be an uncle at an early age. She's making me old!"

He resumed sweeping the floor. He'd promised her he wouldn't tell anyone. *I can't go back on my word. I want to tell somebody, but I can't!* He eyed the telephone miserably. *If I say anything, I'll ruin my relationship with my sister. Then again, we'll always be family—right? Wrong! I'll be forced into exile.*

"Why do I always have to be the first to know everything? Doesn't Tonya realize this is pressure on a brother? I feel like Chris Rock, except it's not about cheatin'. Wanna tell—*can't tell.* Gotta tell—*can't tell.* Damn this is pressure!"

A rap on the door shortened his self-discussion. He knew there was a man standing outside, but he couldn't see his face for the closed sign. After shifting the sign, he saw David standing there with his too-cool demeanor.

This punk was the last person he wanted to see. He thought hard about not opening the door. He pointed to the closed sign and mouthed out, *I'm closed.*

David held his hands out as if saying, *Man, it's me, your boy! You're not going to open up the door?* Reggie unlocked the door and opened it reluctantly.

"What's up? I thought you weren't going to open the door for a minute there," David said cooly.

"For a minute there, you were right," Reggie replied with sarcasm in his voice. "What can I do for you?" He stood aside and let David inside the shop.

"Ah, you know, I just came by to say hello."

Reggie got to thinking about the way things went down between David and Tonya. He hoped David wasn't trying to start something with him because that was a dead-end street. He widened the distance between them.

"Well, it's nice of you to stop by, but I was on my way out in a minute. If you just want to chat or something, you need to call or come by during business hours." It wasn't that he was homophobic or anything, but for some reason, he didn't like the idea of being alone with David.

"Well, actually, I wanted to talk to you about something," David explained.

He better not be trying to make a move on somebody 'cause if he is, it'll be the last move he'll ever make. Reggie jumped to defense mode.

"Oh yeah? And what might you want to talk to me about?" Reggie asked with a clenched fist. *I'll wear his butt out with this broom if he asks what I think he's about to ask.*

David noticed Reggie's defensiveness. "Man, just calm down. What are you all defensive for? I just wanted to talk to you about your sister."

Reggie's posture remained the same. "What about my sister?"

"I just wanted to know if she's truly happy with this guy that she's pregnant by. I spoke with her the other day and she told me she was happy. Somehow, her happiness didn't quite reach her eyes. I know her and I don't think she's telling the truth."

. Reggie's head crooked to one side as his eyes narrowed on David. "Did she tell you she was happy?"

"That's what she said."

"Then, I guess that's what you ought to believe. What did you think you could do—take up where the other brother left off?" Reggie asked.

David shoved his hands into his pockets. He had forgotten how straightforward Reggie could be. Reggie always could push the wrong buttons with him.

"Nah, I just thought I could be there for her. You know, kind of restore my good name."

Reggie busied himself picking up the rest of the trash from the floor. He had to keep busy to keep from slapping some sense into this idiot. He had to give it to the man, he had some nerve!

"So, in other words, this is about you and not my sister?"

"No, it's not at all about me. I care for your sister and if that other guy isn't man enough to be there and take care of his responsibility, I will."

Reggie's anger spilled out of him in the form of a forced laugh. "Man, please! I can't believe you're standing there talking about if that other man ain't *man* enough. It probably would have been different if you had just cheated on my sister. But you cheated on her with *another man!* That makes all the difference in the world right there. The way I see it, that other man is winning because at least he was cheating with another *woman!*"

Reggie went to the door and held it open. "Do yourself a favor and leave my sister alone. She don't want to have nothin' to do with you and neither do I. So make this your last time approaching me about my sister. I don't mind you coming here to get a haircut, but other than that, I don't want to see you."

David shook his head is disbelief. "So you're saying that you can take me as a customer, but you can't take me as family?"

"That's exactly what I'm saying! Money is green and I don't discriminate against dead presidents."

Reluctantly David complied. "Well, you know I'm a firm believer that anything worth having is worth working hard for."

"Well, you should have thought about that before you went bumpin' booties with another brother. Sounds to me like you're just butt out. See ya'." Reggie closed the door behind David and locked it.

He watched as David drove off. He sort of felt sorry for him. It must be hard not to be accepted by anyone. As strange as it was, he and David were a lot alike. Neither he nor David felt as if they belonged anywhere. Both of them were looking for acceptance.

Thirty-four

After her last encounter with Dexter, she began a countdown to the D-day, the wedding day. It seemed that he made it a point to avoid her. If he saw her coming, he would go the other direction. Since wearing regular clothes was becoming absurd, she started to venture into her larger wardrobe. People started to take notice. One girl did a double take when Tonya took some papers to be copied in the copy room. Shyly the girl smiled. "I'm not trying to be funny, but are you expecting?"

Tonya was a little taken aback by the question. "Yes, I am. You don't have to be shy about it," Tonya said, smiling. The girl was probably wondering who the father was. Pretty soon everyone began to offer congratulations. Since Dexter had been incognito, he missed the celebration. She left the copy room and put the copies on her desk. "I may as well go to the restroom now, I don't want to have to come back later," she thought out loud.

She went out into the hall and rounded the corner she bumped into Dexter, *literally*. He reached his arms out to steady her balance. His arms brushed up against her belly. He looked puzzled and stared at her with a strange expression fixed upon his face. She lowered her eyes and he raised his hands as if to touch her again, he let them drop to his sides.

Eight days to the wedding and this happens. He was speechless, as if he knew it was his. It was written all over his blood-drained face. He spun quickly on his heels and strode away. *I hadn't meant for him to find out like this.* How could she begin to explain? What would she say? *Dexter, it was for your own good. No, I can't say that. Dexter, I kept the truth about your baby from you because I thought it was best.* Words didn't seem enough.

Dexter paced around his office like a caged animal. *Is it mine? How could she lie to me the way she did? Just who does she think she's playing with? You should have known, all of the signs were there.* With one long sweep, he brushed his desk clean. Papers and pens flew violently against the wall.

She walked quickly into Rita's office. "Rita, he knows. He knows, Rita. What am I going to do?"

Rita rose quickly from her chair. "Wait, slow down. You can't be getting all upset, honey. Dexter finally knows about it, huh?" She led Tonya to a chair and eased her down.

"Yes, but I didn't tell him anything. He bumped into me and felt it. He knew immediately and he walked away."

"You didn't say anything? You didn't let him know he is the father?"

"No. He didn't give me a chance to do or say anything before he left. What am I going to do?"

"Don't panic. Give it time," she reassured.

"Time isn't something I have a lot of. He's getting married in eight days."

"Don't take this the wrong way. You are the reason for the deadline. If you had taken care of your business in the first place, none of this would be taking place."

"I . . . You're right. How can I fix my mouth to complain about time?"

"Let the chips fall where they may. That's all you can do."

Rita was right. There was nothing she could do about it now.

Tonya was afraid to walk down the hall. *What am I tripping for? He isn't sure it's his.* She had expected to see him in her office, but he never came. Tonya had a lot to think about. The wedding day was approaching fast and still no word from Dexter.

The weekend was a blur and it was Monday again. Kiera's father seemed to be much better, but Tonya wasn't. Only five days left to the big day. Rita burst into Tonya's office during lunch.

"Girl, did you hear the news?" she asked, taking a seat. "Oh wait, let me close your door."

"What news?" Tonya asked in contusion.

"Melissa turned in her letter of resignation today. I guess she plans on being a housewife."

"Congratulations to her," Tonya said sourly.

"Oh, lighten up. Things will be fine. You worry too much over things that are out of your control."

She didn't know why she was disappointed when there was no sign of Dexter. What did she expect? She had deliberately deceived him.

After getting home and showering, she grabbed something to eat. She was getting fat and she didn't like it. She lay on the couch flipping the channels on TV listlessly. Even with cable TV there was nothing to watch. The phone rang. *What now, Mom?*

"Hello," she answered.

"I'll be up in a minute," the familiar voice said. Her heart accelerated. She knew why he was there. It had taken him longer than she expected. He didn't wait for her to answer before he hung up. She jumped at the knock at the door and hesitated, for some reason she couldn't move.

"Open the door, Tonya. You don't want to have to put another one up," he barked.

She opened it slowly. "What do you think I'm going to do—hurt you?" He grimaced. He walked inside and shut the door behind him. She stood there quietly observing him. Mechanically she went to the sofa and took a seat. He did the same.

"You and I have a lot we need to discuss," he said sternly. Anger was written in his features.

"Do we?" she asked aloofly.

"Don't play. Now is not the time. A lot of people have been hurt with your secrets." His eyes blazed.

"Alright, let's talk. What do you want to know?"

"Just to clarify the assumption, because I don't like assumptions. Are you pregnant?"

"Yes." That was all she could say.

His eyes softened. "Is it mine?"

She couldn't look him in the face. It hurt so much to tell the truth. "Yes." He continued to stare blankly.

"Why didn't you tell me? You've had so many opportunities. Why?" he pleaded.

She hadn't expected a show of emotions. This was a total surprise to her. "I don't know why. I've tried reasoning, but I have none. Maybe it was out of fear."

"Fear of what?" he asked softly. She looked down at the carpet. There was a strained silence, yet he did nothing to ease it and waited for her response. She continued to fidget. He sat there on the sofa staring her down. *I can't stand this!*

"I don't know," she answered.

"Yeah, you know. I'm not leaving until I get to the bottom of this."

"Well, after you thought I terminated the pregnancy, you gave me little chance to explain."

"No. You can't use that as an excuse. You saw how much it meant to me, *that* was your opportunity to say otherwise. However, you said nothing," he said condescendingly.

She was not a child. He was not going to talk down to her. "Well, if you recall, I begged you not to leave the way you did. You wouldn't listen." She had to make him understand. Why was everything her fault?

Why is she using all of these excuses? She should have been honest in the first place.

"There were other times when we were alone that you could have told me. Yet, you said nothing. I guess you were going to say it was someone else's baby or go off and have it without saying one word. You were wrong. That's enough of talking about woulda', shoulda', coulda'. We need to start from here," he said gruffly. There was an edge of agitation in his tone.

She knew she couldn't continue to play games with him. "What do you mean *we?*" she asked.

"Just what I said. *We* are going to deal with this. I'm not leaving my child."

What about me? He didn't say he wasn't leaving me. "I see. I won't stop you from being in the baby's life."

"You *couldn't* stop me. Have you been going to the doctor? Is everything normal?"

She couldn't read his face. He was concerned, but it was solely for his child.

"Yes. Everything's been fine."

"Do you know what it is? Have they done an ultrasound?"

"I've had an ultrasound, but I don't know what it is. I don't want to know." She didn't wait to ask if he wanted to see the pictures from the ultrasound. She immediately went to her room and retrieved them.

"These are the pictures," she said, pointing to them. He took them and looked at them. He was amazed at the developing baby. "See, that's the head, the arms and legs."

"It's so small. I can't believe you're carrying something inside this small." Mechanically, he reached out and rubbed her belly. It was so intimate. "And it's mine."

The temptation to hold his hand there was overwhelming and couldn't be resisted. He withdrew his hand. He donned his professional, strictly business attitude.

"I'm paying for all medical expenses. You won't want for anything and you need to find a bigger place to live."

"Hold on a minute. I'm fine living here and I don't want you taking care of all my medical bills. I know you mean well, but I don't want you making any plans."

"Tonya, this is a one-bedroom condo. Where are you going to put the baby? At least stay with me until you have the baby. I want to be there should you need me."

What does he mean stay with him? "I don't think your ex-wife would like that too much, needless to say, nor would I." He had a nerve.

He failed to respond to her comment. "We'll talk about this in detail later. I've got an appointment I have to keep." After glancing at his watch, he stood up to leave.

It was too obvious that a nerve had been struck. Maybe he'd forgotten that he was on the verge of getting married. He showed himself to the door and made a hasty departure.

Thirty-five

Dexter didn't like the idea of telling his father about the baby situation. He wouldn't be happy about it, but there was nothing he could do. This was his child and his father would just have to accept it. He steered the Acura TL down the drive that led to his father's expansive SugarLand house. The colonial style house that he considered his home didn't seem so inviting this time.

All of his childhood memories were there and it would hold memories for his child, too, he hoped. He never felt like a rich kid, even though his family was well-to-do.

There was no point in stalling, his father was expecting him. It still amazed him that he felt somewhat intimidated by his father. Yet, he never backed down from what he felt was right. *This is my life, and I won't let anybody control it but me.*

He turned the knob and pushed open the wooden double doors with stained glass in the center. His dad loved to read in his study and Dexter knew that's where he would find him. He rapped softly on the door and pushed it open.

"Dad, I see you're right where I thought I'd find you. Where's Mom?"

Mr. Freeman looked up from his book and smiled uneasily. Dexter didn't like that look.

"Oh, you know she's down at the country club socializing. What did you need to talk to me about?" He didn't procrastinate.

Dexter took a seat in one of two plush mauve-colored chairs in front of Mr. Freeman's mahogany desk. He could hardly see his father's face for all of the fog coming from his cigar smoking.

"It's about our associate, Tonya Locksley," Dexter said.

Mr. Freeman's eyebrows lifted inquisitively. "Yes, she's a fine attorney. I can see great possibilities in her. What about her?"

"I take it that you have some idea that she and I dated for a while." He didn't want to just spring all of it on his father.

"I wasn't quite sure, but I had some speculations. Dexter . . . where is all of this going? Everything's fine with the wedding—isn't it?"

"Dad, there isn't going to be a wedding. At least not to Melissa." *There I said it. Most of it anyway.*

"What do you mean *no wedding*? What are you talking about?" Mr. Freeman asked in disbelief.

"I'm not marrying Melissa."

"Well, why not? You can't just call off a wedding. Remember my warning to you about Ms. Locksley." His father spat out. He had a way of being melodramatic.

"I remember only too well and I didn't say that I called off the wedding. That's not what I have to talk to you about. What I have to tell you has to do with Tonya Locksley. She's pregnant."

"Well she's pregnant and what does that have to do with you?" Mr. Freeman was becoming upset and he got up from his chair.

"No, Dad, *she's pregnant.*" He hoped his father got the meaning.

"Son, just what are you telling me here? Is it your baby or something?"

Bingo, you hit it dead on the nail. "Yes, that's exactly what I'm saying."

"How could you do this to Melissa—especially right before your wedding? Is that why she resigned?"

He knew his father thought he did it deliberately, so there was no use explaining. "Father, I don't know why she resigned. Maybe she felt it was for the best. As far as the pregnancy goes, I didn't know about it until last week." He got up and started pacing around the study. "She never told me she was pregnant and when I did find out, she had come from an abortion clinic. I was so angry with her because I thought she had gotten rid of it. Needless to say, she didn't and she never told me. She didn't tell me that she was pregnant this time. I just happened to bump into her . . ."

He studied his father's face to look for any expression. He couldn't read it. "Dad, don't think that Tonya . . . Ms. Locksley trapped me into this. She never pursued me, I did the pursuing. The pregnancy was a result of my own doing. We broke up because she thought I was engaged. She found out from a magazine about my alleged engagement to Melissa. If it weren't for that, we would probably still be together."

"What were you thinking? How could you do this to poor Melissa? I know she's hurt by all of this. Son, I never raised you to be a womanizer." Mr. Freeman couldn't believe his ears. Melissa had come from a fine family. He knew her parents well. Her father is a prominent physician in Georgia and her mother is a college professor at Georgia Tech. She was well mannered and groomed to make a man like his son a fine wife. Dexter was messing up the plan. The only thing he knew about Ms. Locksley was what was on her resume. She might be a nice person, but she wasn't enough for his son. There is a such thing as breeding and he wasn't sure that this Tonya Locksley had any. This had to end and that was final.

"My word, son! What will your mother think? Your fathering a child out of wedlock will send your mother to the hospital. On top of all of that, the woman who's pregnant by you is *not* Melissa. What will people say? What will our friends think?"

His father was more concerned about how his friends felt than his own son.

"Don't you see? I don't care about what our friends will think. All I care about right now is my happiness. It doesn't matter at all what people may say."

Mr. Freeman continued without absorbing a word Dexter had said. "Why your mother is down at the country club right now, bragging about your wedding. Bragging about how beautiful a bride Melissa is going to be and how she planned this wedding as a gift to you and Melissa. Are you going to embarrass your mother like that?"

"Father, I can't marry Melissa. I know how much you and Mother think of her, but this is my life and my happiness is at stake here. She seems like a wonderful woman to you, but you haven't lived with her. I didn't want to tell you this, but Melissa never wanted kids. She was pregnant and I never knew about it. The only way I found out was from a receipt she had stashed in the glove compartment of her car." He hoped his father would understand why he couldn't be with her.

Mr. Freeman walked over and stood in front of Dexter. His hand went out to grip his son's shoulder, but he let it hang in mid air. "Are you saying she aborted it?"

Dexter sighed. He wasn't in love with Melissa anymore, but he was still hurt by what she did. "Yes, Father. That's exactly what she did." He sat down and put his head in his hands.

Mr. Freeman was silent for a moment, as if digesting what his son was saying. "Do you expect me to believe something so treacherous about Melissa?"

"I wouldn't make up a thing like this about her. I know

how much you care about her, but you just don't know her. We tried working it out. I forgave her and we decided that we would try to have kids within a year. She let me go for two months thinking she had gotten rid of my baby. After I caught her wrapped up in Jaleel Gregory's arms, she finally admitted that it was his baby."

Mr. Freeman extinguished his cigar. "I . . . I don't know what to say. Jaleel Gregory?"

"Yes. That's the problem I have with him."

"Son, I never knew. Why didn't you come to me?"

"Could I have come to you?"

"Given the previous circumstances, are you sure the baby Ms. Locksley is carrying is yours? I don't want to see you go through the same thing all over again with a different person."

"I'm sure. Tonya isn't like that."

"Do you love Melissa at all?"

"I care about what happens to her, but I'm not in love with her."

"Do you love Ms. Locksley?"

"Yes, I love her. I love her with all of my heart."

"Well, they say home is where the heart is."

"That's true," Dexter answered.

"What are we going to do about the wedding on Saturday? People have already made arrangements to attend."

"There's still going to be a wedding." Dexter smiled.

Thirty-six

On the way to the office she stopped in to see Rita. She motioned for Tonya to come in when she saw her in the door.

"Yes, Mr. Parker. I will, I will . . ." she said, talking into the phone. "Okay, bye, bye."

"Sorry I interrupted. I can come back later if you want me to."

"No need. I had been avoiding that call all week. That man irks my nerves. He constantly calls, wanting to know if there has been any changes in his case. I have to remind him that these decisions take time and it may take another week or so before we can move forward."

"I understand. I'm just getting in from lunch and stopped in to chat and see what's going on," Tonya said lightly.

"I don't know what's going on but, I saw Melissa in her *old* office. I was hoping she was clearing out, but I don't think that's the case."

"Do you think she changed her mind?" Tonya's heart accelerated at the thought. She couldn't handle it.

"I don't know. It could be exactly that. She was happier than usual. I guess those big, fat roses she received brightened her day."

"Well, the wedding is Saturday. He came by my apartment last night. He said that he wanted the baby in his life and even went as far as suggesting I stay with him until the baby is born. I had to remind him that he's getting married. I just don't understand it."

"Maybe this wedding stuff has him in a mental block or something. He's probably excited about the wedding and the baby at the same time. How many men do you know who can do more than one thing at a time?"

"That's low, but I'm starting to believe it. Is Dexter here today?" Tonya asked casually.

"Yes, and he's in an awful mood. He stormed in this morning and locked himself in his office. After Melissa received the flowers she ran into his office, showering him with hugs and kisses. He told her he was happy she liked the flowers, but he had to get back to work."

"That figures. I'm about to go to my office, so I'll talk to you later."

Tonya passed Mr. Freeman on the way to my office and she spoke but, he gave her a rough and dry, "Ms. Locksley" with a nod of his head. When she reached her office she saw a beautiful gold and white envelope lying on her desk with her name printed in script in front. The inside read:

Mr. and Mrs. Tyler Freeman
request your presence
in honor of the uniting in matrimony
of
Dexter Andrew Freeman
and
Melissa Elaine Ferguson.
The ceremony will take place
at six o'clock p.m.
on
Saturday, June 21, 1999
at
St. Mary's Baptist Church
11211 Slater

Houston, Texas 77547
The reception will follow immediately
at the SugarLand Country Club.

Her heart had that familiar sinking feeling. She knew she couldn't expect more. There was a note inside from Dexter asking her to please go. She couldn't watch the man she loved marry someone else. How could he ask her to? *I'm having your child for Christ's sake!* The phone was ringing off the hook before she picked it up.

"Did you get an invitation?" Rita asked.

"Yes, I sure did."

"You are going—right? I mean you have to save face and go."

"I don't think so. I'm not about to walk into that wedding knowing that person going down the aisle should be me. There is no way that's happening."

"Keep your head up. Go to the wedding! I'm going and you should go, too. Show her that you have nothing to be ashamed of." Before she could respond, she saw Dexter in the doorway.

"I'm going to have to call you back. Something's come up."

"I see you got the invitation," Dexter said warily. He didn't wait for her to ask him to have a seat, he helped himself.

"Yes, I did. Why give me an invitation? You can't possibly think I'm going."

"Tonya, I want you to go. This is very important to me. I may be making one of the biggest mistakes of my life. Please be there for me." He looked tired and worry furrowed his brows.

"Dexter, don't you see what you're asking me to do? This is hard, please don't ask this of me."

"Tonya, please. If this is the last thing you ever do for me, please do it. I'm out of the office the rest of this week, so I won't be seeing you anytime before the wedding. I just wanted to clear the air between us. I want you to know that I never deliberately hurt you and I care a great deal about you. I . . . I love you and I'm in love with you. I knew that from the moment I saw you. Someday soon, I'll show you just how much I love you. Trust me." He seemed truly sad. This should have been one of the happiest times of his life and he was sad. "Please come." He turned and walked away and possibly out of her life forever.

She couldn't believe her ears. She had waited all that time to hear him say those words and it came on the brink of his wedding—to *someone else*. Why would he do something like this? He should have never told her. *Why?* Suddenly she realized tears were staining her face. *Why me?*

Thirty-seven

"Come check out my new place," Reggie said cheerfully into the phone. "Can you come by during lunch?"

"I'm happy you called when you did because I was just getting ready to go to lunch. Is your new apartment my surprise?"

"Girl, just wait until you get here."

Tonya took down the directions to Reggie's apartment. When she reached the address, she had to double check to make sure she had the right apartments. They were located in a quiet area by the Galleria. The apartments she drove in front of were nice, *really nice*. They were french style with red brick. The security guard called Reggie's apartment to let him know she was there.

She rang the doorbell and Reggie opened the door. She almost didn't recognize him when he answered the door. There stood Reggie in a nice pair of slacks and a shirt. It was a total transformation. She stood in the open door gawking at him. "Well, are you going to come in or stand out there?" Reggie smiled a gold-tooth-free smile.

"Reggie, what have you done to yourself? Your gold teeth are gone. Oh, my goodness, you're so handsome." She walked in the apartment and looked around.

"Yeah, I had to get rid of my golds. I'm going to miss them, but they had to go."

"I must say that it's an improvement to your looks."

Reggie smiled. "How do you like my place?"

"It's beautiful. It's so big, how many bedrooms do you have?"

"I have three bedrooms and two bathrooms."

"I'll bet this place costs a fortune every month. How long is your lease?"

"I'm not leasing, I'm buying this place."

"Oh, really? Why so many rooms? Are you thinking of moving someone in sometime soon?"

"Well, you never know what the future may bring."

"Be sure to let your manager know that you don't want anyone claiming to be a relative to have a key to your apartment. David went to my apartment manager and told him he was my brother and he was worried because the family hadn't heard from me in a while. The manager gave him a key and he let himself into my apartment. When I got home from a date with Dexter, guess who opens the door and surprises us?"

"He did what? Don't tell me David has turned into a stalker. How is he going to pretend like he's your brother. Which brother was he pretending to be? He must have been pretending to be Kip 'cause he was obviously drunk and out of his mind when he pulled that stunt. I can see right now I'm going to have to have a little talk with David. Damn, Tonya, why do you have to keep digging up these losers? You're making my job as a big brother a lot harder. Fooling around with you, I'll be fighting all of the time."

Tonya laughed. "Reggie, you can change your outside appearance, but you are still the same Reggie on the inside. Look at you, ready to fight at the drop of a hat. I thought you were changing your lifestyle."

"I'm changing, but not that much. You can take the man out of the streets, but you can't take the streets out of the man."

Tonya was genuinely surprised. Her brother was making a move for some stability in his life. "I'm so proud of you, Reggie. Is your little makeover my surprise?"

"This is all included in the surprise, but there's one more thing I want to show you." Reggie picked up an envelope and opened it.

Tonya took the paper from him. "Oh, my goodness, Reggie. You're starting college." She gave her brother a hug. Reggie was off to a wonderful start at changing his life.

"Yes, your big brother is starting college. I know it's not going to be easy, but between you and Regina, I think I can make it through. If you've noticed, I'm attending U of H, your alma mater."

Tonya hugged Reggie. "I can't tell you how pleased I am. I'm very proud of you Reggie, and I know you can do it. Mom and Dad are going to be happy to hear this."

"You know what Tonya? I'm not trying to make Moms and Pops happy. This is for my own happiness. I've spent most of my life trying to win their approval and I've decided that I have to make myself happy before attempting to make anyone else happy."

"Good for you. Does Regina have anything to do with this turning over a new leaf?"

"Regina is someone that I could marry one day. I don't want her hanging out with her sorority sisters and she has to dress up my resume in order to make me look important."

"I'm sure Regina is happy with you as you are. I'm not going to say that a man's line of work isn't important because it is. When any of my sorority sisters say they have a new love interest, the first question we ask is *what does he do?* So, I'm happy you're trying to better yourself."

Reggie looked at his watch. "Well, I know you have to be getting back to the office and I've got to get to the shop. So, I'll call you later."

"Before I go, how did you get away from Ramona?"

"She went gambling in Louisiana with one of her friends and while she was gone, I packed my bags and left. I left her a message on the answering machine telling her I was moving on with my life."

"She didn't go to the shop looking for you?"

"Yes, she came to the shop, talking loud and saying nothing. I politely told her to leave my business establishment and never return or I would call the police. After a few more minutes of trash talking, she finally left. I haven't seen or heard from her since then."

"You think that's the end of her?"

"Probably not. But she better not confront Regina about anything or I don't know what I'll do."

"Don't worry about Ramona, she's a thing of the past," Tonya assured Reggie.

Tonya couldn't have made a bigger mistake than telling Reggie that Ramona was out of the picture. She began stalking Reggie like it was a full-time job. The only time she wasn't calling around for him was when she took a break to eat.

Ramona had gotten so out of control that she had taken to calling Tonya's apartment, letting the phone ring and hanging up whenever she answered. After hanging up on Tonya several times she had the nerve to call back and ask for Reggie. Tonya wanted to lose her religion and curse Ramona out, but that wouldn't have solved anything.

Ramona didn't stop at calling constantly at Tonya's apartment. She called their parents' home also. She had called Mr. Locksley a liar, when he told her Reggie wasn't there.

"I know he over there. Y'all just lying so he won't talk to me. Tell him I'm on my way over there," Ramona told Mr. Locksley.

"Well, you come on over. We'll leave the porch light

on for you. Just make sure you can handle what's coming from the other side of the door," Mr. Locksley had told Ramona.

That girl had lost her mind. Several times she had knocked on Tonya's door looking for Reggie. Tonya was fed up with Ramona's behavior the last time she knocked on her door. She had the nerve to show up at Tonya's apartment wearing something that strippers probably wouldn't wear. Rings on every finger and about eight gold necklaces, cheap gold at that, around her neck. Just nasty!

"Ramona, this is my last warning to you. No more phone calls. No more unannounced visits. As a matter of fact, don't come by at all or I will call the police on you. If Reggie wants to get in touch with you, I'm sure he knows your phone number."

"Do what ya' gotta' do. Just tell him I'm lookin' for him and when I find him, he better not be wit' no other woman—or else!" Ramona said, chewing on a rhinestone studded fingernail.

"Or else what? I know you're not making threats to anyone," Tonya said.

"Or else I'm gon' kill him. That's the or else what. Just let him know that he can run but he can't hide," Ramona called out as she walked off.

That girl was just plain old stupid. She finally stopped stalking Reggie after Tonya called the police on her a couple of times. Actually, Tonya kind of liked the officers the police department sent to her apartment.

Officer Randy was one hunk of an officer and so was Officer Pearson. *That's what I'm talking about! The City of Houston should employ only sexy cops.* She laughed to herself. That would be a problem because more sisters would be committing crimes to have one of those sexy hunks arrest them. Man, the things she had to go through for her brothers!

Thirty-eight

Jimmy Tanzent and his step-father were meeting at Freeman and Reynolds for a mediation. Tonya hoped the mediation went well. If they couldn't reach a settlement agreement, they would go ahead with their suit. The court appointed Leon Horice, a neutral attorney, to mediate between Jimmy and his step-father.

Jimmy's step-father, Doug Williams, was a sweet man. He was in his seventies and full of energy. Mr. Williams and his attorney, Leonard Jackson, waited for Rita, Leon Horice, and Tonya in the conference room. Everyone introduced themselves and started on the business at hand. Jimmy arrived a few minutes after the meeting began.

Mr. Williams seemed genuinely happy to see Jimmy. He spoke to Jimmy, who stuck his nose up in the air and ignored Mr. Williams. He walked right by Mr. Williams and sat next to Rita. "Have we reached an agreement yet?" Jimmy asked in a nasty tone. "I don't have all day to be here. I'm a busy person you know."

Rita scowled at Jimmy. "We've just started the meeting. We haven't had the opportunity to make the settlement offer."

Jimmy looked around the conference room as if he'd lost something. "Where is Mr. Freeman?"

"Mr. Freeman is not going to be here, he's preparing for his wedding this weekend," Rita answered sharply.

"His wedding? Well congratulations to him. But, I don't care about his wedding. I'm paying you people good money to get the job done, not for your personal obligations. I want him here, *now!*" He leaned back in his chair and folded his arms across his chest. His demeanor suggested he had nothing else to say on the matter.

Rita and Tonya exchanged annoyed glances. "Mr. Tanner, I'm quite sure Mr. Horice has more than enough experience handling mediations. Ms. Locksley and myself are more than capable of representing you in this matter. I don't feel it's necessary to pull Mr. Freeman away from his wedding preparations, especially when we have a mediator."

"No one asked what you felt. You are not being paid to feel anything. Either you get Mr. Freeman in here or you lose my business. I'm the client and you do whatever the client tells you. Besides, the client is always right," Jimmy snarled.

"Would you please excuse us for a moment?" Rita asked Jimmy. "Ms. Locksley and I have to find out where Mr. Freeman is."

Tonya and Rita stepped out of the conference room. "Do you get the feeling that Jimmy is gold digging?" Rita asked Tonya.

"Yes, I didn't know he was so rude. He's probably not all that concerned about the future of his sisters."

"Should we find Dexter?"

"Like he said, he's the client. We have to do what he tells us."

Rita told Dexter's secretary to find him and have him call them as soon as possible. Jimmy was determined not to go on with the meeting until Dexter arrived. He refused to listen to any offer of settlement Mr. Jackson offered.

Dexter arrived forty-five minutes later. He spoke to Mr. Williams and Mr. Jackson and next to Jimmy. "I understand there's a problem," he said in a crisp tone. "Is there something that the mediator and my assistants couldn't resolve?"

Jimmy's attitude did an about face. He was much more understanding and even polite. "No, Mr. Freeman, your associates were doing an excellent job, but I wanted to have my full team of attorneys present. There's a lot of money at stake here and I don't want to come out on the short end of the deal."

"What terms of settlement have been discussed?" Dexter asked Mr. Horice.

Mr. Horice had not taken control of the situation and had allowed it to get out of hand. "Well, we haven't had an opportunity to review any settlement offers. I guess now would be an appropriate time to disclose that information."

Mr. Jackson placed a copy of their terms in front of Dexter. "These are our terms. Mr. Tanzent refused to even glance at the offer without your presence. I think my client's offer is more than fair."

Dexter examined the terms line by line. He turned to Jimmy, who was paying little attention to the meeting. "Jimmy, I think their offer is fair. What do you think, Mr. Horice?"

"Whatever you decide is fine with me," Mr. Horice said aloofly.

"Mr. Horice, you are the mediator. Your job is to control the flow of the meeting and to give suggestions. I'm compelled to ask what your purpose is at this mediation if you refuse to do your job," Dexter said sharply to Mr. Horice, who sank further in his chair.

"Maybe you should give them our offer before we consider theirs," Jimmy snapped.

"Mr. Jackson, will you and Mr. Williams excuse us while we confer with our client about this offer?" Dexter asked.

"Most certainly," Mr. Jackson answered.

"Jimmy, this is a substantial offer," Dexter told Jimmy after Mr. Williams and Mr. Jackson stepped out of the conference room. "Mr. Williams has made provisions for his step-children in his will. These provisions will give you and your sisters an enormous amount of money upon his death."

Jimmy looked at the figure written in the settlement terms. "This amount of money is nothing to him. He can offer more than that and, besides, I don't want to have to wait until he dies to receive the money."

"Jimmy, if we take this to court, you could possibly walk away with nothing. The amount of money he's offering you is nothing to sneeze at. Right Mr. Horice?" Dexter asked sternly.

Mr. Horice seemed surprised to be included in the conversation. "Ah, yes, you are exactly right."

"No," Jimmy said curtly. "That's not enough money."

Dexter sighed. "As your attorney, I am giving you advice that is to your advantage. I must reiterate that if we take this to court and lose, you will walk away with nothing or an amount even less than what he's offering you. My suggestion is that you go home and think about it for a couple of days before making any drastic decisions."

"There is nothing to think about. It's our figure or nothing at all." Jimmy paced around the room.

"I think you should listen to Mr. Freeman." Mr. Horice finally had an opinion.

"Jimmy, your actions lead me to believe that there's something you're not telling us here. Is there a reason for you not taking their offer?"

"Okay, I need the money. I've made a few bad investments and I'm on the verge of bankruptcy." Jimmy was willing to drag his step-father through a nasty suit because of a few bad investments.

"Why don't you just ask Mr. Williams for a loan?" Tonya suggested.

"He would never loan me the money," Jimmy groaned.

"Okay," Dexter said. "Why don't we just ask Mr. Williams for half of the money set aside in his will now and upon his death, you will receive the other half? However, your sisters will receive nothing until after Mr. Williams's death. The money you receive prior to his death will be a loan, on which you will have to pay interest. In essence, think of it as paying yourself back. I don't know how much money you need, but half of the amount he set aside in his will should be enough to cover your debts. Honestly, I think that's your only option."

Jimmy seemed skeptical. "Is that the only option?"

"I believe it's your best option. If you were to file a suit, it could take months before any money is awarded, *if* any money is granted. With this arrangement, you could receive your money much sooner."

Jimmy wasn't hot on the idea of having to pay interest on his loan, but he finally came to his senses and agreed. Mr. Williams was pleased with the settlement arrangement. Dexter's secretary drafted the settlement agreement, which Jimmy and Mr. Williams signed.

"I'm sorry we had to take you away from your busy schedule," Rita said to Dexter after the meeting had concluded. "Calling you was the last thing we wanted to do, but Jimmy insisted."

"I understand. You did what you had to do." He looked around for Tonya who had managed to slip away unnoticed.

Rita noticed his wayward glance. "So, how are the wedding plans coming along?"

"I'm sure my father has everything under control. Have a good day, Rita."

Thirty-nine

Instead of going home after work, Tonya went to the hospital to visit Mr. Winters. He was still in intensive care and had been put on a respirator. Tonya wasn't used to seeing Mr. Winters in that condition. It's hard to see someone walking around fine one day and the next they are in intensive care hooked up to a respirator.

Mrs. Winters and Kiera were in the room when Tonya arrived. They were talking to Mr. Winters, who lay motionless.

"How is he?" Tonya asked.

"He's the same, but we're hoping he will make a change for the better," Mrs. Winters said. "I'm going to go home and change clothes. Call me at home if there are any changes."

"Okay, Mom," Kiera said. "We'll keep an eye on Daddy."

"How are you holding up?" Tonya asked Kiera.

"I'm here. If Dad has another attack, that will probably be it." Kiera massaged Mr. Winters hand, frowning at the sore the IV was making. "His hands and feet are so cold. We put extra blankets on him and he's still ice cold."

Tonya's heart started racing. She could remember her grandfather's hands and feet being cold shortly before he died. "Maybe you should have the nurses adjust the air-conditioning."

Kiera continued massaging Mr. Winters hands. She looked at Tonya with mist in her eyes. "We both know that won't help."

Tonya didn't know what to say. Kiera was telling the truth and Tonya could think of nothing to make her feel better. The room was silent except for the sound of the heart monitor beeping.

Tonya's eyes were drawn to the heart monitor. Mr. Winters heart was beating ninety beats per minute. "Well, he has a good heart rate."

Kiera looked at the monitor. "Yes, it fluctuates now and then. I think his heart speeds up when he hears us talking to him. When he doesn't know we're here, it's usually around eight-five to eighty-nine or ninety. The doctor says that's a normal heart rate for heart attack patients."

Tonya didn't want to say anything to Kiera, but she noticed a pattern in Mr. Winters heartbeat. Sometimes it would speed up and when it slowed down, it would be two or more beats less than what it had been. His heart was now beating at eighty-five beats and picked up to ninety-five beats and went back down to eighty-one beats per minute.

"Kiera, I think we should call the nurse because I think something funny is going on with his heart rate." Tonya picked up her purse, preparing to leave the room.

"Nah, I told you that's normal. Where are you going with your scary behind? Don't worry, like I told you, it's normal."

Kiera was acting strange, but reluctantly Tonya set her purse back on the floor. "Okay, I was just wondering if that's normal." Her eyes remained glued to the monitor. Mr. Winters heart rate was at sixty-five. It went up to eighty and back down to sixty. "Kiera, I really think we should call the nurse. His heart rate has dropped from ninety beats to sixty," Tonya said apprehensively.

Kiera looked at the monitor with a touch of worry on

her face. "When a person has suffered a heart trauma like this, that heart rate is normal." She turned to her father. "It's okay, Daddy, if you're in pain and want to rest, just let go."

Mr. Winters wasn't breathing on his own and he had one eye open and the other closed. But Tonya could have sworn that the water draining from his open eye was a tear. Tonya looked at the heart monitor, Mr. Winter's heart rate was at forty. It jumped back up to sixty and went down to thirty. Mr. Winters' eyes squinted and he gritted his teeth. Then there was a flat line. The monitor gave a solid beep. The respirator was still pumping air into his body, but he was gone.

That was Tonya's first time seeing death up close. She ran to Kiera's side who had tears streaming down her cheeks. "It's okay, Daddy, you did what you had to do. I know you didn't want to let go, but I was here for you."

Tonya was unaware of the tears in her own eyes. "I'm sorry, Kiera. I'll call your mother."

The nurses came and asked Kiera to leave the room while they tried to resuscitate him. "No, he's at rest now. Don't try to bring him back," Kiera told the nurses and they complied with her wishes.

The weather outside was dreary but it fit the occasion. The world had just lost a wonderful human being. Tonya was amazed at the strength Kiera had under such bleak circumstances. You never know how strong you are until faced with adversity.

Forty

Tonya had been there for Kiera when her father passed away. That was a time when Kiera needed her the most and she was happy to have been there for her. Keeping in the spirit of her "Be There for the World" mode, she set out to find Kip.

She made a promise to herself and to Kip that she was not going to watch him waste his life away. She was going to give one last effort and after that, if Kip wanted to continue his habits he would be free to do so. After this final attempt, Kip would be on his own.

Kip was in his usual spot under the tree. To her surprise, none of his friends were around. His ever-present beer can was his only companion. He was leaning against the tree as if he were deep in thought.

"Hi, Kip. How are you?" Tonya asked with genuine concern. Kip seemed troubled.

"I'm alright. How about you?" He didn't look in her direction.

"I'm fine. Is it okay if I have a seat?"

"It's not taken."

Tonya sat on one of the makeshift seats. "I guess you've heard about Kiera's dad, huh?"

Kip took a deep breath. "Yeah, I heard about it. It's sad, huh? That man practically raised us all and for him to go so soon is sad. He was a wonderful man."

"You're right, he was wonderful. Straying away from the subject, you've been on my mind."

Kip glanced in her direction uncomfortably. "Don't start with me about my drinking again."

"You know it's a problem. Kip, you drink every day."

"I can quit drinking anytime I get ready. I just choose not to."

"Okay. When was the last time you went a whole day without drinking?"

"What's your point?"

"You don't know when, do you? Having you around is important to me, I want our family to grow old together."

"Moms and Pops don't consider me as part of the family. They don't even try to see how I'm doing."

"Do you ever go to see them without having a reason? I'll bet the only time you see our parents is when you need money. They want to feel like they mean more to you than a bank."

He kicked around a can that was lying on the ground. "I don't know. They never made me feel like anybody, you know. Me and Reggie were like strike one and strike two. If they would have struck out with you, they would have lost the game. You saved our parents from having all nothing kids. They don't care what I do."

"I care what you do. I don't want to watch you drink your life away. Have you seen Reggie lately?"

"Nah, I haven't seen Reggie since he started messing around with some school teacher."

"Reggie is facing the same problems you are. But he's making a difference in his life. He's gotten rid of Ramona, changed his wardrobe, just changed his life. He's even starting college soon. I know if Reggie can make a positive change in his life, so can you."

Kip seemed surprised. "No wonder I haven't seen Reggie." He laughed. "That's good. I'm proud of our big brother." His sullen mood returned. "But that's Reggie.

What can I do to change my life? I don't have a job, no skills, no nothing."

"First of all, Kip, you need to stop drinking. If you can prove to me that you are willing to change, I'll stick my neck out for you and try to get you a job at the firm. It won't be anything glamorous, but it will be a job. You were never a dummy, and you can learn to do something new."

"You would do that for me?" Kip asked seriously. "Why?"

"Because I don't like seeing you like this." She stood to leave. "It's your choice, Kip. Prove to me that you can lay off the bottle and I will help you as much as I can. Besides, I don't want my child to have an uncle who's an alcoholic."

"You don't have any kids, what are you talking about?"

"I will soon. I'm pregnant and I want my baby to have two wonderful uncles."

Kip didn't know whether to hug her or fuss at her. He opted to hug her. "Ah, man, congratulations. I'm going to be an uncle!"

"Yes, Kip. That's all the more reason to get your life in order."

"I don't know, sis. I'll see what I can do."

"All I want you to do is try and if you fail, at least you made an effort. You don't have to worry about me hunting you down after this time. After today, you are going to have to motivate yourself to do better. I'll let you think about it. When you reach a decision, you know where I am or you can go over to Mom and Dad. Talk to you later."

As Tonya drove away, she saw Kip pouring the rest of his beer on the ground and throwing the can away. She hoped that was a positive sign, but knowing Kip, he was probably pouring his beer out because it was flat.

Forty-one

It was the day before his wedding and Dexter should have been happy. He should have had pre-wedding jitters, cold feet, or something. Yet, there was nothing, except for a fleeting moment of uncertainty. Otherwise, he felt nothing, numb. He was taking the remainder of the week to get things ready for D-day, the wedding. Untouched orange juice, bacon, and eggs waited in front of him. The *Wall Street Journal* was still neatly folded by his plate.

He took out his wallet and dialed the pager number. He knew his barber wouldn't be at the shop, so he automatically paged him. This guy, Reggie, could cut his hair perfectly. There was no way anybody else was getting into his head with a pair of clippers. What he liked most about Reggie, was that Reggie would come to him.

After he paged Reggie, he called right back. He told Reggie that he needed a cut and asked if he could drive over to his apartment. Reggie said he would be right over.

Reggie arrived at Dexter's about an hour later. He pulled out his clippers and lined up his guards and edgers. He wrapped a smock around Dexter's neck.

Dexter loved a fresh haircut. He could be dressed in the finest suit and the most expensive shoes, but if his hair wasn't cut, he felt undressed.

"Thanks for getting here so fast," Dexter said.

"Oh, it's no problem. You sounded like you were fiending for a cut, so I rushed right over." Reggie started to cut his hair. "This is a nice place you have here. A very nice bachelor's pad. I recently moved myself."

"Thanks," Dexter answered with little interest. "Well, it won't be a bachelor's pad for long," Dexter said in an unsure tone.

Reggie stopped cutting for a second. "Oh, yeah. What's up with that?" He started back to cutting Dexter's hair.

"Well, I'm supposed to get married this Saturday. That's why I needed a cut today."

Reggie's hand slipped a bit. "Yeah? Gettin' married, huh?" *I know it's not to my sister. Tonya never said anything about getting married to this trick.*

"Yeah, I'm tying the knot."

This time, Reggie let his hand dip. *Oops—a plug!* "Oh, I didn't know you were engaged. How long have you been engaged?"

"Not that long. I don't know." Dexter could have cared less about discussing an engagement. He didn't want to explain the situation to anyone.

"Oh, yeah?" Reggie's hand deliberately slipped again. *Oops—another plug!* The clippers made a noisy sound, like a weed-wacker.

"What was that noise? That didn't sound right," Dexter asked, reaching up to touch his head.

"Aah, man. These clippers are on the fritz again. Say, man, I hate to tell you, but you are going to have to have all of your hair cut off. These clippers done plugged ya'." *That's what you get for playing around with my sister, getting her pregnant, and leaving her.*

"You're not serious right? You're kidding?"

"Nah, man. I don't kid around with the hair. Take a look for yourself." Reggie held up a mirror for Dexter to see several bald spots in his head.

Dexter took one look at his severed hair and muttered several curses. "Man, what happened? How are you going to cut somebody's hair with raggedly clippers? I know you make enough money to keep good equipment."

At this point, Reggie didn't care what Dexter thought. He was about to receive a piece of his mind. "Yeah, man, as a matter of fact, you're right. I *can* afford to have good equipment and I *do* have good equipment. As a matter of fact, I have state-of-the-art equipment. The problem ain't with my equipment, the problem is with me."

"What are you talking about? You just need to fix this mess you've made of my head."

"Oh, yeah, I'm going to fix it alright." Reggie put his clippers down and stood in front of Dexter.

"What's your problem? You seem to need an attitude adjustment or something today."

"I do have an attitude problem and I'm about to adjust it in a few minutes, Mr. Smooth-Talking Attorney. You just can't trust attorneys because all they do is lie. I outta' kick your butt just for the hell of it."

"Man, I don't have time for this! What are you talking about? If you have something you want to say, I suggest you get it off your chest while you have the chance."

"All this time you've been messing around with my sister and now you're marrying some other woman. What was my sister, just a phase or something? What about the baby she's carrying for your sorry butt?"

"What do you mean, your sister?" Dexter pulled the smock away from his neck, eying Reggie with a puzzled expression.

"Yes, Tonya Locksley. Don't look at me like you don't know who I'm talking about. I told her from the beginning that she should have left you alone. I knew something like this was going to happen. I know you're getting married to this other woman on Saturday, but this one— the plugs were for my sister." Reggie looked Dexter straight in the eyes. "I know how my sister feels about you and I wanted her to win for a change. She's been through too many technical knockouts, so I won this round for her."

Dexter was at a loss of words. After a few moments of silence he said, "I know this is going to sound stupid, but I love your sister. I'm very much in love with her."

"You're right, it does sound stupid. I can see how much you love her. You love her so much that you're marrying some other woman. This is my sister we're talking about. I don't let nobody, *nobody* mess over my sister. You either get with my sister or you leave her alone. If you marry this Melissa lady, don't show your face around my sister or our family ever again. She ain't no second-rate woman and I'll be damned if anybody is going to treat her like one. I'm out, my brother." Reggie grabbed his bag and gave Dexter the peace sign as he departed.

Dexter stared as the door closed behind Reggie. There he was, left with plugs in his head and nobody to fix it. *Damn!* Reggie was Tonya's brother, he couldn't help laughing at how ironic the whole situation was turning out to be.

Forty-two

Tonya couldn't stay home and worry herself to death. This was one night she wasn't going to sit around waiting for the phone to ring. The man she loved and the father of her unborn child was getting married on the next afternoon. What did she expect him to do—call off the wedding? She knew there was no chance of Dexter calling off his wedding on the day of the Tanzent mediation.

Mr. Winters' funeral was on that Saturday morning and Dexter's wedding was that afternoon. She knew her place was to comfort Kiera in her time of need. Why should she go to a wedding when the only person who wanted her to attend was the groom?

On that lonely Friday night, the only thing she could do was head to her place of refuge, her parent's house. The light on her parents' porch was a welcome sight. At least she didn't have to tumble in the dark trying to unlock the door.

"Tonya, is that you?" Mrs. Locksley called out.

"Yes, Mom, it's me." She headed to the sitting room where her parents were watching television.

"I'm surprised to see you on a Friday night," Mr. Locksley said.

"Well, I don't have a life, so I came to visit my parents."

"It's nice to know you come to see us only when you're bored." Mrs. Locksley laughed.

Tonya flopped down on the couch beside her mother. "My pleasure."

"What's wrong? I'd know that look anywhere. Are you still upset about Brice Winters passing away? We're going to the funeral in the morning. You are going aren't you?"

"Yes, I'm going to the funeral. I'm upset about that among other things."

"Honey, could you make some coffee?" Mr. Locksley asked Mrs. Locksley.

She gave him a knowing look. "Sure, honey. I'll be back in a minute. Do you want some coffee Tonya?"

"No, I don't want any."

Mr. Locksley poured tobacco into his pipe and lit it. He took a puff. "Honey, what's wrong?"

"Daddy, my world is crumbling all around me."

Mr. Locksley rocked gently in his recliner. "Do you want to talk about it? If you don't I understand."

"It's Dexter," Tonya blubbered, "he's getting married tomorrow."

"I already know he's supposed to be married tomorrow."

"How do you know?"

Mr. Locksley smoked his pipe thoughtfully. "Dexter is a nice young man and I know for a fact that he cares a lot about you."

"How do you know? If he cares so much about me, why is he marrying someone else?"

"He told me himself. He came by earlier this week saying that he didn't want me to hear about his marriage from someone else and especially not from you. At first I was angry with him, but when he explained, I could understand his actions."

"I didn't know he came to see you. Why didn't you tell me?"

"I didn't tell you because I had a feeling we would see

you before his wedding took place. He's marrying this girl because he's trying to protect you."

"Protect me from what?"

"His father threatened to fire you and to tarnish your reputation as an attorney if he didn't marry this woman. He was upset with his father and told him that he wasn't going through with the wedding, but when his father made those threats, he reconsidered. He didn't want to mess up your career, so he did what he thought was best."

Tonya wiped her eyes. "I didn't know he was trying to protect me. I thought he was marrying Melissa because he wanted to be with her."

Mr. Locksley took a puff of his pipe and smiled at Tonya. "He also told me that we're going to be grandparents."

Tonya looked up in surprise. "Why didn't you or Mom say anything?"

"You're a grown woman. What could we do, punish you and send you to your room? Dexter promised to be part of this child's life. He seemed to be excited about the baby."

"I know you had a mouth full of advice to give him. What did you say?"

"Now, that's where you're wrong. I respected him for laying it all on the line. It took a lot of nerve for him to come to me and tell me the situation. Someone else probably wouldn't have said anything and just went about their business. The only thing I did tell him was to follow his heart and he couldn't go wrong. Now, if he marries this woman tomorrow, then that's where his heart is. If his heart is with her, that's where he belongs."

"Dad, I know he's going to marry her tomorrow."

Mr. Locksley took a puff from his pipe. "What if he doesn't? Mr. Freeman will probably try to ruin your career."

"I'm not going to say that my career isn't important, but how much damage can one man do?"

"I'm not sure. Are you willing to risk your career over this man?"

"I don't know, Dad. I just know he's going to marry her tomorrow. Then, it won't matter if I'm willing to give up my career for him or not."

"Would you rather he make a decision to be with you and have his heart somewhere else?"

"You're right, Dad. I wouldn't want him to be with me just for the sake of our child. Enough of this conversation, it's depressing. Mom must be making one strong pot of coffee because she hasn't come back yet." Tonya laughed.

"I'm sure your mother didn't make any coffee. She knew I wanted to have a talk with you."

"On another note, have you talked to Reggie or Kip lately?" Tonya asked.

"No, I saw Reggie last week, but I haven't seen Kip in almost two weeks."

"Dad, I think you and Mom have been too hard on the both of them. They are both starving for love and appreciation from you and Mom. They think they don't mean anything to you."

"What would give them an idea like that? We love them, they are our children just as you are. The only thing your mother and I don't approve of is their lifestyles. Reggie is shacking with that loud-mouthed Ramona and Kip insists on drinking every day. I can't give them praise for their shortcomings."

"Have you ever been to Reggie's barbershop?"

Mr. Locksley shifted uncomfortably in his chair. "No, I haven't seen Reggie's shop."

"Your son has one of the most successful shops in Houston and you haven't seen it."

"Reggie let us down when he dropped out of school. How can you manage a business when you don't have the know how? Half of the time Reggie doesn't even go to work."

"Dad, you of all people know that the best way to learn how to do something is to jump right in and get the experience. That's just what Reggie did and now he has other people working for him. He doesn't have to go to work if he doesn't want to because he's still making money."

"I don't know, Tonya. That boy has been so defiant since he was a kid. He always had to go against our rules."

"We all have minds of our own. You could be very proud of Reggie if you let yourself. I must tell you that Reggie is not with Ramona anymore. He's moved into his own place and it's nice. He doesn't have the gold teeth anymore. He's just made a change."

There was a spark of hope in Mr. Locksley's eyes that was quickly dashed out with pessimism. "Anyone can change their address and wardrobe, that doesn't necessarily mean *they* have changed."

"But he has changed. Dad, he has enrolled in college! He is making a great effort and if you and Mom could encourage him just a little, it would mean so much to him. If you could show him that his efforts mean something to you, I think Reggie could walk away with his degree. He really needs you."

"You really think he's serious, huh?"

"I *know* he is."

"Okay, I'll talk to Reggie. What about Kip? I know Kip is still hanging around with those no good drunks."

"I spoke with Kip this morning and laid it all on the line. I told him that instead of coming to see you and Mom for money, he should drop by to say hello or just to see how you are doing. I promised to help him find a job if he cleaned up his act. When I left, I saw him pouring his beer on the ground. I don't know what that meant, but I took it as a positive sign."

"Maybe you're right," Mr. Locksley said in a guilt-ridden tone. "Maybe I didn't encourage them enough. Instead of pointing out where they fell short, maybe I should have told them how to better themselves. I tried so hard to be a good father to them. I was tough on them because they were growing up to be men. Instead of raising them to be productive young men, I turned them into statistics." He put a hand to his head in frustration.

"You did what you thought was right. You provided us with a wonderful life and taught us the meaning of hard work. Eventually, what you've instilled in us will come out. I see it in Reggie and I know I will see it in Kip. Don't blame yourself, they are just as much to blame as you are."

"I know I've been hard on them and I hope they don't hate me for it. It's just so frustrating to think that all of our hard work has gone down the drain. I would love to see all of our children succeed, but I don't know if they are going to make that happen."

Tonya hugged her father. "Don't give up yet, Dad. You never know what the future may bring. I'm going to bed. I guess my old room is still the same."

"It's just as you left it. Good night."

"Good night, Dad. Tell Mom I'll see her in the morning."

Forty-three

There was standing room only at Mr. Winters's funeral service. There was an overwhelming sadness during the service, but everyone maintained their composure well. There were a few tears shed, but no one fell completely to pieces.

Although the service was on a sad occasion, it was a beautiful service. Mr. Winters's brother, who is a minister, delivered the eulogy. There were so many people who spoke kind words to the family that Tonya lost count. Mr. Winters's fraternity brothers sang their fraternity song as the pallbearers lowered the casket into the ground. Tonya hugged Kiera before she left the cemetery. It was almost as if she was saying good-bye to Kiera for the last time. Kiera wasn't herself and was so stressed that she needed time to get over her father and she didn't know when that would be, if ever.

Most people were going over to the Winters' home for lunch after the service was over. But the Locksleys decided to go home. They would visit with the Winters after things had settled down.

"What should we have for dinner?" Mrs. Locksley asked Tonya.

"I don't know. I don't think you should cook too much of anything unless you and Daddy are hungry. I don't

want anything right now. Maybe we can have a pizza delivered later."

"That sounds like a good idea. Besides, I didn't want
to cook anyway."

"Kiera seemed to be taking it hard," Mr. Locksley said.

"Yes, she is taking it hard. I don't know what I would
do if I lost either of you," Tonya said.

"Well, you don't have to think about us checking out
anytime soon. We plan on being around for a long time,"
Mr. Locksley said as he hugged Mrs. Locksley. "Right,
honey?"

"Right." Mrs. Locksley planted a kiss on his lips.

Tonya was happy that after thirty years, her parents
were still very much in love with one another. They still
went out on dates and did the flower and card thing for
special events.

"How can you two be married for so long and still be
as deeply in love as you are?" Tonya asked her parents.
"What's your secret?"

"There is no secret," Mrs. Locksley stated flatly. "The
key to any successful marriage is a whole lot of hard work.
By that I mean, communication, understanding, compro-
mise, and things of that nature."

"Yes," Mr. Locksley added, "don't think there weren't
any rough times. Instead of giving up, you decide how to
get through the problem."

"Well, I don't have to worry about that for a while,"
Tonya said in a daze.

"Honey, your time will come soon enough. What you
need to concentrate on is having a healthy baby," Mrs.
Locksley said.

"Speaking of the baby, Mom," Tonya said. "Why haven't you made a big deal about me being pregnant?"

"You are an adult and can make decisions for yourself.
I can't tell you what to do with your life. Besides, you

waited until after you finished law school and you can support yourself. What do I have to complain about?"

"Since when did you and Daddy become so liberal? You've been conservative about everything until now."

"We can be liberal now that you're grown. When you were growing up was something different."

Mr. Locksley snapped his fingers. "What time is it? The game starts at two."

"You're about fifteen minutes late. Who's playing?" Tonya asked.

Mr. Locksley frowned at Tonya's question. "What do you mean *who's playing*? The Rockets and the Jazz are playing game four. The Rockets are leading by two games to the Jazz's one. If we win tonight, correction, *when* we win tonight, we eliminate them."

"Daddy, I don't know if we are going to win. You know how we give the game away at the last minute. I hate to doubt the Rockets, but we will probably lose tonight and have to go to Utah."

"I'm not trying to hear the negativity," Mr. Locksley said as he headed to his room. "All anti-Rockets fans need to go home." He laughed to himself.

"Sorry, Dad," Tonya called after her father.

Tonya rubbed her temples and stretched out on the couch. Her head had been hurting since early that morning. "I don't think I want to watch the Rockets get slaughtered this afternoon."

"Me either," Mrs. Locksley said. "Are you feeling alright? You don't seem well."

How could her mother ask her if she was alright knowing the man she was in love with was about to married in less than three hours? "I'm alright," she answered curtly.

"Honey, I wish there was something I could say to make you feel better, but I can't. I know this wedding thing is the reason you're upset and I can't blame you for feeling the way you do."

"Why do I have to be the one to have all of the bad relationships?" Tonya asked sadly. "David turned out to be gay and Dexter was having problems with his ex-wife. Maybe I should stop seeing anyone who has the letter 'D' starting their name."

Mrs. Locksley's eyes widened. "What do you mean David was gay?"

Tonya had let her secret slip in her depression. Her head pounded just a little harder. "That's why we broke up. I was too embarrassed to tell you and Dad about it at the time. I had gone to David's apartment to surprise him with dinner and I heard someone in the bedroom. I called the police thinking an intruder was in the apartment. After the police arrived, they kicked in the door and there was David and Ken in the bed together."

"Dear God! I can't believe it. How could David—sweet David—do something like that? I would have expected him to be with another woman, if anything, but not a man!"

"You can imagine how I felt. Then he tries to pop back up in my life after everything that happened. How could I have possibly gone back to him? The sad part about it is, he doesn't believe he has a problem."

"I'm so sorry, Tonya. I wish you would have told us sooner."

"No, I knew how much you and Daddy liked him. Now you like Dexter and he's marrying someone else. Do you know he had the nerve to invite me to his wedding?"

"I think you should go."

Tonya looked at her mother as if she were insane. "Why? Why should I go watch him marry someone else?"

"I think actually seeing him get married will be closure on how you feel about him. There will be no doubt in your mind that he is off limits."

"I don't need to see him get married to know that it's over."

"Well, I'm a closure kind of person. I have to put everything to an end before moving on to something else. If I know you well, and I think I do, you are a closure kind of person, too. I just think that if you don't go to this wedding, it will be hard for you to move on."

The phone rang, interrupting Tonya's explanation. Mrs. Locksley answered the phone.

"It's for you," Mrs. Locksley said. "It's Rita."

"Oh, I forgot to tell you that I forwarded my phone here."

"Hey, Rita. What's up?"

"Don't pretend you don't know what's up. I know you're going to the wedding."

"I don't think that's such a good idea. I'm pretty sure Melissa would be morbid if she saw me in the audience. She'll probably think I'll make an objection to the wedding."

Rita laughed. "You do object, don't you? Besides, I think you should go because people have been speculating that there has been a problem between the three of you. If you don't show up to the wedding, they will be certain there was or *is* something going on."

"I don't care what they think."

"Girl, yes you do. This is where you have to work everyday. You need to swallow your pride and think about your future at Freeman and Reynolds or start looking for another job. I suggest you put on your best outfit and go to that wedding. I'll come by and pick you up."

"Alright, I guess maybe you're right. My mother seems to think I should go to the wedding to put closure on our relationship."

"I agree with your mother, closure is good."

"I guess."

"So, are your in or out?"

"I'm in. Let me go home and get dressed. I'll be ready about five-thirty."

"Okay, I'll see you then and don't change your mind." Rita hung up quickly before Tonya changed her mind about what she had just committed herself to.

Tonya got up from the couch. "Mom, I'll talk to you and Dad later. I've got to go to a closing."

"Good for you," Mrs. Locksley said. "Are you coming back after the wedding?"

"I don't know, maybe. Talk to you later."

Forty-four

As she waited for Rita to arrive Tonya finished putting on her makeup. Her suit was beautiful. Rita had convinced her to wear something smashing and that she did. It was accented with gold beaded buttons and most of the suit was beaded with tiny beige and gold beads along the shoulders and the sleeves. The skirt was also trimmed with the beads. The skirt was long, and she had to wear high heels to keep it from touching the floor and there was a back slit in it. She willed herself not to change her mind. *I think I can, I think I can* . . . By the time she heard Rita blowing her horn, she had changed her mind.

"What do you mean you're not going?" Rita demanded. "I drove all the way from the other side of town to pick you up. You're going, even if I have to drag you there."

"I can't. I just can't do it."

"You're going to the wedding and that's that. You're not going out like a wimp. Let's go." Reluctantly Tonya got into the car. Rita was right, she was being a wimp about going to the wedding.

St. Mary's was a huge church and there were over three hundred people in attendance. They sat on the fifth row on the right-hand side. There were five groomsmen and five bridesmaids. She had to admit it was nice. It was the typical southern wedding. The bridesmaids' dresses were lavender. It wasn't Tonya's style, but still nice. She didn't know what the problem was before the wedding got started but some of the groomsmen hadn't made it out yet. To her surprise, Jaleel was in the wedding.

Finally, the organist gave the key for everyone to stand and began playing for Melissa's entrance. Oh, she was beautiful alright, just as Tonya expected. Immaculate from head to toe. She glanced at Tonya as she passed by, then smiled her most stunning smile.

Rita leaned close to Tonya and whispered in her ear. "I presume that smile was for you. Maybe, she's finally secure now that she's going down the aisle."

"Yes, that smile was definitely for me. More power to her. What are they going to do—play a song for Dexter to March out to? Where is he?"

"I have no idea," Rita whispered with a light smile on her face.

The minister began. Finally, the minister got to the part where the groom had to respond.

"Do you, Jaleel Gregory, take Melissa . . ."

Tonya began shaking her head from side to side. "This is not right. What's going? Where's Dexter?"

"Apparently, Jaleel is marrying Melissa."

Tonya was in shock. She scanned the church. No one seemed surprised by the switch in grooms. Tonya couldn't help the smile that was playing on her lips. "When did this happen?"

"I don't know," Rita whispered. "I'll bet you're happy you came now, aren't you?"

Tonya nodded. "You bet."

After the wedding was over, Rita and Tonya walked outside to the front of the church.

"Why don't you wait here? It's a long walk to the car. I'll go get it and meet you here," Rita suggested.

"Alright, I'll be here." Tonya's heart was light. She could see the silver lining in the dark cloud that hovered all around her. She squeezed her fists together and mouthed out, *Yes!*

"And just what are you so happy about?"

Startled, Tonya turned to see Dexter casually leaning against the brick wall of the church.

She couldn't hide her embarrassment. "It was just such a lovely wedding."

He closed the distance between them. "Yes, it was a real tearjerker. What do you say to us losing this crowd?"

"Sounds good to me. I just need to talk to Rita before we go."

Dexter and Tonya walked to the parking lot. The sun was setting on a clear evening, which was a drastic change from the morning weather. Dexter stopped walking abruptly.

"What's wrong?" Tonya asked.

"I just remembered that I didn't drive. Did you drive?"

"No, I rode with Rita."

"Maybe Rita will drop us off at my car." Dexter said.

"Sorry guys, I'm already two steps ahead of you," a familiar woman's voice called out.

Dexter and Tonya turned to see Rita walking toward them. "Dexter I hope you can catch."

Dexter seemed confused. "What?"

Rita smiled. "Hold out your hands and catch."

Dexter did as he was instructed. Rita tossed her car keys to him. "I know you need a ride. You can take my car."

Dexter held the keys tightly in his hand. "Thanks. I'll get it back to you in one piece. Can we drop you off somewhere?"

Rita waved her hand. "Nah, my husband is here. I'm riding with him. Go ahead and enjoy yourselves."

Tonya hugged Rita. "Thank you so much. I owe you one."

"And I'll remind you of it." Rita smiled. "Go ahead,

call me later and give me all of the juicy details." Rita hurried off to her husband's car.

She took Dexter's hand and walked to Rita's car. "So where are we going?" Tonya asked. Tonya was elated to be at Dexter's side once again.

"I have a couple of people that I have to see." Dexter smiled. "But, I have to drop you off at home first. After I've tied up these loose ends, I'll come back to pick you up. I shouldn't be more than an hour or an hour and a half."

"That's fine. I understand you have things to do. I'll just go home and get changed. By that time, you should be back."

"No, don't change clothes. We're going out to celebrate."

"Celebrate what?"

"We're going to celebrate me taking control of my life. That's what we're going to celebrate."

Tonya couldn't help but wonder if he was talking about Melissa. Maybe he had to smooth things over with his family. She knew it was something that he had to deal with, so she forced herself to understand.

"Sounds like a wonderful reason to celebrate."

Just as he promised, he was back in an hour and a half, still driving Rita's car. Tonya was anxiously waiting.

"It didn't take long for you to come back. Did you get a chance to tie up those loose ends?" Tonya asked.

Dexter smiled mysteriously. "Yes, I did manage to take care of those things. I told you I would be back shortly."

"Where do you plan on celebrating?"

"Maybe we can play it by ear. We could drop in on your parents and if they don't have anything planned, then we could all go to dinner. I also want to know if the Rockets eliminated the Jazz, maybe your dad and I could go to a playoff game."

"I'm sure Daddy would love that. We can visit my parents if you like."

Dexter drove with a smug expression on his face. "I like. I wonder who won the game."

"Ask my dad when we get there. I'm sure he'll give you all of the sports highlights and you already know who won. More than likely it wasn't the Rockets."

"Look at you." He took his eyes off the road to look at her briefly. "I thought you were a die-hard Rockets fan."

"I am. I just know when to face the agony of defeat instead of holding on to a small shred of hope."

"You're such an optimist," he said sarcastically. "I didn't think you were the type to give up so easily."

"I'm not, but I do know when to take a reality check."

Dexter eased the car into the Locksley driveway. "And what did your reality check have to say about me?"

Tonya chose not to answer his question. She noticed that her parents had a yard full of cars. Some of the cars were parked along the street. "What in the world are my parents doing with all of these people over?"

"I don't know," Dexter answered. "Maybe they invited a few friends over for the playoff game."

"You could be right, but Daddy has never invited so many people over before."

They walked to the front door. Dexter rang the door bell and smiled at Tonya. She smiled back at him, and he planted a kiss on her lips.

"Doesn't it seem like we've done this before?" Tonya asked.

"What, kiss on your parents door step?"

"Yes."

"We have. I want you to keep something for me."

"What?" Tonya could hear her mother's footsteps coming toward the door.

Dexter reached into his pocket and pulled out a small,

black, velvet, box. He opened the box to reveal a dazzling diamond ring. "How long you get to keep that depends on what your answer is."

Tonya could hardly contain her excitement as her finger caressed the cool stone. "You didn't ask me a question," she smiled.

"You're right. I guess I may as well do this right, huh?" He removed the ring from the box and bent down on one knee. "Tonya Locksley, will you please make me one of the happiest men in the world by saying you will marry me?"

Mrs. Locksley opened the door just as Dexter slid the ring on Tonya's finger.

"I thought you would never ask. Yes, I will marry you." She placed a passionate kiss on his lips.

"I'm so happy you said yes," Mrs. Locksley said to Tonya. "Now, everyone is here."

"What's going on?" Tonya asked.

Dexter interrupted before Mrs. Locksley could explain. "I asked your parents to invite everyone over, including a minister. I was praying that you would say you would marry me because I want to get married to you on *this* day. We've been through so much and I want to make everything right for you, our child, and myself. We deserve to be happy. We should be a family and raise our child the right way."

Tonya's mother hugged her with tears in her eyes. "I'm so happy for you."

Tonya's joy matched her mother's. "Well, it seems we have a wedding to attend."

Reggie walked up to Dexter. "Man, I heard what you were doing for my sister and I respect that. I'm sorry about what I did to your hair."

Dexter's hand automatically went to his head and he rubbed it absently. "That's okay. I understand how you feel about your sister because I feel the same way."

"What did you do to Dexter's head, Reggie?" Tonya asked.

Reggie began stuttering. "Ah, well . . . let's just say that I'm the reason his head is shaved clean."

Tonya looked to Dexter. "He had a good talk to me yesterday. He told me to shape up or ship out."

Tonya kissed Reggie on the cheek. "Thank you, Reggie. But you didn't have to cut all of his hair off."

Reggie smiled. "I didn't and you don't want to know the rest. Let's get on with this wedding 'cause I'm ready to get my drink on. Where's Pops? He has to give the bride away."

"How about I let my big brother give me away? Would you mind walking your sister down the aisle?"

"I'd be more than honored to. What about Dad?"

Tonya looked at her father, who was busy directing everyone to their places. "I don't think Dad will mind. He's busy organizing things."

"Can I be your maid of honor?" Kiera asked.

"And I'd like to be a bridesmaid," Rita said.

"You knew about this? Both of you knew and wouldn't say anything." Tonya laughed.

"It was so hard keeping this a secret," Rita laughed. "You know I can't keep water to myself."

"Well, let's get this party started."

"I'm with you." Tonya laughed.

Dexter and Tonya were married in the gazebo in her parents' backyard. On that day, she became the happiest woman in the world. She became Mrs. Dexter Andrew Freeman.

She had always wondered what her wedding would be like. She had also wondered what her husband would be like. Now she had the answer to both of those questions. If there were any way for her go back and change her wedding, she wouldn't have done a thing to it. In her eyes, her wedding day was perfect—well, almost perfect. It was the perfect surprise.

Dexter made a promise to himself to make Tonya forget all of the pain he had brought to her. He wanted to focus on their new life together and the promises tomorrow would bring. Every day they shared together would be special. Those special moments began with a honeymoon in Hawaii. It was then that Tonya fell in love with Hawaii. Being there was like standing at the edge of the earth watching the ocean meet the sky. They did everything from frolicking in the clear blue water to spending lazy nights on the beach under the open sky.

On one of those star-filled nights, Tonya gazed at her husband and thanked God for sending him to her. No, it wasn't a relationship that was worry free, but she was thankful for it anyway. They sat in perfect silence on the secluded beach, watching shooting stars streak across the sky.

Dexter wrapped his arm around her. Tonya noticed that familiar far-off look in his eyes.

Tonya pointed to a shooting star overhead. "Make a wish. Maybe one day it will come true.

Dexter studied the sky for a moment before placing a lingering kiss on his wife's lips. "All of my wishes came true the moment when you became my wife." His hand rubbed the bulge in her belly. "And now with junior coming along, I couldn't ask for anything more."

"How do you know the baby's going to be a junior? It could turn out to be a girl."

"Nah, there hasn't been a girl born to the Freeman family for years. That's why our baby is going to be a boy."

"Alright, mister, don't be too sure of yourself."

"I can't help but be sure of myself. It's just a fact that our baby is going to be a boy."

"Don't say anything when *she* gets here. Do you think your parents are truly happy about us and the baby?" Tonya asked.

"I honestly don't know." He didn't want to put a damper on his honeymoon by discussing such complex issues. "They are in their own way. They still have to get over the truth about Melissa."

"Have you spoken to either of them?"

"No. I haven't spoken to either of them since the wedding." Dexter watched the white foam on the surface of the water come in and disappear.

"Do you plan on calling them?" She almost felt as if she was prying into an issue Dexter didn't want to share. His relaxed disposition became tense.

Dexter sighed. "When we get back. Can we change the subject? Believe me, my parents are the last thing I want to think about on my honeymoon."

"You never told me how Melissa and Jaleel ended up getting married."

"Oh, that." Dexter smiled. He could smile about the situation now that he was finally with someone he loved. "When Melissa and I were married, things just didn't turn out the way we planned. I wasn't happy and she wasn't happy. We found out that we were complete opposites. I threw myself into my work and so did she. The one thing I would have changed for was a child. She was dead set against children. To make a long story short, she aborted a baby that I thought was mine. It turned out that she had been having an affair with Jaleel Gregory and it was his baby. That is why we divorced."

"I know that was painful for you. That was two low blows." Tonya gave his hand a reassuring squeeze.

"I never told my father why Melissa and I divorced. I wanted her integrity to remain intact. Both my mother and father believe that I was the reason for the divorce. Melissa's father was pushing from her end and my father vas pushing from my end for us to get back together. I iterally had to tell him what happened between Melissa and me before he could see my side of things."

"And what did he think after you told him the truth?"

"He didn't fight me on not going through with the wedding. It was then that I had a talk with Jaleel and Melissa. Jaleel had made it clear that he still wanted Melissa and Melissa had feelings for him, too. It was simple. There could still be a wedding of two people who wanted to get married. After that, it was just a matter of calling up the guests and thinking of a creative way to tell them that I wasn't the groom."

"And then?" Tonya urged him to continue.

"And then, I spoke with your mother and father and told them my plan to marry you. They took everything from there. That's how all of your friends and family ended up at your house. And we live happily ever after."

Who said that there was no such thing as the perfect man? She had living proof of the perfect man, wrapping her in his arms. Even with all of his faults, he was perfect for her.

Epilogue

It had been almost two years since Tonya and Dexter were married. A lot of things had changed in her life. The birth of their daughter, Janet, brought new meaning to their lives. Janet, who was about to turn one, had yet to meet her grandparents on Dexter's side of the family. Mr. Freeman couldn't face the fact that he was wrong about Melissa. He wished Dexter luck with his marriage, but chose not to interact with them. Tonya didn't think he could admit that he'd been wrong.

It bothered Tonya that their daughter hadn't met her grandparents. She was annoyed that Dexter was content with his parents not being in Janet's life. Since she and Dexter left Freeman and Reynolds to start their own firm, Freeman and Freeman, they hadn't seen Dexter's parents. Tonya knew that deep down inside, Dexter missed his parents, but he would never admit it. Dexter didn't seem bothered about them not being in his life at all. He was being just as nonchalant about the situation as his parents were. Tonya sent them cards on special occasions, only to have no response. Tonya decided to give them one last opportunity to become involved in Janet's life. She and Dexter were giving Janet a birthday party for her first birthday. She signed the card, *from your grand-daughter, Janet*. If they didn't respond to this invitation, she was giving up.

Other than the problem with Dexter's family, everything was great. Tonya and Kiera decided to let bygones be bygones and wiped the slate clean. She and Kiera had resumed best friends status once again and Kiera was one of Janet's godmothers, Rita was the other. Yes, Tonya now had two new best friends. After Freeman and Freeman was started, Rita left Freeman and Reynolds and joined Tonya and Dexter in their firm. They now had over thirty attorneys employed at Freeman and Freeman. Kip had proven to Tonya that he could stop drinking and Tonya gave him a job at their firm as their chief of security.

Reggie stayed in school and was a junior at the University of Houston with a B average and his shop was doing better than ever. He and Regina had been married for six months and seemed to be very much in love.

Melissa and Jaleel moved back to Atlanta. She no longer practiced law. She became a housewife and raised their new baby boy.

David finally gave up on Tonya. He decided he had to focus on his own life and struggled to find his identity. Was he gay or straight? Only David could tell. Rumors had it that he finally came to grips with himself as a homosexual and he was marching proudly at the Gay Day Parade with *Ken* at his side. But you know how rumors are. More than likely if you hear the same story from three different sources, it's true.

Ramona, well . . . what was there to say about Ramona? She was still Ramona.

The family had come to an agreement that Janet's party should be at her grandparents' house. It turned out to be a beautiful Saturday afternoon. Tonya, Dexter, and Reggie had just finished the task of stringing up balloons. Everyone stood back to observe their finished work. They had taped balloons all around in the backyard. "I'm going inside to get a drink, you two want something?" Dexter asked Tonya and Reggie.

"If there's some lemonade in the fridge bring me some," Tonya said.

"Me, too," Reggie said over his shoulder. He turned to Tonya. "You know, sis, Pops has been coming by the shop pretty regularly for the last few months. I cut his hair at least once a week."

Tonya looped her arm through Reggie's. "That's good Reggie. After all of these years, he finally went to see your shop. That was a big step for him."

"Yeah, now everybody knows who he is. He plays dominoes with some of the men every now and then and he keeps Mrs. Zellermyle busy. He thinks her burgers are the best on the north side of town. It's kind of nice having him around. I never knew he and I could have a relationship like this."

"I'm glad Dad decided to see your shop. I knew he would like it if he gave it a chance. So, you see him every week, huh?"

"Yep, Pops drops by often, even when he doesn't need a haircut. Did I tell you what he did for me?"

"No, what?" Tonya asked.

"He made an arrangement with the barber college down the street from my shop. All of the top-of-the-line students will have the opportunity to work at my shop if I have any booths available. I let the students come in and I see how well they cut. If I like what they can do I'll offer them a job. I also let the students help around the shop and see how shop life is, you know, like an internship. I have a student chair set up and those customers who are willing to take a chance, will let students cut their hair at a discounted rate. But, everything has been going well and for once in my life, I can actually say that I'm happy."

"I'm happy for you, too, Reggie. I'm also happy that

Kip is all straightened out and my life couldn't be any better right now."

"Yeah, I'm proud of Kip. It's almost like he's a different person. He goes to work faithfully and stopped drinking. He has really made a change for the better. I can't believe he left those wino's alone long enough to hold down a job. Where is Kip anyway? He can't miss his niece's first birthday party."

"He's at the office. We've installed a new security system and he's training security personnel on the new system. He said he would be here as soon as he finished."

"I can't believe Kip is at work on a Saturday. The world must be coming to an end."

"You are one to talk. It wasn't all that long ago that you were doing the same thing."

Dexter returned from the house and gave each of them a glass of lemonade.

"What took you so long?" Reggie asked Dexter. "You must have had to grow some lemons and then make the lemonade."

Dexter laughed. "Very funny, Reggie. You are drinking Dexter's homemade lemonade."

Reggie took a sip of his lemonade. "Man, this stuff is a little tart, don't you think?"

"I think it tastes fine," Tonya said to Dexter. "It just needs a little more sugar."

"Don't try to sugarcoat the truth, Tonya." Reggie laughed. "This lemonade is just plain old sour. It doesn't need a little more sugar, it needs a lot. Tell the truth."

"I never claimed to be a Betty Crocker. Let me see you do better." Dexter told Reggie.

"Nah, I can't bless you with a sample of Reggie's lemonade today. I don't want to embarrass you." Reggie winked his eye at Tonya.

Tonya went into the house and brought out Janet's

cake. After everyone had arrived, they lit the candle and sang the birthday song to her.

"Now make a wish and blow out the candle." Tonya instructed Janet. Tonya made a wish herself and helped Janet blow out the candle. Everyone clapped and brought their presents for Janet to open.

The doorbell rang as everyone was snapping pictures of Janet. Dexter put down his camera. "I'll go inside and get the door. Do we have a knife for the cake?" he asked Tonya before going into the house.

"No, bring one out with you when you come back."

"Alright." Dexter went to the front door and opened it. He stood motionless as his mother and father stood out front with presents in their arms.

"I hope we're not too late," Mr. Freeman said.

Dexter stepped aside, waiting for them to come inside. "No, we're just about to cut the cake." He tensed up at their presence.

Mrs. Freeman touched her son on the cheek. "I've missed you so much, Dexter. You don't know how much I've wanted to call you. I just didn't know how you would receive me." She held out her arms to Dexter, wanting to hug him.

Dexter was reluctant to comply, but he realized that he missed his parents, too. He hugged her close to him. "I've missed you, too."

"Son, I don't know how to say this. It took a long time for me to get over what happened. I had no right to try to dictate how you should live your life, and who you chose to love. I was wrong and I hope you can find it in your heart someday to forgive me. I hope Tonya will forgive me, too. I've suffered because of my selfishness." He held out his hand to Dexter.

"No handshakes this time, Father, you deserve a hug." Dexter took his father's hand, pulled him close, and hugged him. "I forgive you Father and so does Tonya.

Let me take you out back and introduce you to your granddaughter."

The noisy crowd out back was silenced when the Freemans stepped out. Everyone was frozen in their positions.

"Is that who I think it is?" Reggie whispered to Tonya.

"Yes, silly. Will you be quiet? They'll hear you."

Tonya was the first to break the ice. "Mr. and Mrs. Freeman, I'm so pleased you could make it." She escorted them out to the gazebo.

"Thank you," Mr. Freeman said. "We're happy to be here."

Tonya introduced the Freemans to her family and introduced Janet last. "This is your granddaughter, Janet Elaine Freeman." She picked up Janet and held her in her arms. "Janet, this is your grandmother and grandfather." Janet smiled and quickly hid her face in her mother's arms.

"She's beautiful," Mr. Freeman said. "May I hold her?"

"Sure." Tonya gave Janet to Mr. Freeman who touched her face and hair.

Pretty soon, the laughter and chatter continued and they all enjoyed Janet's birthday party as a family.

Dear Reader,

I hope you enjoyed *For Love's Sake* because it was such a pleasure writing it. I have loved to write for as long as I can remember. It was a wonderful feeling to bring each character to life with the stroke of my keyboard. The most rewarding feeling is the fact that I had the opportunity to share my story with you.

I would love to hear from you. If you would like to share your ideas or comments please E-mail me at rlee231429@aol.com.

About the Author

Rochunda Lee lives in Houston, Texas. She is a graduate of the University of Houston with a degree in Social Sciences. She has always enjoyed writing because it allows her to be creative and use her imagination to the fullest extent. She enjoys going to the movies, visiting with friends and relatives and traveling.

Coming this Holiday Season from Arabesque Books . . .

WINTER NIGHTS
by Francis Ray, Shirley Hailstock, and Donna Hill
    1-58314-039-5 $4.99US/$6.50CAN
Christmas wishes, Kwanzaa kisses, and New Year's near-misses—holiday romance has a magic all its own. Now three of Arabesque's most beloved authors bring you the joy of this very special time of year, when dreams of desire really do come true . . .

NO GREATER GIFT by Geri Guillaume
    1-58314-040-9 $4.99US/$6.50CAN
Kira Dodd couldn't believe it when her mother impulsively settled on a Texas ranch with her new love. After flying out to get her, Kira finds herself fantasizing about a sexy cowboy and all of a sudden, her mother's runaway love affair doesn't seem so crazy after all.

SOMEONE LIKE YOU by Jacquelin Thomas
    1-58314-041-7 $4.99US/$6.50CAN
When an African American newspaper publishes an unflattering article about Blythe Bloodstone, she hastily confronts the handsome publisher. She soon realizes that he is a man determined to teach her the meaning of Kwanzaa . . . and a very important lesson about her heart.

MIDNIGHT PASSION by Kayla Perrin
    1-58314-044-1 $4.99US/$6.50CAN
Jade Alexander's two New Year's resolutions were to reopen her hair salon and never to trust a man again with her heart. But her old flame shows up at a party and as the clock strikes midnight, Jade can feel her resolve weakening—and her desire kindling—under his piercing gaze.

Please Use the Coupon on the Next Page to Order

OWN THESE HOLIDAY ROMANCES
FROM ARABESQUE BOOKS

Coming in December From Arabesque Books . . .

THE LOOK OF LOVE by Monica Jackson
  1-58314-069-7 $4.99US/$6.50CAN
When busy single mother Carmel Matthews meets handsome plastic surgeon Steve Reynolds, he sets her pulse racing like never before. But he and Carmel will have to confront their deepest doubts and fears, if they are to have a love that promises all they've ever desired . . .

VIOLETS ARE BLUE by Sonia Icilyn
  1-58314-057-3 $4.99US/$6.50CAN
Arlisa Davenport's impoverished childhood never hurt more than when she caught Brad Belleville, her young love, mocking her. A decade later, when her pregnant sister is kidnapped, she must turn to Brad for help and soon discovers that their desire is far more alluring than she'd ever imagined.

DISTANT MEMORIES by Niqui Stanhope
  1-58314-059-X $4.99US/$6.50CAN
Days after realizing her Hollywood dreams, Racquel Ward finds herself tragically disfigured and near death. With her abusive ex-husband at her bedside, she places her fragile trust in Dr. Sean KirPatrick. Now they must both overcome overwhelming obstacles to believe in the power of love . . .

SPELLBOUND by Deirdre Savoy
  1-58314-058-1 $4.99US/$6.50CAN
Ariel Windsor is insistent that heartache will never crush her again . . . until she meets irresistible Jarad Naughton. He is intrigued by her beauty and by the rumor that she's the last in a line of witches who can make men fall in love with them in six days . . . now, they're both playing for keeps.

Please Use the Coupon on the Next Page to Order

OWN THESE NEW ROMANCES FROM ARABESQUE BOOKS